# RAGE

A Love Story

Julie Anne Peters

# RAGE

*A Love Story*

Alfred A. Knopf

*New York*

THIS IS A BORZOI BOOK PUBLISHED BY ALFRED A. KNOPF, INC.

Published in the United States of America by Alfred A. Knopf, a division of Random House, Inc., New York.

Knopf, Borzoi Books, and the colophon are registered trademarks of Random House, Inc.

Visit us on the Web! www.randomhouse.com/teens

Educators and librarians, for a variety of teaching tools, visit us at www.randomhouse.com/teachers

Library of Congress Cataloging-in-Publication Data
Peters, Julie Anne.
Rage: a love story / Julie Anne Peters. — 1st ed.
p. cm.
Summary: At the end of high school, Johanna finally begins dating the girl she has loved from afar, but Reeve is as much trouble as she claims to be as she and her twin brother damage Johanna's self-esteem, friendships, and already precarious relationship with her sister.
ISBN 978-0-375-85209-1 (trade) — ISBN 978-0-375-95209-8 (lib. bdg.) —
ISBN 978-0-375-89358-2 (e-book)
[1. Family problems—Fiction. 2. Lesbians—Fiction. 3. Homosexuality—Fiction. 4. Sisters—Fiction. 5. Dating violence—Fiction. 6. Child abuse—Fiction. 7. Orphans—Fiction.] I. Title.
PZ7.P44158Rag 2009
[Fic]—dc22
2008033500

Printed in the United States of America

September 2009

10 9 8 7 6 5 4 3 2 1

First Edition

*To Alyson Lacoste, who asked me to write this book*
*and I said, "No. Absolutely not."*
*Alyson is a very persuasive young woman.*

# RAGE

## A Love Story

# *Joyland: Take 1*

I'm wearing ultra-lowrider camo pants that barely cover my crack and if she looks she'll see the strap of my thong. This filmy beige crop top where, if I get a chill, my nipples will be my most outstanding feature. My hair looks sexy hanging in my eyes. My walk is killer. She can't not notice me.

I enter her field of vision, she does a slow double take, then stops talking with her clique, the LBDs, mid-sentence. Her eyes scrape me, skim me. Scratch and burn me. I feel her drink me in and salivate. I don't look. Not yet, not yet. My eyes shift slightly. ZAP. ZING. She's hooked. I smile her in.

She's mine.

．　．　．

## Joyland: Take 2

Same sexy me. She detaches from the LesBo Dykes, or Les Beau Dykes, and follows me to the parking lot. She gets in her car, stays close to mine, runs a yellow light. She tracks me to the bank of the river, to the edge of Fallon Falls. We park and get out. I step on the slippery rocks, arms extended, balancing across the rushing water. I spring to the shore, knowing she's on my scent. Around the side of the boulder, I duck into a cave and wait. The smell of burnt sugar tickles my nose. I hear her. She enters and steps in front of me— reaches out a hand, both hands, and moves into me, slides her arms around my waist, my bare skin, where nerve endings spark and snap. There's no time to blink or moisten my lips.

"Hi. I'm Johanna."

She kisses me long and hard, awakens the ache of longing inside me. Her lips are metal, then melon. Finally, finally she lets me go. I gasp for breath and she smiles, a one-sided, sliver-

*moon smile, and says, "Now that we have the introductions out of the way . . ."*

. . .

"Johanna, dear?"

I jerk to the present.

"Mrs. Arcaro has passed," Jeannette says.

I missed it, the last breath of her life. A pang of guilt for daydreaming at this critical time stabs at my heart, but I chase it away. I give Mrs. Arcaro's frail hand a gentle squeeze and lay it on the sheet. I feel Mom smiling down on me from heaven.

As I'm leaving Memorial Hospice, I feel uplifted. I meant something to someone. Even if Mrs. Arcaro was a stranger, I'm the one who was there for her at the end.

I'm the one who stayed.

# Chapter 1

I locate the room on the first floor where Mrs. Goins asked me to meet her. She was desperate, she said. So many seniors on the verge of not graduating, she said. Would I please tutor this one? A special one who needs special help with the senior project, she said.

I guess I'm meant to feel special, but I have my own stuff to finish—like that damn Film Studies class Novak talked me into.

I peek in. The classroom's empty. Did I get the room wrong? I've been losing whole blocks of time lately, spacing constantly. Where does life go when it's lost to you?

My backpack slips off my shoulder and a note falls out of the front pocket.

"I'm dropping Film Studies," Novak wrote.

An old note from the beginning of term. At the time I thought: Thanks. Abandon me, like everyone else has.

I hear Mrs. Goins coming before I see her. She's . . . rustling? Maybe her thighs are rubbing together or something. Since the first of the year, she's put on, like, twenty pounds. A lot of people call her Meaty Loins.

I would never do that.

The person behind Meaty Loins materializes.

"Johanna, this is Robbie Inouye. Robbie, Johanna Lynch."

*Oh my God. Kill me now.*

Robbie Inouye scares the hell out of me. He might be retarded, or challenged, or whatever terminology you use to dance around the truth. He's definitely messed. His eyes aren't symmetrical, or could it be his head's on crooked? The corners of his mouth are always caked with dried-up spittle and he lumbers, drags his feet like Frankenstein. He's not big. I'm five eight and he's shorter than me, but he *seems* huge.

Once upon a time, slow-moving Robbie would get jostled in the hall. I'd see people cut in front of him, making him stumble. Then came last November, right before Thanksgiving. I remember because Novak had been dumped by her boyfriend, Dante—again—and it was taking longer than usual to stanch the internal bleeding. We were in the restroom by the cafeteria. I got her past the point of slitting her wrists by reassuring her that she was an idiot for staying with him. "If I wasn't so fucking irresistible," she hiccuped, swiping at her nose, "I wouldn't attract vermin." "Exactly," I replied. I was late; I couldn't stay to hold her hand. "I'm better off without the asshole." "Too true." I had a midterm in trig and I'd blown the last quiz.

"Thank you, sweetie." Novak hugged me. "What would I do without you?" She held me so hard I couldn't breathe.

So I'm charging out of the restroom, dodging bodies and wedging through the mob of people exiting the cafeteria. Late bell rings and my class is two flights up. Then I hear this cry, more of a keen or wail. I look over and see a blur of skin, bone, and loose spittle, bared teeth. It's Robbie.

Someone had taken the instrument case he carries around. A guy was swinging it over his head and Robbie was lying on the floor like he'd been jumped. His books and papers had spilled down the stairs and one of his shoes was off.

Without warning, he rose up like Atlantis emerging from the sea, like Goliath in a rage, fists flailing, screeching and bellowing so loud my ears squinched. The guy with the case passed it to another guy, then a girl, a guy, the girl again. Robbie went crazy. He started swinging in all directions, clawing to get that case. He let out this high-pitched hawk screech, along with foam and spit, then busted the girl right in the chops with his fist. I felt the impact as she screamed and dropped the case.

The first guy made the mistake of retaliating for his girl-friend, hooking Robbie's neck from behind. Robbie whirled and smacked the guy's head into a brick wall.

I heard—*felt*—the crunch of bone.

I don't know why I did it, but the case was only about two feet away and I bent to retrieve it. Robbie grabbed the case and swung it up. The corner smacked me in the chin and slammed me into the stair rail.

His face came inches from my face, then his eyes rolled back into his head and he hauled off and whacked me on the

shoulder. I crashed, tumbling down the stairs, feeling verte-
brae crush.

My shoulder was dislocated. This was before my sister,
Tessa, moved back home, so Novak took me to the Urgent
Care Center.

The guy Robbie clobbered had a concussion, and his girl
a fat lip, but none of us pressed charges. Unhappily ever after, Robbie plodded the halls and people steered clear. Especially me.

"Robbie, why don't you find a seat?" Mrs. Goins says.

Franken Psycho's case brushes my leg and I jump back.

Before I can get a squeak out, Mrs. Goins lowers her voice
and goes, "Thank you for doing this, Johanna. He needs to
graduate."

So do I. "Mrs. Goins, my work schedule changed. I just
found out today, and now I have to go in at two. Um, every
day, I think." My eyes shift to Robbie and I see he's helped
himself to the teacher's desk and is rolling in the office chair.
He pulls open the top drawer and removes a stapler.

Mrs. Goins looks at me over her granny glasses. "I thought
I could count on you."

My face flares. She sponsored the Youth Service Club
when I was in it, before Mom got sick. . . .

"You're the first person I thought of." The pleading in her
eyes. Or is it desperation?

"I—I guess I can change my schedule back."

She rests her hand on my forearm. "Thank you, Johanna."

"Get out of my chair, Robbie," Mrs. Goins orders him.
He's stapled together a bunched-up wad of his t-shirt, and as
he yanks it apart, staples ping the window.

She motions him to a desk up front and he grabs his battered brown instrument case. It's the size of a trombone or saxophone.

"Robbie, Johanna is going to get you through the senior project so you can graduate with your class. She'll be tutoring you. Do you know what 'tutor' means? It means—"

"I know what it means," Robbie says in this sluggish monotone. Robotically, his head rotates, and his eyes fix on me.

A streak of phantom pain shoots through my arm. *Please don't hurt me.*

"He has the essay to finish. I'm not sure he's even started it. Robbie," she carps at him, "have you even started writing the essay?"

He doesn't answer.

*Chill. Don't piss him off.* She removes a sheet of paper from her messenger bag and waves it at me. Robbie extends his legs in front of him so I have to step over them. He raises them enough to make me half trip.

*Asstard.* Wait, I feel bad calling a retard an asstard. Wait, not really.

Is that a smirk on his face?

Mrs. Goins glances at her watch. "I have a student conference in five minutes, so I'll leave you to it. He needs to have the essay finished and handed in to the English department by next Friday." As she bustles by, she adds, "Robbie, do this one last assignment and you're out of here. Cooperate with Johanna."

I skim over the sheet. Oh yeah. I'm familiar with it. Name. Date. In no less than a thousand words, describe your best moment and your worst moment in high school and what each taught you about yourself.

We found out what the senior project would be last September at our first senior assembly. They told us we had to have it in by April first to graduate. It's already May.

"Cooperate with Johanna," Robbie says.

"What?" When I glance up over the sheet at him, he eyes me warily. I move behind the teacher's desk to put something solid between us. "Did you bring any paper?"

His arms fling out to the side and I lurch back, jamming into the whiteboard tray. Ow.

He smiles vacantly.

*What's with this guy?* I flop into the rolling chair and it almost tips over. He sniggers. "Do you have anything to write with?" I ask.

"Cooperate with Johanna," he says.

I tug open the top drawer of the desk and find a green mechanical pencil. There are sheets of white copy paper in a lower drawer, so I remove a few and click out a length of lead on the pencil.

Robbie watches me the whole time, mesmerized. I get up and hand him the paper and pencil. He holds the pencil up to his nose and sniffs. He does the same with the paper.

Weird.

*Can he read?* Well, hopefully, since he's a senior in high school. But half the jocks can't read. *Bad Johanna. Shouldn't stereotype.* Robbie has probably been mainstreamed, or whatever you call it.

I read to Robbie, "In no less than a thousand words, describe your best moment and—"

"Your worst moment of high school and what each taught you about yourself," he drones.

I give him the xeroxed copy of the senior project. *Can he write?*

"Johanna, Johanna, Johanna," he deadpans. He straightens in the desk and prints a series of words across the page. I peer over to see what he's writing.

He covers it up. Not before I catch a glimpse of my name. He's spelled it "Joe Hana." He wrote something bigger at the bottom of the page.

He lifts his arm so I can see. Two words: FUCK YOU.

Tutoring session over. I snatch my backpack off the desk and head for the door.

"Hey!"

I don't stop.

"Hey," he calls louder. The desk creaks.

"What?" I whirl.

He blinks fast. "I didn't mean you." His eyes bounce around for a second, then focus on something behind me.

I pivot. All the blood rushes to my face. My head and brain and ears explode.

It's her.

How long has she been standing there?

"What are you doing?" she asks.

I open my mouth to speak, to say the first words I've ever spoken to Reeve Hartt. Then realize she isn't talking to me.

Robbie says, "Cooperate with Johanna."

Reeve's eyes flash on my face for a second. It's fleeting, but I think she actually notices I'm here.

"We have to go, Robbie," she murmurs, and takes off. Not far. She stops and waits. I could reach out and touch her. I could take her hand. . . .

Robbie scrabbles to stand and snags his case. He trundles over to me at the door and I step aside to let him pass. He thrusts out the paper and pencil.

"Later, dude," he says. His arm clips my shoulder, and that phantom pain flares through me.

Reeve takes off with Robbie tramping behind her. At the end of the hall, at the intersection, he says something to her and she spins around and slugs him in the chest.

I flinch and squeal. Reeve shoots a dark look my way.

I leap back into the classroom as my heart gallops in my chest.

So close. I clench my pack to me and try to catch my breath.

What's their connection? I wonder. She knows him. They can't be together. Please. Robbie's retarded. Reeve's gay.

And mine.

But only in Joyland.

So far.

# Chapter 2

I know I locked the door before I left for school. I'm positive.

Novak's sitting at the table, her laptop open and papers spread out. "Hope you don't mind. Tessa let me in."

It's still strange to have Tessa back. Sort of like old times, but not.

Novak doesn't even glance up as I sling my backpack to the floor and go, "You won't *believe* what I have to do—"

She sticks up an index finger, like, Hang on. She keys rapid-fire.

How long has she been here? Her knitting is strung from the divan to the coffee table. She glances over her shoulder, gets up fast, and gathers the yarn and needles, shoving them into her bag.

"What are you making?" I ask.

"A chastity belt."

"Better use steel wool."

"Oh, caw. It's actually something for the baby."

She returns to the laptop and I sprawl out lengthwise on the divan. I dig in the cushions for the TV remote and punch the power button.

Novak says, "Wait. I can't write with that on."

I remote it off. I twist my head to watch her, her arching back, her long hair streaming down over her shoulders, all silk and shine. A catch in my stomach makes me ache and I turn away.

Maybe once, I wanted her.

"How was hell?" she asks, still keying.

"You'd know if you showed up occasionally."

"I'm almost done. I just have this one paper to finish and I'm out of there."

I can't stop looking at her. The ache slithers up between my—

*No. Stop it. You're just lonely.*

"I brought your mail up," Novak says. She motions with her chin to a stack on the counter. I get up and sift through it. No college acceptances. Credit card apps and magazine subscriptions, all of them for Tessa or Martin.

Novak's reading over what she wrote. She looks up and air-smooches me. I stick out my tongue in a gag. We have this running game where she pretends she's into me and I fend off her disgusting advances.

It was always fun—until Dante.

"Mind if I turn on the TV now?"

She holds up a hand, then lowers it. Permission.

This low divan is the only piece of furniture I bought for myself. Tessa took the sofa bed when she moved out of the apartment to go to college in Minnesota. She brought back a husband.

I surf around, hit a movie in Spanish. A scene where these two are doing it under the sheets and moaning. It catches Novak's attention and she says to me, "Horndog."

"Speak for yourself."

"I am."

She resumes proofing.

*Me and Reeve.* God, she looked hot today. The outfit I'd conjured up in Joyland is the kind of thing Reeve wears. Lowriders and transparent tops, miles of exposed skin. I'd never even go without a bra. Once I wore a thong to school and felt uncomfortable all day, like rope was riding up my butt. I was scared everyone could tell by the way I walked.

The guy flings off the sheets and says something in Spanish. The señorita is *muy bonita.* She has on this filmy negligee. Thick mascara and eyeliner. I just love the way Reeve does her eyes. Some days she paints on eye shadow with stripes and patterns, like animal prints or abstract art. I choose my seat in the cafeteria so I can consume her at lunch. She has these wide anime eyes.

I've figured out that her moods are all in her eye art. If she's happy, there are pastel skies and rolling waves. Anger is jagged storms, big black slashes. One day she drew a teardrop below each eye and glued a blue jewel inside.

*Is it hot in here, or what?* I caterpillar back far enough to reach the doorknob and crack open the door. Below, in the main house, I hear the sliding door to the patio roll open and closed. Hurried footsteps. A car door slams and the engine starts. "What was Tessa doing home?" I ask Novak.

"Hmm? Oh, she says she was really nauseated today. You know."

I found out about my possibly future niece or nephew when I was down in the garage doing laundry. Martin came in with an armload of towels and said, "You can congratulate me now."

"For what?" I said. "Being dorky?"

He dumped the load on my head. "I assume Tessa told you."

"That you're a dork?" I said, digging out. "Nope. Figured it out all by myself."

"We're preggers." His smile lit up the night.

"Cool. Congrats," I said. I almost added, I hope it takes this time. God. I almost said that.

Novak comes over and lifts my legs to slide in under. A tingle spreads through my belly. "What are you doing?" she asks.

"Watching air circulate."

Novak sighs. "I swear, I'm going to hook you up."

I cast her a lethal glare. "It'll be your last act on Earth." The one time, the only time, she fixed me up was with this shaved and pierced feminazi chick who ranted all night about taking down the patriarchy and reclaiming her uterus.

Novak's quiet.

"What?"

"Can I ask Dante over?"

"Now?"

She hunches her shoulders to her ears.

Fuck-fest time. I need to get out of here anyway. "Keep it down, okay? Tessa will be on my case for running a whore-house."

Novak smiles. "I can take care of Tessa." She pulls out a crochet hook and slits it across her throat.

When we were younger, Tessa tried to teach me how to knit and crochet too, but I'm a spaz. I couldn't even cast on, or whatever it's called.

I push to my feet and Novak adds, "Thanks. Oh, by the way, you might be getting a call from Amanda Montero."

"Why?"

"I told her about your place."

"Told her what?"

"Well . . . she'll pay you."

It takes me a minute. "I'm not pimping my apartment. Novak—"

"Okay. I just thought you'd want to earn a little extra cash."

"I don't." Not like that. I head for my room.

"You could watch. At this rate, it's the only action you'll ever get. Just kidding," she calls. "Not really."

I say under my breath, "Fuck you."

"You know you want to."

I close my bedroom door. It's so hard being gay—I don't care what anybody says. Being gay and a virgin is just stupid and wrong. When I told Novak I was a lesbian, she was, like, "So, what's your point?" We were fifteen, just starting high school. Mom hadn't been diagnosed yet, and Tessa was gone. I came out to Novak the same year Tessa lost her first baby.

Why am I thinking this? There's no connection.

I wade through the piles on my floor for a clean shirt.

This is Tessa's second pregnancy.

I change into my skinny jeans and slip on checkered Converses. In the living room, Novak is lying on the divan, her arm flung across her eyes.

"Don't smoke, okay? Tell Dante that." Last time it reeked of pot in here for a week. Like living inside a bong.

"Love you, Johanna Banana. You juicy fruit." Novak lifts her arm and kiss-kisses me.

I should tell her, Game over.

I snag my backpack and keys, figure I'll hang at the mall for a while. No, not the mall. I'll go to the hospice. The stack of mail is still on the counter, so I scoop it up.

The apartment steps are wood and warped; they sag with the slightest pressure. Mom and Dad had big plans for fixing up the apartment over the garage. Then life had different plans, like them dying.

I draw open the patio door and slip inside the main house. The shades are drawn; it's dark and chilly, and the paint fumes make me cough. Martin keeps the thermostat at Polar. Tessa's painting the living room purple. Excuse me—aubergine. *Should she be painting when she's pregnant?*

I set the mail on the table and spot the slim stack Tessa's collecting for me. My car insurance. Bank statement. A twenty-dollar bill.

I keep telling her she doesn't need to give me money. I leave it. I drop the mail into my pack and head out. A flash of red ribbon in the trash can by the counter catches my eye and I fish it out.

· It's the loop of the ribbon that was tied to the cast of my handprint. A piece of the cast—my right pinkie—is now a shard. I dig out a bigger chunk, the palm and thumb. On the counter, I puzzle all the pieces back together. I made this in kindergarten. I can still feel the cold, squishy mush of the plaster of paris between my fingers. That cast has been hanging on the wall in our dining room forever.

Tessa comes back into my life just when I'm over her bailing. And she trashes my handprint. I run my index finger across the tiny fingers, the smooth palm, and this lump rises in my throat. It's just a handprint.

I made it for Mother's Day.

I sweep the plaster pieces over the edge of the counter into the trash. As soon as I can afford my own place, I'm gone. *You hear that, Tessa? Me. I'll be the one who leaves.*

# Chapter 3

Robbie shuffles in ten minutes after the last bell, looking like he has no idea where he is, who he is, what he is. I know the feeling.

I wonder if people like him can remember stuff.

People like him. *God, I'm so mean.*

He crosses the room and stands at the desk. This bubble of spit clings to his lower lip and I want to clue him, lick my lip where the spit is so he'll wipe it off or suck it in.

"Do you want to sit down?" I ask.

He spins a full circle and spirals into a desk. Wow, that was kind of . . . balletic? Except for his case smashing into the desk beside him. The thud pongs around the room and lands in my chest.

From his pants pocket he withdraws a wad of string and shakes it out. He starts threading it through his fingers.

This is *so* not getting the essay written. I get up and hand him his paper and pencil. I brought lined paper and a regular pencil. A pen too.

He winds the string around and through his fingers.

"Hey!"

He jerks aware, untangles the string and lowers it to his lap. I set the essay on the desk.

"Your best moment," he says, staring at the paper and writing utensils.

"Right. Start over."

He glances up. "No. Yours."

"What do you mean?" *If he's going to be belligerent or something . . .*

"I mean," he says slowly and deliberately, "what was your best moment?"

"I lied on my essay."

He cracks a grin. "What did you write?"

I think back. "I wrote about this time I studied really hard and got one hundred percent in AP Physics. I can't even spell AP."

The grin widens.

"See, it doesn't matter what you write. Just not . . . my name. Or 'fuck you.' I have to hand this in to Mrs. Goins."

"Meaty Loins," Robbie says.

I suppress a smile.

"In no less than a thousand words," he adds.

"Right."

He peers down at the paper and scrunches his forehead. I return to the desk. I can feel him staring at me. He doesn't actually ever make eye contact; more like fixes on my mouth.

"What's your best moment?" he asks.

Didn't we just have this conversation?

Robbie says, "Don't lie."

Brain freeze. Seriously. I can't think of anything.

Robbie waits and waits. My mind seizes. Finally a thought breaks free, but the only words that form are "I don't think I've had a best moment."

He nods once. "Me neither. I have a worst moment," he says. "I have a whole bunch of worst moments."

"Good. I mean, not good. That you have bad stuff in your life. Start with the worst. Pick one of those."

He centers the paper on the desk, turning and twisting until the corners are equidistant and squared, for God's sake, then takes a year to decide—pencil or pen? Pencil or pen? Pen! I watch him write his name in the upper-right-hand corner. He has nice handwriting for a guy. Is that sexist? Martin's writing is completely illegible, which I only know because he wrote me a note once: "You're going to be an aunt! I'm calling you Auntie Mojo."

That was the first time, right after Tessa moved home.

Robbie scratches his scalp behind his ear. "How do you spell 'murder'?"

"What?"

He writes something.

"Who got murdered?"

Robbie raises his head a fraction of an inch. "My mother. I killed her."

The back of my head smacks the whiteboard as the chair slips. It must bruise my brain, because when I come to, I'm sidestepping out the door, telling Robbie, "I forgot something in my locker. I mean, my car. I mean, I'll be right back."

I bolt. My projectile body smashes into another moving object and the collision sends us both flying.

"What the hell?" Hands press against my shoulders. "What the hell!"

*Oh my God.* My mind and muscles engage. I've knocked over Reeve. I'm . . . on top of her.

I clamber off. My voice catches somewhere between my stomach and throat. *I touched Reeve Hartt, full body contact.*

I jump to my feet and hold a hand out to her. "Sorry."

She twists away and pushes to her feet.

"Really," I say. "It's . . . it's him. He's . . ." My eyes dart back into the room, where Robbie is still sitting, hunched over, writing. "He says he killed his mother."

"What?" Reeve's face contorts. She leans forward to peer into the room and for an instant I think she'll rush me, storm in, maybe bump me, ignite me. Her feet stay planted. "He's a head case," she says. "Did you think he was serious?"

I open my mouth. Suck up air.

All these years. All my imagined scenes and stimulations. The almost dreamlike quality of her, her skin all milky translucence. The rise of her breasts over the low-cut string camisole. My attention wavers. We lie together, on the hallway floor. She gazes into my eyes.

I swallow hard. "He wrote it," I say, "on his senior essay."

Reeve's eyes slit. "Butt nugget!" she calls into the room. "Get your dumb ass out here."

Her eyes meet mine again and hold. She seems to ratchet down a notch. Or I do? I smile. And hiccup.

Robbie's essay flaps in front of my face. "It's not done," he says. "A thousand words is ten times ten times ten."

I take it from him and skim the three sheets he's filled, front and back. He wrote a lot. A sentence fragment jumps out at me: ". . . cut up her body into bit size peeces and ate it."

*Oh my God. He is a psycho.*

Reeve says, "You told her you killed our mother?"

I look from him to her. *Our?*

A grin sneaks across Robbie's face but is snatched away when Reeve grabs his shirt, balls a fist, and punches him in the face. Hard. I feel the floor tilt.

"He's a liar," Reeve says to me. "Don't believe anything he tells you." She's twisting his shirt in her fist, choking him. "What else did you say, you dickwad? If you said anything about me . . ."

"He didn't." I reach over and press down on Reeve's wrist. "He didn't say anything about you."

She stares at my hand on her arm. "Why'd you do that?" She jerks away.

"I . . ." But she's not talking to me. Her eyes have resettled beyond me, on Robbie.

He recites, "Cooperate with Johanna."

Reeve backs up a step. "Time to fly." She pivots and charges down the hall, the frayed hem of her jeans sweeping the floor. Robbie lingers, like he wants to say something else. I want to ask if he's okay. Reeve turns and screeches, "Shut up, Robbie!"

Bling's is packed with tweeners. I swear they get younger and meaner every day. If I say, "Can I help you?" they give me this look, like, *Pleez. You? You suck.* My job at the mall is, basically, trolling for shoplifters. I clock in and immediately spy a clique of streaky blondes who are all dressed in coordinating outfits, trying on bracelets and fingering necklaces, removing earrings off the rack as they spin it. To cause distraction. So obvious. One of them drops two cards of gold hoops into her purse.

I mosey over. "Can I help you?"

She lunges toward the aisle. I block it. Frantically, she scans for her buds, who've scattered. *Nice.*

Adjusting the earring cards on the table, I lower my voice and say, "You won't get out the door. Everything is marked with an antitheft code. The alarm will go off and you'll get busted."

Her lower lip quivers.

I add, "When I look away, you're going to put the earrings back."

I retreat a step and hear her purse unsnap.

They aren't always so dumb. I mean, *come on*. Who'd pay to code six million pieces of junk jewelry? I catch her in my peripheral vision, skittering out the door.

I can't wait to go to college so I never have to work again. The biggest sale I ever rang up was $16.12. I wish I could spend all my spare time at the hospice, but volunteer work won't pay for tuition.

The mall closes at ten, and Shondri, my boss, says she'll clear the register and do the deposit. On my way past the food court, the smell of Chinese makes my stomach grumble. Dinner was a snarfed bag of chips.

But I know one place where there's always food—and socially redeeming work.

\* \* \*

25

The hospice never closes. When Mom was here, I sat with her all night, every night, until the end. "Hi, Johanna," Jeannette greets me from the front desk. "You're here late."

"Couldn't sleep," I fib.

She's eating a burrito the size of a blimp. My eyes must glom on to it, because she says, "There's plenty in the kitchen." Jeannette dabs her mouth with a napkin. "Miguel's donated tonight."

Local restaurants are always bringing leftovers to the hospice. It's sort of weird to think about—there's never a food shortage for people who mostly can't eat.

I wander through the empty cafeteria to the kitchen, where one of the nurses is chowing down a chimichanga while reading a paperback. He glances up and smiles. "Johanna, right?"

Yikes. I don't remember his name. "Hey . . . you," I say lamely. The badge on his scrubs is covered by a jean jacket. He's either coming in or going out.

A tray of taquitos warms on the stove behind him, and as I lift up the foil, his cell rings. "Babe," he speaks into it. "Where are you?" He gets up and leaves with his chimichanga.

*Solo mío.* I find a plate and help myself. Jeannette wanders in. "I'm sorry about Mrs. Arcaro," she says. "I know you were close."

I nod and swallow. Mrs. Arcaro came to the hospice during the time Mom was here. I could've cared for Mom at home until the end, but Tessa decided I wasn't capable. Even though I'd been doing it by myself the whole time she was sick.

"Frank's been agitated all day." Jeannette pours herself a cup of coffee. "Maybe you could drop in and see him?"

"Sure," I say. Frank's this grizzled old guy about ninety years old who has dementia and diabetes and I don't know what all. He doesn't have any family, or at least no one who cares enough to visit. Too many people die alone in this world.

On my way to the ward, I stuff the rest of my taquito into my mouth. Frank's laid out in bed, masturbating.

*Ew.* "Frank?" I say softly. "It's Johanna."

He rubs his wanker. It's dark and wrinkled. "Frank?"

Nothing is really happening. No hardening of the, you know, arteries. For privacy, I pull his blanket over his lap. His eyes are far away and he has a quirky smile on his face.

It makes me smile inside.

*Go for it, Frank.*

# Chapter 4
## *Joyland: Take 3*

We're in this amazing bed, naked, spinning around and around—because the bed is round. Reeve is kissing me and I'm all over her, running my hands through the hair on her head and between her legs. She's soft and firm and arching into me.

She says, "Johanna. I love you. I want you."

"I want you too," I say. "I want you bad."

The bed spins and spins. We spin harder and faster, out of control. She screams, "Don't stop!"

"I won't. I promise."

She expels a breath like she's emptying her lungs or cleansing her soul. I breathe her in and out. I run a red silk scarf over her flat belly and around her breasts and in between them. She unties the red ribbon in my hair to unleash my ponytail and my hair splashes like a waterfall over her face. She holds it back and I kiss her. I kiss her so soft and gentle it's mist and fog. It's spray. The beating of my *heart is constant and steady, sharp as knuckles on wood and metal and pounding on wood and pounding, pounding. . . .*

. . .

Knocking? Someone is knocking.

What time is it?

I hold myself for one last surge, then stagger out of bed to answer the door.

Dante looms behind Novak, grinning like the fool he is. "Hey ya, Joho," he says.

I hate that he uses Novak's nickname for me.

"Hi, sweetie." Novak kisses me on the cheek. "We came to say hi. Hi." *She's* high. She slides past me into the apartment and I consider shutting the door in Dante's face. He's tall and thin, with razed hair and a shadow beard. His clothes are always the same—tight black tee and loose jeans that creep down his butt. One eyebrow is pierced.

I loathe this jerk for all the hurt he's laid on my friend. But she loves him. I have to honor that stupid fact.

"What time is it?" I check my watch. 7:46—p.m. I vaguely remember deciding I'd skip Film Studies to sleep in.

Dante tramps to the refrigerator and yanks it open, removes a can of Fresca. My Fresca. He pops the top and slugs it down.

Novak rests her head on my shoulder. "I love you, Johanna Banana," she says.

"Give me a minute," I tell her. "I'll bail."

"You don't have to." Novak snuggles in tighter. She's too close and I'm too needy.

I'm also hot and sticky. I beat a path to my bedroom to

change from my drawstrings into jeans, wishing, not for the first time, that my bedroom door had a lock. Novak knows it's off-limits, but I don't trust Dante.

When I emerge into the living room, Dante has Novak's shirt up around her neck and her bra unlatched. I snatch a hoodie off the divan and yank the door shut behind me.

The door whooshes open. Novak says, "Johanna," breathing hard. She wrestles her shirt down over her boobs and hands me something. "You can borrow it," she says.

They're keys to her Crossfire. "You're kidding."

She smiles weakly. "What would I do without you?"

"Get a hotel?" I say.

She blows me a kiss and shuts the door.


I sit in the Crossfire for two or three minutes, swooning, scared to crank the ignition. Plus, I don't know where to go. The hospice? The tweenie town mall? What a waste of a hot car.

Slowly, carefully, I shift into first and inch away from the curb. I drive around the neighborhood, getting used to the gears, the feel of the clutch and brake. The Crossfire was Novak's eighteenth-birthday present from her parents. My parents didn't quite make it to mine. The interior is white leather, no backseat. Too cramped for sex. But there's an MP3 player, GPS, OnStar.

Mickey D's is all lit up, a queue of cars at the drive-thru, honking and flashing their lights. Someone moons out the top of a convertible.

I idle at a red light, accidentally gunning the engine. A guy hollers, "Novak, you cunt! Suck my bone!"

I auto the window down and flip him the bird. Guys are so . . . typical.

An idea springs loose and I zip into the far-left lane, gunning for the Interstate.

I only know about Rainbow Alley from a flyer in film class. The Gay/Straight Alliance was hyping this horror-movie night at Rainbow Alley. I was too gutless to join the GSA, mostly because I knew Reeve was in it. Reeve and the other LBDs. Those girls, their tribal unity, intimidate me. Reeve doesn't just scare me. She terrifies me. It gets worse every day, this smoldering want, my crushing need. I think I've been in love with Reeve Hartt since the first time I saw her.

Why can't I just approach her, talk to her? The ache I feel every time I see her. It's killing me.

In downtown Denver, I drive past 1050 Broadway three times. No neon pink triangles or flashing rainbow flags. But there is an actual alley behind the building, so I veer into it.

Suddenly, the night opens up like Narnia. Lights glow, music blares.

Two people come racing down the alley, one squealing, the other chasing her with a pump water gun. They run in front of me and the guy with the gun thunks on the hood of the Crossfire.

"Hey!"

"Sorry." He holds the water gun over his head and sticks his face in my open window. "Tight wheels."

"Thanks."

He streaks off again.

I take a deep breath. Okay, I can do this. Now or never? Now. Cars and SUVs hog the cramped parking lot. The back door to the two-story building is propped open with a chair, and voices and music float out. On the fire escape stairs, a couple of girls are cuddling and kissing.

*Can I do this?*

*Yes! Dammit.*

I lick my dry lips. *Will I see her?*

The door to the Crossfire opens and my legs swing out. The girl from the chase-down says, "Bitchin' car." Her shirt's soaked.

"Thanks," I say. "It's not mine."

Her eyes waffle. "You jacked it?"

I stare at her nipples. "It's a friend's."

She eyes the interior over my shoulder. "Bitchin' friend. Introduce me."

I laugh, and so does she. She's a boy dyke, or whatever, with a shaved head and hairy legs. Not really my type, but what *is* my type? I have only one: Reeve Hartt.

"You here for the karaoke?" she asks.

"Um . . . I guess."

"Starts soon. I'm Tiffany." She extends her hand. "T."

"Johanna," I say, shaking it. She holds my hand longer than a simple greeting requires. Testing, feeling out the possibilities.

I loosen my grip.

T sighs and says, "Come if you're coming."

*Am I?* The lock on the car door clicks. I guess I'm coming.

The kissers on the stairs part to let us through. They nod at Tiffany and check me out. What do they see?

Tall girl, broad shoulders, average weight, longish, straight hair, tight jeans, sleeveless shirt. Converses. God, I should've dressed more sexy. I should've put on makeup.

T slows at the top of the stairs and leans against the door to let me pass. She checks me out the whole way. My eyes avoid hers as they soak up the scene.

A rectangular room, painted all different colors, a mural on the far wall. I can read the letters: PRIDE. There are two long couches and armchairs, people lounging. A girl sitting on a boy's lap. A guy fiddling with a microphone in the center of the room puts his mouth to it and says, "Pick up. Shut up." People begin to claim folding chairs and scrape them around to sit closer to the karaoke machine.

T touches my back. "See you," she says, and takes off.

People are talking and laughing, flipping through the karaoke notebooks. Reeve materializes out of the mural. She's playing pool with two other girls behind a beaded curtain.

She bends over to line up her shot and I can see clear down her halter. One of the girls with her I know from school. Brittny? Britt? She and Reeve were together last year, then they weren't.

Someone nudges me and I gulp a can of air.

"In or out?"

A kinetic surge draws me in, toward her. I stall under a string of twinkling lights.

I can't see if Reeve makes her shot. Her eye makeup tonight is dark and heavy. She's intense. Guarded.

Britt saws her cue stick back and forth over her hand

three, four times, and strikes the white ball. It smacks one of the striped balls, sending it careering into a side hole. Britt whoops.

Reeve's expression doesn't alter, even when she glances up and catches my eye. Or does it?

Does she recognize me? She circles the table, her back to me, and lines up her next shot.

## Joyland: Take 4

She turns slowly toward me. Her eyes, they drink me up. She closes the distance between us and asks, her voice low and sultry, "Do you play?"

I smile. "I never have," I say.

She knows the truth when she hears it. "Do you want to learn?"

My smile widens. "I do."

I sweat and shiver at the same time. She doesn't speak, but the vibes between us are fingernails on a chalkboard, increasing their pressure and volume until my ears whine and my teeth hurt.

She leads me to the table. Hands me her cue stick and slides around behind me. All eyes in the room are on her—us. All the girls want her, and some of the guys too. She takes me in her arms and I drop the stick on the floor.

*She laughs. So do I. I retrieve the stick. She sets it on the table.*

*Her lips start out hard as molded plastic, then turn soft as padded felt.*

*She runs her hands up under my shirt and the twinkling lights explode.*

. . .

"Excuse me." A guy touches my arm. "I have to use the john."

I step aside to let him pass.

The karaoke blares and I'm swarmed; I lose sight of Reeve. As the crowd clears, I see her kissing a nameless girl. The girl has no face, no arms or legs or physical presence. No meaning to me.

A sharp edge gouges my arm.

"You want the book?" a guy asks. The black three-ring binder. The karaoke songbook.

"No, thanks."

Everything's tilting, listing in place. I refocus.

*Where is she?*

I scan, but don't see her. Maybe what I saw was a . . . projection? The person she was kissing was me, the girl I want to be.

The cue sticks are on the table, as if her game was interrupted. There, at the top of the stairs leading to the exit, I catch a glimpse of her ice blue halter.

A mob of people cram the doorway, all coming in for karaoke. I murmur, "Excuse me. Excuse me. Sorry," as I maneuver my way through. "Ow!" a girl yelps when I step on her foot.

"Sorry." I wince.

She smiles. "That's okay. Hi."

Reeve is bounding down the stairs, the other two girls ahead of her. She leaps from the bottom step, throws back her head, and cries, "Yee-ow-eeee!" at the top of her lungs. She smacks each of the girls on the back, sending Britt stumbling forward into an SUV and the other girl tripping. Reeve dances in a circle.

Britt hollers, "Reeve, dammit! That hurt."

Reeve laughs and laughs.

I stand on the landing, at the railing, breathing in her laughter. She slows near an SUV and pounds on the hood, as if she's beating out excess energy.

Britt goes, "What is your problem?"

Reeve says, "You."

The other girl, who isn't anyone, who isn't even there, unlocks the car door. Reeve dances over to her and grabs a clump of her hair. She yanks the girl's head back, gazes down into her face, and kisses her. I black out.

When I come to, Reeve is staring at me.

"Butt brain!" she yells. "Move ass."

Robbie emerges from under the stairs. He ambles to the car. Tossing his case over the seat to Reeve, he squishes into the back with her.

As the car pulls away, Reeve's head pops up through the moon roof. She cups both hands around her mouth and calls, "Cooperate with Johanna!"

OMG. She knows my name!

# Chapter 5

The apartment door is hanging wide open. I barrel up the stairs and stop. There's a tall, shadowy figure in the kitchen, behind the refrigerator door.

Retreat? Go downstairs? Call 911? Scream? The guy leans back. It's Dante, buck naked. He shuts the refrigerator door and says, "Joho." He hitches his chin at me, then guzzles the beer. My apartment reeks. He burps. "Whassup?"

"Where's Novak?"

He notices he's dangling all over and steps behind the counter. Novak appears in the hallway, also naked, tossing her hair over one side of her head with her arm.

She's illuminated by light filtering through the hall from the bathroom. Her eyes meet mine, but I can't hold them. She has smaller breasts than I imagined, probably because she always wears push-up bras. Her hair is reddish blond . . .

down there. She drops her arms and straightens her back, like she doesn't mind me looking, like she's *inviting* me to look.

Dante skitters past Novak, covering his privates, clipping her arm and spinning her sideways.

"You were in my room," I say.

Novak crosses her arms over her breasts.

*Fuck*, I mime. My glare reams her out.

"Hang on." She backs up and disappears into the room— *my* room—behind Dante. I fling my pack on the divan. *Damn. Damn her!*

In a moment Dante comes out dressed, Novak cowering behind him. "Later, Joho," he says to me.

"Don't ever call me that."

He saunters past, taking his sweet time. I plant my feet and stare at Novak.

She bites her lip, nears me, shoulders hunched. "I'll buy you new sheets?" she offers.

God! I clench my jaw and turn away. Novak stops me, her hand extended.

"What?"

"My keys?"

I dig them out of my pocket and smack them into her palm. She goes, "Johanna, you just don't understand. You've never been in love."

"You just shut up. And leave."

She looks stung.

*She's* hurt? How dare she invade my bedroom? The place where Reeve and I . . . Where Reeve and I . . .

What? There is no Reeve and I. But one day . . . there might . . . *Will.*

"Johanna . . . I'm sorry."

She made my bed, which makes it worse. I never make my bed. Bundling the sheets in my arms, I storm downstairs to the garage, stuff the sheets in the washer, and dump a heap of Cheer on top. It's jammed wall to wall in here. Mostly Mom-and-Dad things. Tessa said I should go through them and I said she should.

As the washer fills, I flip over a full laundry basket and plop on top, elbows on knees, staring into the abyss. My face drops to my arms, then hands, and I feel it. The longing.

I miss Mom so much. Dad had Parkinson's and died of complications when I was twelve, but he was never all that present in my life. Mom and Dad met late in life and didn't start having kids until they were ancient. After Dad died, Mom sank into this deep depression. No one could lift it. Certainly not me. She just deteriorated, then she got sick and I got stuck.

*No.* Not for one moment do I regret a single second I got with Mom. The service club, chorus, all my extracurricular activities, time I might've spent with friends—I don't feel I sacrificed anything to make Mom's life easier at the end.

*Don't think about it, Johanna.*

Think about how hot Reeve looked tonight. In that faded baby blue halter with her destroyed jeans that sit so low they expose her sharp hip bones and smooth belly. She's so small, tiny. Lately she seems even leaner. I bet I could get one hand around her upper arm. I'd like to take both of them and pull her into me. Kiss her, meld her lips to mine. Her lips aren't small. They're her most distinguishing feature. Lush. Her eyes and her legs, her hips, waist, breasts. She has bigger breasts than Novak, I bet. Reeve tests the limits of the school dress code, for sure. She always wears these revealing tops with plunging V's, or string camis to show off her breasts. Why not? They're . . . scrumptious. She doesn't need a damn push-up bra.

That's Reeve, always flaunting it and proud to show it off.

Wish she'd flaunt it at me.

"Johanna?"

My elbows buckle and I wobble to my feet.

Tessa pushes her bangs back and a shock of hair sticks up in front. "Why are you doing laundry at this hour?"

"Did it wake you up? I'm sorry."

"Nah, I was up."

She still has her name badge on from work. She shakes off her fatigue, or whatever, and says, "If you get the urge . . ." Her arm sweeps across the ocean of laundry at our feet.

"I'm not feeling it," I say.

She cracks a smile. It's the most genuine exchange we've had since she moved home. Since Mom asked her to come back to handle all the financial affairs. Even though I could've done it. Tessa had been starting grad school; she flew home every other weekend, then flew back to be with Martin. I could've quit school and easily gotten my GED. I *told* Mom that.

Tessa and I stand for a long minute looking at each other, then it gets weird and we both look down.

"Martin has solemnly promised to go through all his boxes. He's such a pack rat. He won't throw anything away that has sentimental value."

"Good thing you don't have that problem."

Tessa gives me a funny look.

My eyes stray to her belly. There's maybe a bulge?

Why'd you leave Colorado? I want to ask. Why'd you have to go all the way to Minnesota? Didn't you get my letter? I want to ask. The last one, the important one? Does Martin hold you at night and tell you he loves you? Does his skin feel warm and does he make love to you when you want him? Is he there for you when you need him? The way you weren't there for me? And still aren't?

Tessa yawns, then does this thing with her jaw where she shifts it left and right until it pops.

It's always annoyed me.

She says, "Don't stay up too late."

I want to say, Talk to me. Will you please just talk to me about the letter?

Seniors have off-campus privileges and most drive to Pizza Hut or Mickey D's, but Reeve always stays in for lunch. She sits with the LBDs.

She stays, so I stay. There are separate blocks of designated tables, like ethnic neighborhoods. The gays and lesbians don't even associate much, since gay guys eat with their straight girlfriends.

When Novak's here, we sit with the stoners and skaters, like today. She sets a tuna fish sandwich from the machine in front of me and slides in across on the bench. "I owe you so much," she says. "You're my BFF forever."

"Redundant," I say. I sit so I can see Reeve. So I can bore my eyes into her soul and hope she feels me.

Novak rips open a bag of Doritos between us. "Dante says thanks, by the way, for use of the hospitality suite."

My gaze wavers long enough to fire a flare at Novak. I take a bite of sandwich. Reeve's spearing green beans onto a fork. There's a girl between her and Britt, some other nameless and faceless lesbian, jabbering away, telling a joke or something. Everyone laughs. Except Reeve. She bites each end of bean off the fork and chews, then holds the rest between her teeth.

I concentrate hard: Look up, Reeve. Look at me. See me. Feel the purity of my love for you.

". . . next Friday. And maybe Saturday too?"

Reeve raises her head a fraction of an inch and I think, Here!

Novak kicks my leg, diverting my attention.

"Are you listening to me?" She shakes the Doritos bag in my face. "Eat."

I remove a chip. Reeve returns to stabbing beans.

"So, do you mind?"

Reeve stands with her tray and I almost shoot up in reflex. "Mind what?"

"Letting us use your place both nights? Note how I'm asking you in advance?"

Reeve dumps the remaining contents of her lunch into the garbage, stacks her tray on top, and takes off. Where does she go? It's the same routine every day.

"Earth to Lesbo."

I turn on Novak. "Don't fuck Dante in my bed. Stay out of my room, I'm warning you. Don't bring beer or pot to the apartment, and be gone when I get home."

Novak flinches. Then she bats her eyelashes and salutes. "Yes, sir. Could you post the rules, sir? I'm a little slow, sir."

She must feel my rising simmer, because she reaches across the table and runs her fingers under my jaw. "Johanna, whatever you want."

I falter. I want it bad. Then I remember this is Novak.


Robbie doesn't show after school. I wait forty minutes, sitting at Mrs. Goins' desk, facing the door, watching the hall. Forty-two. Forty-three minutes.

He's not coming. Neither is she. A curtain of despair draws closed inside me.

# Chapter 6

The veg girl's mother is leaving the hospice as I walk in. I shouldn't call her that. Carrie—that's the girl's name. I've only seen her once, when I was delivering flowers to the private ward and her mother was carting in luggage.

Carrie was in a car accident. She was speeding, joyriding after a party, and the other three people in the car died. Carrie lived, if you want to call it that. Her family decided to take her off life support, hoping for the best—the best being that she'd pass quietly and quickly.

It's been five months. People stopped coming by after the first month. Now the only person who visits regularly is the mother.

She complains about everything. Carrie's room, her bed, the linens, the room temperature, the level of attention Carrie gets. Nothing the hospice workers do is enough. I think at the end of life, enough is enough.

Jeannette's on the phone and I don't want to stand around being useless. There's harp music streaming out of one of the private rooms and it pulls me down the hallway.

Carrie's door is cracked, so I stick my head in and see she's covered to her chin, her sheets tucked in so tight she couldn't budge an inch if she did regain consciousness. Which she won't.

I slip in and sit in the chair beside her bed. Her face is like molded wax. Her hair has been curled and makeup applied. Her mother can't even let her die in a natural state.

Carrie's head is bent at a stiff angle and I relax her chin. Better. Her lips look dry. I open her bedside table to find her lip gloss. She has one kind, a favorite flavor, I'm guessing. Strawberry mango. I squirt a dab on my index finger and smooth it across her lips.

She doesn't move, doesn't react, doesn't alter her breathing. "I'm here," I say softly, pressing on her shoulder. "You're not alone."

Mom always said I was such a comfort to her—when she was still verbal. It's how I know what I'm doing here matters.

Carrie has her own bed linens and down comforter. I remove her hand from under it, loosen the sheets, and crook her elbow so her arm will rest comfortably while I hold her hand. Her fingers are cool. I rub them. She wears a class ring, engraved gold with a garnet. I run a thumb over the loose ring. Carrie is shrinking.

Her cheeks are caving in. She's beautiful, though. Even now.

## *Joyland: Take 5*

She eases open my bedroom door and slices through the darkness. Opaline edges outline the contours of her body. I can't see her face, but I know it's her.

"Johanna," she whispers in the night.

"Reeve," I whisper back.

"Do you want me?" she asks.

"You have to ask?" A finger of electricity tickles the back of my neck. She doesn't move, but her eyes fix on me, weld my soul to hers. She says, "How much?"

I can't express in real numbers the depth of my desire for her. "Reeve," I say. "The universe and beyond."

She laughs a little. There's a hint of nasty in that laugh. In a sexy, smoldering way.

"Come here," I say. She notices that I'm naked on the bed. "Please?"

*"Show me the money."*

*"It's all here."*

*She rushes in and flings herself across me, making me squeal and clasp my arms around her back. She starts kissing me on the cheek and eyes and nose. Her face is poised inches from mine.*
*"Made you beg." She grins.*

*Made you mine, I think.*

. . .

Mrs. Goins stops me in the hall on my way to class. "How's Robbie's essay coming?" she asks.

"He's working on the second part. About the worst thing." I know it's not cool to rat him out, but my motives are ulterior. "He didn't show up yesterday."

Mrs. Goins' eyes narrow. "I'll make sure he gets there today. If you've gotten him to write anything, you're a miracle worker. Thanks again, Johanna." She smiles. Something in that smile reminds me of Mom. Then it's gone.

She pats my arm. "It'll all be over soon."

I don't need it all to be over; I need it all to begin.

An impulsive, instinctive need to know compels me to follow Mrs. Goins into the staff room. "Can I ask you something, Mrs. Goins?"

Her head swivels.

"About Robbie."

She surveys the area and her eyes light on an empty table. "Over here." She motions me to follow.

There's a teacher at the Xerox machine. He says, "Morning, Paige. Counting down."

"Fourteen days," she says.

A knot of panic clenches my chest. Fourteen days. I'm running out of time.

Mrs. Goins says to me, "I'm retiring."

"You are?" I sound shocked. I guess I am. I thought teachers kept going and going until they died at their desks grading papers.

"What is it you want to know, Johanna?"

I wait for the other teacher to collect his copies and leave. "What's wrong with him?"

"Wrong?" Mrs. Goins pours herself a cup of coffee. "He has a slight deficiency, if that's what you mean."

Slight?

"Although it's puzzling," she says, dumping in about a pound of creamer. "He isn't mentally challenged, according to his IQ test. He's been termed a 'highly functional autistic.'"

Termed? Were we all "termed"?

Mrs. Goins adds, "I'm not really at liberty to discuss his case."

Like you just did? The bell rings and I jump.

"Do you need a hall pass?" Mrs. Goins asks.

I shake my head no.

As I race up the stairs to class, I think, Robbie's a case. What does that make Reeve?

Fourteen more days. No time to waste.


Robbie's head is down and he's writing away, hunched over his paper. He brought his own paper and pen and finger string and the instrument case, of course. It's perched precariously on the edge of the desk beside him. As I pass, I reach out to balance it. Robbie clenches my wrist.

His hold is insistent but gentle. He lets me go.

"What's in it?" I ask.

"M16," he replies.

"Is that a saxophone?"

"Cruise missile," he says. "Set to detonate on impact. The slightest movement and . . . KABOOM."

I flinch.

He shoves the case under the desk beside him. It unnerves me, the way his eyes suddenly retract and die. He resumes scribbling. He's not that bad-looking. From this angle, I mean, if he shaved or got a decent haircut. He has a round chin with a divot in it, same as Reeve. Her face is more chiseled, though. Her dimple is only noticeable to someone who notices her every amazing detail. Robbie has dark patches of stubble on his chin, down his neck. If you squint and blur his features, like Impressionist art or something, he's kind of cute.

His eyes, though. Empty holes. No emotion behind them. Is that the autism?

I slide my pack on top of the teacher's desk and sit in the chair. "What are you writing?" I ask.

He doesn't hear? Or the distance between us is so vast my words don't reach him, or his brain, his highly functional autistic—

*She's here. I feel her.*

I get up and glide in her direction. She's close.

*Six, five, four feet away.* There's a moment when my curtain seems too heavy to lift, or part. What's on the other side?

Fear?

Anticipation?

No.

Need. Desire. My arms extend, press against the curtain and . . .

She's sitting on the floor in the hall, huddling against the brick wall, her knees to her chest, head buried. She's clutching her legs so tight her arms lock. She's . . . shivering?

"Reeve?"

She jerks her head up and scrambles to her feet. We stand for a moment, face to face.

Close enough to notice her dimple. A solid wall of fire combusts between us. Does she feel it?

"Is Hell Boy ready?" It takes a moment to absorb her words, the fact that she's talking to me. When she cranes her neck to peer into the room, her head is an inch away from my arm. "Come on, we're going to miss the last bus!" she calls to him.

Robbie's pen lifts. His thought seems to suspend in midair, then evaporate.

Reeve steps away from me.

I step toward her.

Her head shakes from side to side as she keeps moving back.

Robbie barrels out the door, nearly knocking me over.

They're gone.

I rock on my heels and grind my palms into my eye sockets. Time bleeds away behind my eyes. Fourteen days left. All the time wasted. As I trudge back into the room to grab my pack, an object snags my attention. His case.

He forgot his case.

But if it *is* a bomb . . .

*Stupid.* It's *not* a bomb.

But if it's motion-activated . . .

I pull it out from under the desk and pray for the end to be quick.

A city bus crunches to the curb and they get on. I note the bus number, then sprint to my car.

The bus veers onto I-70 and exits at Vasquez, heading into Commerce City. Two stops to let people off, then Reeve and Robbie descend. I tail as inconspicuously as possible, ducking down every time I see Reeve look over her shoulder. Which she does a lot. She and Robbie turn up a gravel driveway and I swerve across the street to park.

What if they're just cutting through a yard? As I'm checking my side-view mirror to merge back into the street, I see Reeve through a picture window. This is her house. I twist off the ignition.

The yard is fenced with chain-link, sections of it sagging or bent to the ground. It's really just dirt and weeds. The houses here are old, crumbling, with flat gravel roofs.

Her yard is littered with trash. A garbage bag has burst open and spewed its contents across the yard and into the neighbor's.

I lock my door and sit for a while, psyched—I know where she lives.

One corner of her porch is caved in, like someone took a sledgehammer to the concrete. Upstairs there's black paper covering a window. Her room?

A van rumbles up the narrow street and takes a wide arc, almost ramming me. It squeals around me into the driveway. A guy jumps out and screams, "You *whore*! Don't you ever fucking run out on me again! I'll kill you!"

I cower down inside my car. He storms around the front of the van and wrenches open the passenger door. "Get out, cunt."

He reaches in and drags this lady out *by the hair*. As she flails her arms to detach the guy's hands from her head, he throws her down face-first in the driveway.

*Oh God, oh God.*

"Get up."

She struggles to her knees.

"Get the fuck up." He kicks her.

What should I *do*?

The woman curls into a fetal position.

The guy's hair is slicked back and his piercing black eyes cut so deep they hurt. I know this because he's looking right at me. When did I open my door and get out?

The guy knees the woman right in the face. I gasp as her head flies back and blood spurts from her mouth or nose. *Call 911! I don't have a phone.* The maniac is starting toward me!

I launch back into my car. As I switch over the ignition, he stops, pivots, and saunters back.

I turn the car off and slide down into the seat. I should . . . get out! Help that lady! Call the cops!

I can't. I'm paralyzed.

Reeve comes out, yells, "What'd you do to her?"

I sit up straight. The guy's disappeared.

Reeve bends to the woman and lifts her up. The front door

of the house crashes open and the guy appears on the rickety porch. He's guzzling a longneck beer, peering down the street at me. Salutes me with the bottle.

I shrink in my skin.

Reeve balances the woman on her hip. "Bastard!" she screeches at the man.

The beer bottle corkscrews through the air, narrowly missing Reeve's head, but hitting the lady square in the back. She lurches.

"Stop!" Reeve yells.

*Now.* My eyes graze the corner of Robbie's case on the seat, and I reach for it, then catch a glimpse of Robbie near, the van. He scans the lady and Reeve says something to him.

Robbie smashes over a section of chain-link fence.

Reeve screams, "Robbie, no!"

He rushes the guy.

"No!" Reeve cries. "Robbie, no!" She shoves the woman against the van and charges after Robbie, who slams the guy down on the cement and starts to strangle him. Reeve jumps on Robbie's back, pounding and screeching.

Now I'm bolting from the car and racing to the porch. Reeve is trying to pry one of Robbie's hands off the guy's neck. I take the other.

Her eyes lock on mine.

The guy chokes and coughs. Robbie's so strong. I snake my arm around his neck and yank back. That loosens his grip enough for Reeve to lodge between them and push Robbie off.

Up close the guy's face is greasy, pockmarked. He clamps on to Reeve's arm and she fists him in the face. "Don't touch me," she says. "Don't you fucking touch me."

I have Robbie cuffed by his arms in back, but I know I'm not really holding him. He's wheezing.

The guy crawls to the edge of the porch and over the side. He says to Reeve, "Just ask your mother if she was using."

Reeve snarls, "If she is, I know who set her up." She looks at me. Her eyes become veiled and she curses under her breath.

Robbie twists out of my grasp and clomps toward the driveway.

The guy retrieves his beer, throws back his shoulders, and grins at me. "Bull dyke to the rescue."

Reeve just fixes on me and this fleeting expression crosses her eyes. Pain? Anger? She flings open the front door and disappears.

Leaving me outside alone. With *him*. His grin widens.

My brain informs my feet to move! I back down the walk, then turn and run. A shudder shakes my whole entire body.

He isn't coming after me, thank God.

That look on Reeve's face haunts me all the way home. It went beyond horror and humiliation. I shouldn't have interfered. But I had to.

I'd do anything for her.

# Chapter 7
## *Joyland: Take 6*

Snow sifts through the branches of our wild juniper, catching on needles and frosting berries. It's the middle of summer and the snow brings a welcome relief from the heat. We can have snow in our summer, anytime we want it. She's lying next to me on a towel, catching snowflakes on her tongue. A fluffy crystal lands on the tip and she curls her tongue at me. With my lips, I accept the offering.

A wind kicks up and blows so hard it yanks the branches. One breaks away and slams down on Reeve. I'm strong; I hike the branch and launch it. She's unhurt, smiling up at me.

Her eyes are blue-black, glittering diamonds of winter summer solstice. She snaps her fingers and casts a spell on me. We're in a snow globe, glitter raining down on us and sticking to our silver skin. She looks at me and says, "You saved me."

I say, "I always will."

• • •

Joyland dissolves and all that remains is flat terrain. I want to fall asleep so I can dream. But it's late, time for school.

The senior lot is full, so I park across the street. A van careers in front of me, backs up, and rams my bumper. Glass shatters.

Robbie surges out the passenger side and checks the damage.

"Your headlight's broke," he says as I leap out. To Reeve he goes, "You broke her headlight."

Reeve strolls off toward school.

"It's . . . okay. It was already broken," I call to her.

She crosses the street.

"Reeve!" I shout. She doesn't stop.

Robbie says, "You should get that fixed."

"Yeah, thanks." I reach in the car for my backpack. When I straighten, Robbie's in my face.

"She's sorry."

I gaze after Reeve. "I can see that."

He turns and hustles after her.

Damn. I should've given Robbie his case. He got me all rattled with his care and concern about my headlight.

Reeve isn't in the cafeteria with the LBDs. Where is she?

I buy a croissant sandwich from the machine and head out to my car. The van is gone. Chunks of busted headlamp remain. Message received, Reeve. Thanks.

I'd parked so the morning sun beat directly on my windshield and now the interior is stuffy and, oh, about two hundred degrees. I crank down both windows to catch a cross breeze, then lie with my head on the passenger door armrest, legs extended out the driver's side window.

Last spring Novak wanted me to fly to California with her to check out UCLA and UC Berkeley. At that time I'd been so consumed with Mom dying, I hadn't had time or energy to even think about college. Novak and I always talked about going to the same college, rooming together—before Dante.

When Tessa was in college, I wrote to her religiously once a week. She wrote back, but more sporadically. After Mom got sick, while she was on morphine and sleeping a lot, to pass the time I'd write this one letter to Tessa over and over. In my mind I'd see her read it and call me immediately. I got the letter, she'd say. I'm coming home. You don't have to, I'd counter, but she'd already be on the plane. Eventually I finished it. Sent it. And nothing. Most of the drafts are still in my spiral under the bed, along with the love letters I've never given to Reeve.

Letters from Joyland. Love, Johanna.

On the way to class, I make a pit stop.

She's in the restroom, refreshing her makeup, drawing heavy black liner over and under her eye. My stomach jams up my throat.

*This is stupid. We've been through something. We need to talk about it.*

"Hey, do you have any gum or breath mints?" I ask.

Her eyes fix on mine in the mirror, then away.

I move toward the sink and she steps back, like I'm contaminated. "I didn't brush my teeth this morning and the sandwich I ate for lunch was, like, pure onions." *Shut up, Johanna*. I twist on the spigot and thrust my hands under freezing cold water. Did I just tell her I didn't brush my teeth?

She looks like she either wants to say something, or kill me. I turn off the water. The paper towels are behind her and my hands are dripping.

She leans aside.

"Thanks," I say. I can't believe how controlled my voice sounds. "God, I need some gum."

"I don't have any gum," she says. "What were you doing at my house?"

I rip off a square of towel. "Robbie left his cruise missile and I came over to give it back to him."

"His what?"

"Whatever he carries in that case."

"He told you it was a cruise missile?"

"An M16 or something. A motion-detector bomb."

A slight smile cricks her lips. "And you believed that?"

"No. But what *is* in there?"

She ignores the question and turns to leave.

"Look, about what happened at your house—"

A trio of girls bursts through the door, giggling, shattering the fragile connection we're establishing. They jam into a stall and light a cigarette. It gets hot and crowded.

"Where is Robbie's bomb?" Reeve turns back.

"In my car."

Time passes. Babies are born. Old people die.

Reeve says, "Well?"

"Well what?"

She blows out an irritated breath. "Can we go get it?"

"Oh, sure." *We.* She said *we.* My feet move.

Reeve floats beside me and I feel huge, monstrous next to her. Uplifted and weighty both. I hold the outside door open for her.

We don't speak all the way to my car. All the things I can think of to say are weak. Or crucial.

Reeve stands aside while I get the case. As I hand it to her, she says, "Thanks," and our fingers touch. Nerve endings spark.

She turns away. Then turns back. "What you saw yesterday? You didn't see it."

"Okay," I say.

Her gaze drifts down the street.

"I did, though," I say.

She shakes her head.

I have the strongest urge to reach out and touch her. Just . . . touch.

She flinches, as if I had. She says, "No." I let her get away. For the last time.


Robbie bounds into the room a few seconds after me. Doesn't say hi or hello or no or "cooperate with Johanna." Slides into his desk, pulls out sheets of crumpled paper, and starts to write.

I want to ask, How's it going? Though I now know his life sucks on a very serious level.

He has his case with him, I notice. "Um, let me know if you need help, okay?"

Scritch-scratch of pen on paper.

I pull out my checkbook and thumb through the register.

Some fool has entered amounts with no notations of where she spent the money. At the end I wrote in a negative number. What is that? My bank balance? Last month I was overdrawn by more than a hundred dollars, and this month my car insurance is due.

I'm calculating how much I'll make if I work at Bling's every night, all weekend, all summer, every day for the rest of my life when I hear, "Aren't you done yet?"

My head shoots up. Reeve's resting a shoulder on the doorframe, her arms crossed.

"Hi." God. My voice is three octaves higher than usual. I clear my throat. "What time is it?" I check my watch. It's flashing 12:00. Cheap Bling's watch.

She saunters into the room and glances up at the big clock over the door. "Twenty after."

Oh yeah.

Her eyes shift to me. "What is he writing?"

"His memoir. Expect a call from Jerry Springer any day."

Reeve casts me a death look.

Shit! "I'm kidding. It's just the essay. The senior project."

Sometime during the day she had finished her makeup. Mood: murderous. "He won't have any trouble finding a worst moment," she says. "Choosing one, maybe."

"Really," Robbie mumbles.

"What's your *best* moment, asstard?" Reeve asks him.

Robbie stops writing and raises his chin. He doesn't look at Reeve. Or me.

Reeve says, "I bet I know."

Robbie gazes up at her and this powerful emotion passes between them—love or hate or what? It's a communion.

Reeve moves her lips. Robbie shakes his head. She motions with her chin and Robbie stands, cramming his papers into his back pocket.

"Wait." I almost knock his case out of his hand. Reeve has stopped right outside the door; impaled herself against the brick wall, looking like she's bracing for an attack. "What were you doing?" she asks.

"What?"

She rolls her eyes. "You ask that a lot. What? When? Who? You should develop better listening skills."

"Better what?" I smile.

She smirks. "While rat boy was working, what were you doing?"

"You mean, balancing my checkbook?"

"You have money?"

"No. That's the problem."

She holds my eyes. "You have a job?"

"Yeah. At Bling's. In the mall?"

"Career minded." She nods. "I like that in a girl."

"You do?"

Reeve opens her mouth like she wants to say something, like she's *aching* to say it. I know the feeling.

Robbie emerges and she grabs him, tugging him along after her. At the hall intersection, she slows and twists her head around. Robbie keeps going. Reeve reaches in her pocket and tosses me something, which I snag one-handed.

It's a pack of Orbit.

# Chapter 8

I'm feeling energized, euphoric. After an evening at the hospice. After making contact with Reeve. I take the stairs to the apartment two at a time and see there's a note pushpinned to my door: "We need to talk. Come see me if you get home by 9."

Tessa's handwriting is tiny and cramped. My watch face is blank now. Inside, the clock on the cable box reads 9:48. Oops, too late.

I strip and climb into bed.

Sleep eludes me. I taste peppermint from the gum, all of which I chewed. *Reeve.* How she actually remembered and got me gum. The meaning in her eyes, the understanding between us, her gravitational pull toward me. She wore that short stretchy vest that ties under her breasts, over a skimpy tank. She doesn't own a lot of outfits, but she can wear that one every day for me. Her hair is black on top with that blond underlayer. How does she achieve the two-tone effect? Does someone do it for her? Britt maybe. Britt's hair is always highlighted or streaked.

No. I won't associate Reeve with Britt. Or anyone. Only peppermint. I can chew on that all night.

Heaven forbid Tessa should go to bed one minute after nine. She couldn't say, Come talk to me. Anytime.

I roll over and curl into myself. That letter, the one I never should've sent, it changed things between Tessa and me. I don't think . . . she loves me . . . anymore.

She used to call and say, "Do you want me to move back? Because I will. Just say the word." I'd always tell her, "No, everything's fine. Mom can still get around." Even when Mom couldn't, I didn't want Tessa to have to quit college. Tessa would say, "You're so strong. I don't know if I could handle it day after day." She meant watching Mom die.

I'm not strong, Tessa. It's just, some things in life, you have no choice.

I throw off my tangled sheet and pad out for a glass of milk or something. When I open the carton, the odor staggers me backward.

My stomach heaves as I pour the curdled gunk down the sink.

I have to get out of here, go somewhere. Back to the hospice. I throw on jeans and a hoodie. The misty air is heavy with the smell of burning wood. Who's up at this hour building a fire? Reeve and I would, if we lived together. We'd lie in front of the fireplace and make love all night.

Halfway to my car, I stop in the dewy grass. I'm barefoot.

Can you be wide awake and unconscious?

Martin and Tessa are both home, their cars parked side by side in the driveway. I slide open the patio door as quietly as possible. The lights are out, and dark shapes moving in the living room freeze me in my tracks. Martin steps behind Tessa, their silhouettes converging. He holds her around the middle, his hands spread across her tummy. Tessa's hands come to rest over his.

Martin says, "Hmm. Yes, I'm definitely seeing blue. Blue dots. Blue measles. We should name him Spot."

Tessa bops her head off Martin's chest. "Do you really hate the name Martin? We could go with Marty. Or Martina."

Martin says, "Let's stick with Spot." He asks, "When are you going in for your next ultrasound?"

She doesn't answer.

"We're twelve weeks now." Martin smoothes her bangs back from her forehead. "Right?"

The quiet wraps around them. Their last baby died at twelve weeks.

This is my cue to leave. I step back—on a squeaky floorboard. Their heads swivel in unison.

"Mojo?"

"Hey, guys." I wave weakly.

Martin lets go of Tessa but slides his hand into hers and raises it to his lips. "Word up, homie?" he says to me as he kisses her knuckles.

"I got your note," I say to Tessa.

"Oh, right. Don't let your car insurance expire."

"That's it? Gee, thanks for the sisterly advice." I head for the refrigerator.

Tessa follows me. "I mean it, Johanna. I won't let you drive without insurance."

Their milk is fresh. I drink right out of the carton because I know it galls her.

Tessa's cell phone rings in her bag. She fishes it out as Martin sneaks up behind me. He goes to tip up the carton in my face and I twist away. He did that once and I got a milk bath. I chased him out the front door into the street and pounded him good. Martin asks, "What are you doing up at the witching hour, Mojo?"

"Casting a spell on my evil bro-in-law." I wiggle voodoo fingers at him.

Martin smacks his cheeks and ovals his mouth in horror. It cracks me up. He's wearing this t-shirt that says: INTERNET ATE MY BRAIN.

"Geek," I say as I pass him.

"Gangsta." He yanks on my hoodie.

Tessa rushes out of the dining room into the living room. "I just put in a twelve-hour shift," she says into her cell. "Can't you find someone else?"

I say to Martin, "Spot, huh?"

His whole face crinkles in a grin.

I add, "For a middle name, how about Ted?"

Martin bursts into laughter.

My future niece or nephew: Spot Ted Däg. Yeah, I'm *good*.

I'm about to leave when Tessa sweeps back in. She lifts her carryall off the counter and tells Martin, "I have to go back."

"You just got off," he says.

"We're short-staffed. One of the new interns fell and broke

her ankle and Cody has strep. People are lined up around the building."

Martin cocks his head.

"Well, I'm sorry," Tessa says.

"No, it's okay."

God, he's understanding. I'd probably say, How about some me time? Some home time? Tessa works in a free clinic downtown as a nurse-practitioner.

Martin says, "Your jacket's pretty bloody."

Tessa scans the front of her lab coat. "Shit. We had a bleeder today." She drops her carryall and charges through the living room to the bedroom.

Martin expels a long breath. He turns to me. "Spotted Däg goes, 'Woof.'"

"Arf," I say.

*Joyland: Take 7*

*We race across the granite path, tossing off our shoes and shirts. I'm chasing Reeve to Fallon Falls. She's agile and her small, angular body fits between the crevices as she slithers through the rocks to the river.*

*I'm laughing, my hair whipped by the stiff wind, and I'm breathless from chasing her and being this close to catching her.*

*"Reeve!" I call. "Wait up."*

*"Hurry. The show is starting."*

*Firecrackers from nowhere dazzle the sky. It's night and the falls reflect the blue and red and gold, streaks of rainbow water cascading over the edge.*

*Reeve ducks behind the falls, then splits the water, lifting her arms to take the power of the river. She cries out, "Ahweeeeeeeeee. Johanna, come and get me."*

*I'm close, a hand touch away.*

*Then the water sucks her up and she vanishes.*

• • •

By Thursday all seniors are supposed to have reconciled their student fees and fines and cleaned out their lockers. We were advised a month ago to pick up our graduation announcements. The list of graduating seniors is posted on the wall at the guidance center and we have to check the spelling of our names for our diplomas.

I stay home and think off to Reeve.

The ringing phone jolts me aware. Still tingling all over, I straggle out of bed, but I don't get there in time. Novak leaves a message: "Johanna, where are you? I thought we were going to the senior picnic."

That was today? I squint at the clock on the TV. 4:38, p.m.?

"Hey, lesbo. I miss you. Call me as soon as you get this. And, Dante and I are still planning to use your place tonight, right? Okay? Call me. You didn't miss anything at the picnic. You had to bring your own meat, so I took Dante. Caw."

Did Reeve go to the picnic?

I'm starving. If I go grocery shopping, I'll have to write a bad check. I'm not scheduled to work until Saturday, but I call Bling's on a whim. Shondri says, "I got tonight covered."

Figures.

She adds, "That new girl just quit on me, though, so I'll need someone tomorrow night. Maybe all weekend."

"Put me down," I tell her. Yay. I get to eat.

Shondri says, "Is that more than thirty hours? I can't pay you overtime."

"I don't care. I need the work."

"We have to keep it under thirty hours, but plan to be here by four tomorrow and stay till closing."

"You got it."

She hangs on. What?

"You're the most reliable kid I've ever known." Shondri disconnects.

Wow. First of all, I'm not a kid. Second, what's wrong with me that I stay and no one else does?


Novak falls into my arms at the door. "So wasted," she slurs. Her breath exceeds the legal limit. Behind her, Dante smirks.

Detaching from Novak, I grab my bag off the chair and mumble, "Have fun." I want to add, Don't foul my sheets.

Dante says, "You don't have to leave."

"What?"

Novak teeters a moment, then flops onto the divan.

Dante raises an eyebrow.

What is he suggesting?

My eyes fix on Novak. She didn't. She wouldn't tell him. Dante doesn't know I'm a lesbian. But that smirk on his face . . .

*Ew.* Ickiness crawls under my skin.

I stomp out the door and down the stairs. Novak, how could you? I trusted you. And how could you sink so low? This one service project we did as juniors was going around to sixth- and seventh-grade girls, talking to them about the pressures they'll face in high school, the perils of dating. Our group would do role-plays to show girls how to get out of risky situations. Novak was better at it than me, since she'd had experience. Her closing line was always, "No means no. Respect yourself. Protect yourself. Just. Say. No."

In real life, how many times has Novak actually said no to guys, about anything?

All the way to Rainbow Alley, I think about it—her. Novak's been dating since she was twelve; hard dating by middle school. I don't know how many times she's asked me to buy her pregnancy kits.

I'm still shuddering and feeling sort of tainted when I turn into the alley. Does he want, like, a three-way?

Do people actually do that?

Maybe they do.

I'm only looking for a one-way—a one-on-one way.

Fewer cars are parked in the lot, and no kissers or smokers occupy the fire escape. I take the metal stairs two at a time and hit the landing. Posters collage the door—an ad for an indie-band fest, a poetry slam. Music and voices seep into the night from inside. I pull the door open and step in. A bunch of people are sprawled on rugs and pillows in front of the TV—movie night? Robbie's there, sitting on his case on the floor. If he's here . . .

My heart pounds.

She's lounging on a long couch, flipping through a zine. She doesn't see me come in—or does she? She drops the zine on the floor and scoots to curl up against the armrest, hugging her knees.

Nameless girl sits down beside her. She says something to Reeve, smiles and laughs, and nudges Reeve a little on the shoulder. Reeve lashes out an arm, clubbing the girl in the face.

*Geez*. What'd the girl say to her? Because Reeve definitely said NO.

The girl staggers to her feet and starts to cry. Reeve unfolds herself, springs upright, and embraces the girl. She places her hands on either side of the girl's face and kisses her.

I don't see that. It's not real.

Reeve's *mine*. She's saving herself, her *best* self, for me.

I exit the way I came in, clomping down the stairs, tracing the route to my car. A roar in my ears drowns the static and I take off.

My head hurts. My heart hurts. She's everything, everyone I want and need.

Why do I continue to allow myself to believe we're a possibility?

Blindly, I drive into the school parking lot. I don't hear the other car drive in, or the door open, or the footsteps. I don't see it coming. My passenger door swings open and a guy climbs in beside me.

I have the presence of mind to scream.

# Chapter 9

The night swallows me whole as I fling my door open and am submerged in darkness. An SUV swerves into the lot and almost hits me. Brakes squeal. Or is that me, screaming? Headlights flood the interior of my Tercel and the guy gets out. He limps away.

Reeve springs from the SUV. "Who was that?"

I crush her in a hug. "God, if you hadn't come . . ." My arms tighten around her.

She goes stiff and I loosen my grip.

"Who was it?" she says again.

"I don't know. Some guy. He just got in my car."

She searches my face. "I didn't do anything with her," she says.

"What?"

"She's not my girlfriend."

I'm shaken, confused. "I'm sorry." I reach for her. "I mean, I'm glad."

Her lips part and a shallow breath escapes. I'm still hyperventilating, so I draw in a deep breath and exhale hard.

Reeve is here. Close like this, she seems fragile, like a dragonfly.

"What are you doing here?" I ask.

Her eyes flit around the parking lot. "Saving your ass from getting raped?"

"Yeah," I say. "Thank you."

We stand for a moment, looking at each other, into each other. Reeve saw my pain; she saw me run out, ran after me.

She says, "Did you know you were screaming?"

"Was I?"

"I'm deaf, aren't I?"

I grin. She smiles.

She adds, "Why did you come here?"

I check out the lot. "I don't know. It seemed like a safe place to go?"

She just looks at me. "You're kind of weird, aren't you?"

"Possibly."

She tilts her head. "That's a total turn-on for me."

All the blood rushes to my face. Thank God it's dark.

Her eyelids droop. They're painted silver and gold tonight, dazzling and reflective in the moonlight. This night, and that moon, and Reeve.

"Do you have any Orbit?" she asks.

"Will you go out with me?" The words just belch from my brain.

She blinks. "Now?"

"No. I mean, sometime."

"Why not now? Are you hungry?"

"Always."

"You have a cell? We'll call for pizza. Have it delivered here."

My eyebrows arch. "To the parking lot?"

"Hey, it's where you go," she says.

God, she's here, joking around with me. Flirting? I hate to admit I can't afford a cell. "I have a better idea. Let's go get a pizza."

She doesn't say yes or no. It's a stupid idea. "Or—"

"You drive," she says.


The closest pizza place I know is Montoni's, three blocks from the school in this melting pot–ish neighborhood— Italian, Middle Eastern, Vietnamese. Our service club used to meet here.

"I've seen this place," Reeve says as we pull to the curb. "I've never eaten here."

"I have. It's good." I reach for the door handle and Reeve clenches my arm. "I want this to be the first," she says. "For both of us."

First what? Date? Orgasm?

"What about there?" Reeve points. "Have you eaten there?"

My eyes follow her finger across the street to the Ishtar Café and Hookah. "No."

She takes off and I'm sucked into the wake of her comet tail.

The inside of the café is smoky, amber lamps diffusing the haze. There's no hostess or wait staff in sight. Reeve chooses a booth by the lotto machine.

A waiter appears out of nowhere and drops off two menus. He says, "You want hookah?"

Reeve and I look at each other. "Sure," we say together.

The waiter leaves.

Reeve picks up her menu and studies it for a moment. She catches me staring.

"What do you see?" she asks, lowering the menu.

The urge is strong, but I don't jump the table between us. "Two eyes, a mouth, a nose." Real poetic, Johanna. God, I'm freaking out here. I'm with Reeve Hartt on a date.

She smiles. A smile so tender and sad, I want to go to her, hold her, caress her face, kiss her lips, her eyes, nose, throat.

She resumes scanning the menu.

Something stops me from asking the same question of her. No doubt she sees a pathetic, desperate, freaking-out freak. The waiter sets a brass-and-glass urn or vase or goblet thing on the table and sprinkles these round, flat charcoals into a bowl. He lights the charcoal and says, "Shisha?"

Reeve and I go, "What?"

I giggle hysterically. She levels a stare at me.

The waiter says, "Eighteen?" pointing to me, then Reeve.

"Yeah. Do you need ID?" I ask.

He waves me off. "What flavor you like? Apple, melon, mint, cherry, banana, mix fruit . . ." He rattles off a dozen more.

Reeve looks at me and I shrug. We both say, "Cherry."

I smile into my chest. She lets out a small laugh.

He opens a wooden box and selects a square package. Tobacco, I guess. We both watch intently as he fills bowls and assembles the hookah urn. Snaking out from either side are long, skinny hoses covered in braided cord.

The waiter picks up one pipe and mimes what we're supposed to do. He hands me the hose, while Reeve takes the other. The waiter vanishes.

Reeve says, "It's like a bong."

There are mouthpieces at the ends of the pipes and Reeve inserts hers into her mouth. I copy. I suck a little and nothing happens.

I've smoked before with Novak. Not from a bong.

Reeve's eyes rest on me. "Are you getting anything?"

"Dizzy."

She cricks a lip. "Any smoke?"

"No. Are you?"

She shakes her head.

We must not be sucking hard enough, I figure. I try again and water bubbles in the clear globe of the urn. Smoke fills a chamber, and a second later I feel it on my tongue. A bite. It tastes like bark. Or burnt candy.

Reeve's eyes widen.

Oh wow. This is nice.

I inhale and the smoke tickles my throat. It isn't harsh, like cigarettes. Cool, I think. Warm. My muscles and bones and shoulders relax. Reeve closes her lids and inhales.

Her eyes are beautiful tonight. She looks like an angel. Or a water nymph. Provocative pastel eyes. She removes her mouthpiece and smiles.

That smile is total surrender.

"Oh, baby," she says. "So fly."

I'm soaring, all right. Is this legal?

The waiter comes to take our order and we both quickly scan the menu again. I don't know what most of this stuff is. Hummus, I've heard of. Reeve says to the waiter, "Number nine?"

I close my menu. "Same." The waiter leaves.

Reeve picks up her pipe. "Nine's my lucky number."

"Yeah? I'll remember that." We both inhale. Breathing out my last knot of nervousness, I ask, "Why?"

Reeve holds the cherry smoke in her lungs, then expresses a long, visible stream of breath. "That's how many girls I've fucked."

The shock registers only slightly, in my conscious brain. I suck in on the hookah extra hard, filling my chest cavity.

Reeve lowers her pipe. "What do you see now?"

Defiance? Daring? For a moment, though, she lets down her guard. "Two eyes, a nose, a mouth."

Reeve looks away.

"I see nine girls who didn't know what hit them."

A smile curls her lips. "You got that right."

I wave my pipe in the air. "Hookah!" I say.

She laughs, this silky, serpentine laugh that ribbons down my throat.

The waiter sets two football-sized plates in front of us filled with skewered meat and rice and globs of purplish goo. He uncovers a basket of pita bread.

Reeve sets her pipe beside her plate. "I hope you're paying," she says. "I don't have any money."

"I asked *you* out, didn't I?"

She spreads her napkin in her lap. "Thanks," she says. "Seriously."

"Hey, you saved my life. It's the least I can do."

She picks up her skewer of meat and sniffs, then nibbles the tip.

The meat is both chewy and tender. I'm not sure if you're supposed to just eat it off the stick, but that's how Reeve's doing it, so I do too. It's good.

We eat in silence for a minute, testing everything. Reeve says, "So what are the best and worst moments you've had in high school and how has each changed your life?" She dips her skewered meat into the purply gunk. "For extra credit, who gives a shit?"

"Really." Not me. Not now.

Reeve says, "Since you're having difficulty nailing it, I'll go first. Best moment? The day my dad left. Worst moment? The day my dad left."

I feel my forehead furrow.

"He's not the biggest asshole in the world." She lifts her pipe. Her hand is trembling a little when she adds, "There's always someone worse. At the time, you can't imagine who . . ."

We've spiraled into this deep discussion without warning. The urge to reach across and take her hand is overpowering, but my reflexes are slow and my arm won't move.

"Do you have one?" she asks. "Let me rephrase that. Is there an asshole in your life?" She blows out smoke.

My first thought is Dante, but he's *not* in my life. Then the door opens and a guy staggers in. His rheumy eyes graze the booths and glue on me. My stomach lurches. It's the guy who got in my car.

"You don't have to answer," Reeve says.

"No, I . . ." He slumps onto a barstool, turning his back to me.

I refocus on Reeve. "My dad is dead. When he was alive, he wasn't an asshole."

Reeve concentrates on my face. "How'd he die?"

"Parkinson's. Pneumonia, actually. He was older."

Reeve asks, "Well, is your mom a bitch at least?"

My eyes fall. "She's dead too. I live alone."

"How?"

"Cancer. She was—"

"How do you live alone?"

I look up. What does she mean? Like, how do I manage?

"Never mind," she says. "I'm sorry. I have to go."

"What?"

She's scooting out of the booth.

"Reeve—"

"I left Robbie all alone."

"Reeve!" I throw down my skewer. Scrambling to move, I snag my bag and slide out of the booth.

I have to dodge a drunk woman who stumbles off her barstool, then stop at the door because . . . we haven't paid.

I don't have any cash on me, and my checkbook's at home.

Reeve slips out as a man and woman come in. I insert myself between them to follow her. The guilt will gnaw at me later. I can come by tomorrow and pay. I will. But now—

She vanishes in the night. The sidewalk is empty, the street deserted. "Reeve!"

Her slim figure zips between parked cars across the street and I dash after her. The sharp night air is sobering.

My legs are longer and she isn't running very fast, so I catch her and spin her around. She shoves me. She pushes me so hard I fall on the asphalt, crunching my tailbone.

"Don't," she says. "Don't come any closer." Her voice sounds threatening. "I mean it."

I push to my feet, slowly. "Reeve, I . . ."

She backs up a step, then turns and flees. Over her shoulder, she yells, "Don't follow me!"

My heart screams, Go after her! Don't let her go! But my head rules. It always has.

I drag to my car and sit inside, stunned. My butt hurts. What just happened? What did I say, or do?

And what's that on my windshield? I open the door and get out to remove the paper from under my wiper blade. A fifty-dollar ticket for a busted headlight.

Fuck. Can I just catch *one* break?

# Chapter 10

My brain won't stop remixing the scene from last night. Rewriting the ending: Reeve falls in love with me; Reeve comes home with me.

Reeve running from me—that doesn't play in Joyland.

I need mind-numbing activity. Today is senior ditch day, so school won't work. I decide to clean the apartment. It's the first time I've swept under the refrigerator. Entire ecosystems are destroyed.

The phone rings, but I don't get there in time. I haven't bothered to brush my hair or teeth yet, and I'm still wearing the oversized t-shirt I wore to bed. Do I stink? Maybe that's what scared Reeve away. I strip in the bathroom, and as I reach to crank on the shower, the phone rings again. I sprint to the living room to pick up.

"How does a lesbo spend senior ditch day?"

"Scouring the shit from her life?"

Novak is quiet. Then she sniffles.

I didn't mean her. "Novak, I—"

"Everything's fucked," she says. "Can I come over?"

"I have to be at work at four." Kind of cold, I think. But I'm not feeling all toasty warm toward her, not after last night.

"I won't stay long."

I don't say anything.

"Please?"

I realize I ran out here naked and now I'm all goose pimply.

"Yeah, okay. Sure."

Novak's father is an international investment banker. The drive from Countryside Commons, where she lives, is fifteen minutes if you book it.

I take a quick shower and put my tee back on. In the kitchen I've removed everything from the cabinets. What was I thinking?

Was I thinking my life is an empty cupboard? Restock it. There's a can of cream of celery soup that must be left over from when Tessa lived up here in high school. After Tessa left and Mom got sick, I pretty much did all the grocery shopping. Mom would make a list. Until she was forced to leave her own home, she was making grocery lists. A knock sounds on the door.

"It's open!" I yell.

I'm restacking Tessa's Corelle plates as the door whooshes open. "You don't lock your door either?"

I spin around.

"I bring gum." She holds up a pack of Orbit.

My heart does a backflip.

Reeve takes in the chaos and coughs. "Sorry." She fans her face.

Lysol fumes. "I'll open the windows." I rush past Reeve to crack the front window.

"So this is your crib," she says, looking around.

"What?"

She slugs my shoulder. "I'm going to smack you every time you say that."

"Say what?" I smile and she balls a fist.

"Is this how you get high on ditch day?" she asks, dropping the gum on the divan. "Sniffing Scrubbing Bubbles?"

"Yeah, I'm a huffer. Actually, this is the first time I've ever cleaned this place."

Her face lights up. "And I get to share?"

I exaggerate a grin. "Epic."

She smiles back. That warm, tender smile I melt under.

She has on shorts and a faded pink crop top. Her hair's ruffled and loose and her high cheekbones glow with sparkles of glitter.

I haven't even combed my hair. "You could've come earlier," I say, sweeping my mess of tangles over my head. "To share in the first scouring of Terrifying Toilet Bowl."

"Oh snap," she says.

I measure the distance between us, allowing it to close in. Mentally I spin a web around us. No escape this time. She isn't struggling to free herself, just standing here surveying her territory.

I take a step toward her. This is my territory.

"I came to see how you live alone."

Another step.

She tenses, then propels herself across the living room to the dining room, which is the same room, though it suddenly seems larger.

"How did you even know where I lived?" I perch on the arm of the divan. Give her space, I think. The door is close enough that I can block it if she bolts.

Reeve turns and looks at me. Her eyes scan my front and settle on my thighs.

My naked thighs. I realize I don't have anything on under the shirt, which has ridden up. Can she see? Do I want her to?

"How do you afford this?" she asks.

I shrug. "I'm an heiress, sort of."

Her eyes bounce around. "Is there a john?"

"Yeah. He's in the bedroom. You came at a bad time."

She sees I'm joking and grins.

God, I love her smile. I point. "It's down the hall."

Reeve heads that way. My heart is in my throat. Reeve is here, in my apartment. "Wow, you have two bedrooms?" she calls.

I move to the end of the short hall, where it splits into two rooms. "No," I say. "Only one." The other room is a storage closet.

She peers into the cramped closet that's packed with junk. Tessa's sewing machine and skeins of yarn, her dolls and stuffed animals. Maybe that's why this apartment never felt like mine. Too much of Tessa left behind.

"It's a walk-in closet. If you *could* walk in."

Reeve snaps, "You don't know what a closet is." She charges me, bumps me backward, and shuts herself in the bathroom.

I've said the wrong thing—again?

My skin sizzles where she touched me. Water runs in the sink, and I think, Touch everything, leave fingerprints.

Thunks on the stairs draw my attention and Novak suddenly bursts in. "Johanna." She literally throws herself at me.

I remove her arms from around me and flatten them to her sides. Her face disintegrates.

"What?" I say, even though I know what. Make that who.

Novak bites her lip and twists her hair over her shoulder. Her hair is thick and luxurious, the kind of hair you see in shampoo commercials. "I'm sorry about last night," she says. "I didn't know Dante was going to do that." She tries to hold my eyes but can't. "Okay, we talked about it."

My jaw drops.

"You wouldn't have been forced to do anything you didn't want to. You could always say no. And you did." She shrugs one shoulder.

"Yeah. I guess I respect myself."

Novak swallows hard. "It wasn't my idea. We were talking about you and I told Dante you were a lesbian and he thought that was cool. He asked if I'd be willing to do it with you so he could watch."

"You *did* tell him."

I don't know what shocks me more. That she betrayed my confidence about my sexuality or that she agreed to the plan.

"Hey," she adds, "you should be flattered. Guys want you. Girls want you. You don't even have to choose. You know I'd sleep with you, even without Dante."

Our eyes meet and lock.

Novak's intense gaze breaks off and her eyes shift over my shoulder. "You didn't mention you had company," she says flatly.

Reeve is standing in the hallway. How long has she been there? She ducks around Novak and beelines for the open door.

"No!"

She's past me. I race out the door and down the stairs to catch her. "You don't have to go, Reeve. Don't go."

She slows and turns. Her eyes have lost their luminescence. They lift up to the landing, where Novak is slumped in the doorway, separating her split ends.

Reeve heads toward the van that's parked at the curb. I'm not going to let her get away.

Crushing grass in my bare feet, I step into a patch of goathead thorns and yelp. I hop on one foot, trying to brush off the burs as I make my way to the end of the yard, where I stub my toe on the broken sidewalk. "Reeve. Reeve!"

The van door slams shut.

I lunge for the handle. "It's only Novak," I tell her.

Reeve starts the engine. Exhaust coughs out the tailpipe and I have to raise my voice to be heard. "She's just a friend." The window's open an inch, so I know Reeve can hear me. "Please. Whatever you heard . . ."

Reeve meets my eyes. Hers are dark, and deadly.

"Can I call you?" I ask.

A flicker, a trace of uncertainty flashes across her face. She shifts into gear. I press my forehead against the metal trim over the window and ask, "Will you call me? Please?"

She doesn't jam her foot on the gas.

"Do you have something to write with?" I say. "I'll give you my number."

Reeve checks the rearview mirror and drives off.

I storm past Novak on the landing and fling myself onto the divan. A bur is embedded in my foot and I pull my ankle up chest high to dig it out. "Thanks. Your timing sucks."

Novak doesn't say anything.

I glance up to see her checking out my privates. I spin away and stretch my shirt down over my knees.

"Reeve Hartt?" Novak comes over and perches beside me. "You have to be kidding. She's such a skank."

I whirl on her. "Shut up."

Novak flinches. "God. Are you sleeping together?"

The bur pops out, and I throw it at Novak. "That's none of your business." I stand. "That's all you know, isn't it? Not every relationship is only about sex."

Novak says, "I love Dante." She picks up the pack of Orbit beside her. "I'd do anything for him."

*Yeah, like betray your best friend.* I snatch the gum out of her hand.

She sits back and makes herself comfortable. "Can I live with you?"

I glare over my shoulder. "No." *Hell, no.*

"Mom kicked me out."

"Wh-what?" My voice falters.

She drops her head, finds the pricker on the cushion and rolls it between her fingers. "She says I can stay until graduation, then I'm out. She says she knew what was going on all these years. She's always known."

She can't know *all* of it.

"It'll only be for the summer." Novak bends forward, sets the bur on the table, then presses her hands between her thighs. "Please?"

She can't be serious. "Why don't you live with Dante?"

"I can't."

"Why not?"

"His mother hates me." Her head twists to face me. "Every time I come over, she looks at me like I'm a blight on her darling baby's butt. She doesn't even say hello to me."

"Get a place together," I say. "He works. You could work." She's never had to work in her life. Dante works construction part-time, which has to be good money.

Novak sits up and arches her back, raking fingers through her hair. "We want to save our money for the future."

"So you figure you can live here for free? Move in and leech off me?"

She casts me a withering look. "Did I say I wouldn't pay you? Did I say anything about living here for free? I fully intend to pay you rent."

Sure. It's getting warm, so I cross the room to put distance between us.

"Johanna. Please."

No, I think. Don't do this. "What about Dante? You know he'll end up staying here too."

"He'll contribute his share."

Like hell. The three of us living together? "No way. It won't work, Novak. I'm sorry." I head down the hallway.

The divan creaks and I feel her rush up behind me. "Okay," she says. "It's okay. I understand. This won't affect our friendship."

She gives me a hug from behind and my breath catches.

Novak says softly, "Because I am your friend, I have to tell you." She comes around in front of me. Lacing her fingers with mine, she presses down. She's so close I can smell her sweet breath. "Don't get involved with Reeve Hartt. I mean it, Johanna. You'll be in over your head."

## Joyland: Take 8

*We walk along the sandy beach. We're barefoot. We step on glass.*
*Back up.*

*We mount horses and ride. We ride bareback. We canter along the shore. We've both chosen enormous Thoroughbreds. Lacquer black. Only Reeve is willow white. Her legs hang free and her slender thighs press against the horse's flanks. She laughs, high and light, her happiness dispersing in a spray of seawater caught by the wind. Extending her arms to either side as far as she can reach, she spreads her fingers like wings.*

*I ride up beside her and touch her wing tips to mine. We close in, steeple our hands. In silent communion, we interlock fingers and press our palms together.*

*Slowing to a steady lope, we ride in mirrored strides. Our horses bump rumps and snigger, nuzzling like lovers.*

*We telepath our thoughts and feelings.*

*Reeve: Let's ride to the rocks.*

*Me: You're on.*

*I jam my heels into Black Beauty's flanks and the horse spurts ahead. Behind me, Reeve whoops a war cry. She gallops past and heads straight for the water.*

*Danger. "Wait, Reeve." My head drops and my thighs clench hold. I grip my horse's mane and urge her on. "Catch them. Catch Reeve. Don't lose her in the waves. Don't let her drown."*

*Reeve cries again. She's under.*

*Reeve!*

*I call to her, "Hold on, baby. I'm coming."*

*The last thing I see is a spray of black foam.*

• • •

# Chapter 11

Saturday, on my way to work, I stop by the Ishtar Café. No one even remembers we were there. Did I dream it? But I can still taste cherry tobacco at the back of my throat, so I leave money for our unpaid bill.

Eight hours at Bling's, then to the hospice. Carrie's mom is throwing a fit about the cleaning people moving Carrie's pictures so they can dust. She'll do the cleaning and dusting, she says, and she doesn't want that male nurse anywhere near her daughter.

Bitch. Sad bitch.

On the way to Frank's room, I have to pass the room Mom was in. I'm usually okay, but today my knees feel wobbly and my throat constricts. I wish I would've told Mom about me, about who I really am; wish she could've seen me with a girlfriend, being happy. She loved Dad so much. I want love like she had with Dad, like Tessa has with Martin. Why can't I have that? I can, and will.

I sit with Frank, watching professional poker on cable. His eyes are open, but he doesn't see, or doesn't comprehend. He falls asleep around midnight.

There's a manila envelope shoved under my door at home, sealed with tape, no writing on the front. I unclasp it. Five twenty-dollar bills. LATE NOTICE screaming out in big red letters on my car insurance.

Tessa has attached a sticky note: "We need to talk."

Where were you when I needed to hear from my sister so much it almost killed me? Answer that, Tessa Marie Däg.


Robbie shuffles around the bend in the hallway as I watch from the classroom door. He's alone.

"Johanna, Johanna, Johanna," he goes. "I am here to cooperate."

"Where's Reeve?"

He edges past me into the room, not answering. Locating his seat, he drops his pack, positions his case precisely in the middle of the desktop beside him, and sits with his hands folded in his lap.

I linger at the door, hoping, praying, she might be a step behind, riding through the fog on a horse.

The only fog is in my brain.

"Where's your essay?" I ask Robbie, tossing my pack onto the teacher's desk.

He cocks his head. "You don't have it?"

Do I? I dig through my pack. So much crap in here, I can't find anything. I dump the contents onto the desk.

"Just kidding." Robbie whips the pages out of his back pocket. He grins.

Hilarious.

His pages are folded lengthwise and he runs his jagged thumbnail down the crease, then makes a major production out of smoothing the pages over the desk.

"Do you need a pen?"

He produces a pencil from his shirt pocket and, touching his tongue to the sharpened lead, says, "Let us begin."

I study him as he writes. And writes. He has Reeve's intensity of purpose—is that autism?

The clock over the door ticks. Twenty more minutes of babysitting. Wish I had an iPod or cell. Maybe I could find something to read, or clean out my pack.

I feel impatient, restless.

"Can I see what you've written?" I engage Robbie. I get up and walk over to him; extend a hand.

He stops writing and lifts his head. His eyes blip around the room. I sit at the desk beside his, wiggling my fingers.

He drops his arms and slumps. I have to reach over and get the essay.

"March 12," he wrote. "I was born." Brilliant.

"May 23 I kill my mother.

"May 24 Ikilled myfather. May 25Ikilledherfather."

I glance sideways at Robbie. He says, "The plot thickens."

I set the first page aside and begin page two.

When he locked the closet me and Reeve hid in there and he found us. dark is no cover. Reeve says don't say anything she told him no don't. but he didn't lissen .evry night Reeve made me go in and we shut the door and waited in the dark and it was dark and cold and ther were bugs and roches skorpions and spiders in the dark and he'd come and say wer'e playing hide and seek kids and Reeve woud whisper don't say anything don't cry he won't find us in the dark. but he always did. He took me first and Reeve begged him, No take me. In the dark I heard her.The dark is no cover. she didn't cry or scream I screamed. that once. and Ihit him. and after that he took me first.

I force my eyes from the page, my heart hammering in my chest. I look at Robbie. He's staring into his lap, playing with his string.

God, if this is true . . .

**darkdarkdarkdarkdarkdark . . . covercovercovercover**

The rest of this page is filled with that. Then there's a third page.

I cot my mom shooting up and she says get out. I told Reeve she didn't believe me. I get the needle and Ishow Reeve and she takes it.She tells me forget it and stay out of moms way.She keeps the needle. I find it and I smell it smells like viniger. We hide in the closet. Evrynight we

**hide in the closet he finds us. We disappear we cover oursells with all the cloths it's hot and suffcating dark. darkdarkdarkdark we covercover. Reeve says does he hurt you? I say no She says he hurts me. He burns me with his cigarette. He burns me too but I don't tell Reeve.**

I shut my eyes, but the next line has already wormed its way in.

**Reeve cuts. She doesn't know I know . . .**

My stomach hurts. I can't—

I fold the pages together, hoping the words will fester, pop, ooze down the crease and off the page.

I turn to Robbie. "How much of this is true?"

He says, "Negative zero."

Is he lying? I lied on my essay. Everyone lies.

God. I can't turn this in to Mrs. Goins. She'd have social services or whatever all over them. But what if she should? Or what if it's a bunch of bullshit?

Does Reeve cut? I've never seen scars, but I never get past what shows—her face and breasts and legs and eyes. Especially her eyes.

"Where's Reeve?" I ask Robbie again, swinging out of the desk. "Is she coming for you?"

"She doesn't come for guys." He exaggerates a grin. "Do you want me to keep writing?"

"You know what?" I round the teacher's desk. "I think this is enough. Maybe tomorrow we can start on the best moment."

"We?" Robbie asks.

I have cramps. Head and stomach cramps. "You," I say. "I meant I'd be here for you."

He stands and scrapes his case across the desktop, then saunters to the door. He says, "I'm going to meet her now. If you want to come."

She sits cross-legged on the grassy knoll in front of the school, gazing up at the sky. Twisting her head slightly as Robbie tromps down the hill, me behind him. When she sees me, she springs to her feet.

"Hi," I say.

She looks the way I feel: dismantled. We lock eyes. Robbie plops on his case on the grass.

Reeve mumbles, "I need to get Robbie home by four."

"No, you don't," Robbie says.

Reeve fists his temple.

I wince. Does she have to hit him so hard?

She peers up the street. "There's our bus."

"I'll give you a ride home," I say.

A look of horror streaks through Reeve's eyes. "I don't want you coming to my house. Ever. Again."

"Okay. Then I'll drop you at the corner."

She levels me with her stare.

*Reeve, please,* my eyes plead. *Let me help you, be with you.* "Later, then?" I say. "Can we meet somewhere?"

Her eyes lose focus. "Not tonight. I can't tonight."

"Sometime? Anytime."

A long moment passes. I hear the bus grinding to a stop

and she goes, "You don't want this. You don't need me in your life."

I take a step closer to her. In a lowered voice, I say, "Yes. I do."

She can't help but look. Her breath seeps out between her lips.

A hand touches my arm and I flinch. Robbie says, "You know what I want? A grilled cheese sandwich."

Reeve and I go, "Shut up." This makes us laugh.

Reeve hugs his head to her and answers, "Okay."

Okay? To meeting me? Or to the sandwich? The bus door opens and we all tear down the hill. Robbie gets on, then Reeve. I watch through the filmed, scratchy windows as they take seats together near the middle.

The bus pulls out. Reeve turns to look out the window at me. Her eyes hold the longing I feel.


Blaring music in the background amplifies Novak's rant. "If she thinks I care that she's kicking me out, she's delusional. I just can't believe Dad's on her side this time."

She's talking fast and loud. Where is she? I can hear voices and laughter behind her.

"Johanna, are you there?" she screeches.

"Where are you?"

"It's like child abuse, you know? Neglect. They're throwing me out on the street."

Except you're not a child, I want to say. And they've given you everything.

Novak says, "She won't even let me use the pool."

"Well, fuck," I say.

"I *know*. Bitch. I was going to invite you guys over for a party. You could stay the weekend, like you used to. Except instead of sleeping with me, you'd be fucking Reeve Hartt." She coughs a short laugh. "And I'd watch."

"I'm hanging up."

"Come on, Johanna. I didn't mean that," she says in a rush.

The last time I stayed over at her house was Thanksgiving. Tessa and Martin had flown to Minnesota to be with his family, and even though Martin had asked me to come, I knew he was only being nice. But Tessa could've insisted.

We spent the whole weekend at Novak's in the greenhouse getting wasted. Then she and Dante had a fight. She wanted to ask him for Thanksgiving dinner, but her mother said not now, not ever.

"I love you, Johanna Banana," Novak says softly, then hangs up.

Novak. She drives me crazy. But I don't know what I would've done without her, especially this last year.


"What would you do if you knew someone who was in an abusive situation?" I ask Jeannette. We're sitting at the crafts table, molding Play-Doh with Mrs. and Mr. Mockrie. They have Alzheimer's, which I think is kind of sweet, both of them losing their minds together.

"Who?" Jeannette asks. "Who's in an abusive relationship?"

"Someone. A friend. It's a family situation."

97

Mr. Mockrie rolls a fat snake.

Jeannette stops pounding her Doh and looks hard at me. "Is this someone I know?"

"No." I see what she's getting at. "It's not me. It's a friend of mine."

Mr. Mockrie grunts and I help him dig off another glob of blue Doh to mold. Jeannette moistens her lips. "How old's this friend?"

"Seventeen. Eighteen."

She says, "You know this for sure? That there's abuse?"

"I know. But, I mean, I don't have it on film."

The buzzer sounds up front and Jeannette scrambles. "If that's Evelyn . . ." Her jaw sets. Evelyn is Carrie's mother. "Don't get involved." Jeannette scrapes back her chair and stands.

"What?"

She smashes her Doh back into the container. "You don't want to get involved in someone else's family business. Believe me."

What I believe is I want to be so deeply involved in Reeve's business there's no way out.

# Chapter 12

A message on the closed door reads: NO CLASS TODAY. PICK UP YOUR REPORTS IN MY BOX. I don't care about the Film Studies report, except for everyone else in class seeing my grade.

My grade is 73. I spent at least an hour thinking about narrative structure and "how non-narrative short film applies the structure in the way documentaries don't." The note under my grade says, "You didn't credibly prove your point." Did I have one?

I stuff my report folder into my pack and head for my locker. As I round the bend, I'm obliterated by Reeve, slamming me up against the wall and saying, "Is this a good time for you?"

Her hand is splayed on my breastbone and I wonder if she can feel my heart exploding. "Absolutely," I say.

She hitches her head to the left, then takes off. My lungs empty as I peel off the wall and follow her.

We pass the band rooms, the practice studios and recording lab, and zip into a zigzagging hall. I've never even been in the new Arts wing of the building before. "Down here," Reeve says over her shoulder. She wrenches open a steel door marked B2 and holds it for me.

My eyes adjust to the red emergency light glowing halfway down the wall where more stairs descend.

When the door slams, Reeve pinches my arm.

Ow. "What is this place?" I ask as she brushes by, hip-checking me into the railing.

"Robbie calls it the pit of Acheron," Reeve says.

God, she's fast; I have to run to keep up. She has on this really short skirt and platforms, the pink crop top. Such a beautiful blur.

"Robbie found this place, like, the first week of school and we've been coming here." Reeve's voice echoes. "Nobody knows."

A burst of excitement jets up my spine.

Reeve flips on a light switch and an underworld labyrinth illuminates. Fluorescent bulbs flicker and buzz; metal glints. Tubes and aluminum boxes and vertical poles; horizontal vents snake and maze across a mile of concrete flooring. It's the school's heating and cooling system.

"Here!" Reeve calls. Her voice bounces. She ducks behind a floor-to-ceiling steel column, and when I circle it, she's gone.

"Over here." Reverberation. I twist.

"No, this way."

I spin around.

She laughs.

"Reeve."

I hear her plats clopping.

"Back here."

I suck at hide-and-seek.

Between two coffin-like units I come out at a drainage pit. Reeve jumps off a pipe and lands behind me.

I yelp.

She clasps her hands around my waist and turns me around.

*Don't let go.* I grab her hands and hold them there. We hook eyes.

"Come. This way." She breaks free and we navigate through a sea of aluminum poles, boxes, vents. At the farthest end is a door. "It was locked," Reeve says, "but Robbie fixed that."

He fixed it by bashing in the door until it splintered and the latch broke loose.

Reeve palms the door open and steps inside. She curls her index finger at me. As I move up next to her, her finger touches the tip of my chin. I think she might pull me in and kiss me, but instead she flips on the light.

I squint at the sudden brightness.

There's a short sofa, like a loveseat, with the foam popping out. A couple of plastic tubs shoved together for a table. Reeve's eye-shadow kits and eyeliner pencils, mascara, brushes, paintbrushes in all different widths and textures, glitter and beads and sequins.

Reeve says, "It's awesome, isn't it?"

With her here, yeah. But basically it's a pit.

She takes my hand and twirls me around under her arm. I have to duck to make it. She pushes me onto the loveseat, then hovers over me. "You're the only one I've ever brought here," she says.

*Thank you, God or whoever.*

She lowers herself to sit next to me. "I don't bring my girls down here."

"So . . . I'm your first?"

A smile tugs her lips. "You wish." Her head angles up at me and we hold eyes so long it almost becomes a contest.

I blink first.

"What did you want to talk about?" she asks.

I hate to break the communion, or whatever this is. "Robbie."

She drops her eyes. "What about him?"

I want her focus back on me—us. "I just need to ask you . . . to show you . . ." My backpack traveled with me through the labyrinth, it's such an appendage. I fish out the spiral with Robbie's essay in it and pass the folded pages to Reeve.

"I'm sorry you got stuck with him," she says, taking the essay. "He needs to graduate."

"No, it's all right. He's . . ."

Her eyes slit.

"Funny," I finish.

"In the head," she mutters. She shifts on the loveseat to pull one leg underneath her. "He almost died when he was a baby."

"Really?"

"No, I'm lying. You can't believe a word I say." Her one plat clunks to the floor and she pulls off the other. The pages rustle in her lap. She reads aloud: "'May 23 I kill my mother. May 24 I killed my father.'"

Reeve stops. "Nice."

"That's only the beginning." I remove the first sheet.

She reads the second page to herself, and the third. Her eyes dance across and down the pages and she doesn't breathe. She bends at the waist and her hair falls across her face so I can't see her reaction. When she gets to the end, she says, "You should correct his spelling and punctuation."

"What?"

"He has an IQ of a hundred and sixty, you know."

"Really?"

She clicks her tongue, like, Yes, you should know. What do I know about autism?

Reeve rereads something. As she does, she plucks eyelashes out of her eyelid. I notice then how almost all the eyelashes on her right eye are missing.

"Is any of it true?" I ask.

"It's Robbie's interpretation," she says.

"What's your interpretation?" What did she write in her essay? "Is he . . . Are you . . . ?" God. How to ask this? "Are you guys being molested?"

Reeve laughs.

My face flushes.

"I'm sorry." She claps a hand over her mouth. "It's just . . ." She laughs silently behind her hand.

She's laughing at me. My eyes skim up and down her arm, any square of exposed skin I can see. What do cutting scars look like? I just blurt it out: "Do you cut?"

She stops laughing. Releasing the leg from underneath her, she arches away from me and says, "Johanna, you can't begin to understand."

Is she right? Because I *don't* understand any of it. My own tragedies are so . . . ordinary.

"Don't ever ask me questions you can't handle the answers to." She stares down at Robbie's essay.

She thinks I'm naïve. Which, okay, maybe I am.

I reach over and place my hand on her leg. "I want to know you."

She sucks in a breath, like my touch burned her, or my words did. I remove my hand and she exhales. "All that stuff happened in the past," she says. "It's shit from Robbie's childhood. Nice childhood, huh?"

It was yours too, I think. "So," I say, "it's over?"

Reeve pushes to her feet and the essay sails to the floor. "The asshole's gone. He's been gone for years." She drops to her knees by her makeup, picks up a tube of mascara, and unscrews it.

"But who's that guy at your house?"

"What guy?" She opens a lighted mirror.

"That guy who beat up your mom."

She slaps the mirror down. "Is that all you wanted to talk about? My crappy home life?"

"No."

"What else?"

The tension crackles. "Us."

She shakes her head. "There is no *us*."

"Not yet," I say. "But I want there to be."

The atoms between us charge and split. Reeve says slowly, "Can't you hear? Did I not point it all out? You can't handle me."

"You don't know what I can handle."

"Fine," she says.

"Reeve." In one breath, I let out the life I've been holding in. "I want you. I don't care what baggage you bring. I've—I've got stuff too."

This shakes her visibly. She pushes to her feet and heads for the door. I shoulder my pack. "Don't forget Robbie's memoir." She points to the floor and I stoop to reassemble the strewn pages.

"He's supposed to write about high school, isn't he? Make him start over."

"Okay," I say. We'll start at the beginning. You and me, Reeve. Let's begin.

"Will you toss me my shoes?"

I do better than that. I gather the pair of plats and kneel in front of her to slip them onto her feet. I clasp her right ankle and her toes curl under. I run my index finger across the bridge of each toe.

She closes her eyes and opens her mouth.

I rise to face her and the light extinguishes. She says, "Forget it."

"No." I take her hand. "I know what I want, Reeve." Enough wasted time. "I know what I can handle."

# Chapter 13

"Johanna, there you are." Tessa sits up in one of the lawn chairs out back, crocheting a square of pink and purple yarn. Her yarn bag overflows with similar squares, like she's making quilt blocks. I check out her stomach to see if there's a change. "Come over here," she says.

I almost say, You come here. I know what she's going to ask.

"Your graduation"—Tessa continues to work—"is on May twenty-third, right?"

"Um, yeah."

"Do you want a party?"

"A what?"

"If you want, we can plan a graduation party."

We, as in you and me? Or you and Martin? "That's okay," I say. "Novak's having one." Novak's mom is planning this extravagant celebration. Now that Novak's being evicted, though, are the party plans canceled?

"So, you could have one too," Tessa says.

Who would I invite? Novak'll be busy that day. Reeve? Would Reeve come to my party?

Tessa glances up, shielding her eyes from the sun. My eyes laser into her belly. I think the bulge looks bigger, which is a relief. The miscarriage happened right before she flew home to talk to Mom about "making arrangements." I never got to tell her how excited I was about becoming an aunt, getting a niece or nephew. I love babies.

Thank God I didn't say anything then. It was like Tessa was avoiding me, anyway. Novak had brought over a knitting project she said wasn't turning out right and she needed Tessa's help. They were in the dining room when I came out of Mom's bedroom. Tessa was bawling her eyes out. Novak said to me, "She lost the baby."

Novak hugged Tessa. I went over to be with her too, but Tessa got up fast and left. I ended up consoling Novak.

Tessa shoves her crocheting in her bag and stands. "We're coming to your graduation."

"You don't have to," I say.

"We want to." She starts past me.

I scrape my foot in the dirt. "I don't even know if I'm going. Hardly anyone goes." That's probably not true. Everyone is talking about announcements and rings and the slogans they're painting on their caps. Novak complained about the limited number of tickets she got for family members because all her aunts and uncles and cousins are flying in.

Tessa snipes, "Well, let me know, okay? I already put in for the day off. And so did Martin."

I snarl behind her back, "Oh, you'll be the first to know." Believe me, I'll send you a *personal* announcement.


Reeve says, "Hi." It stops me in my tracks. She adds, "I thought I'd find you here." She's seated at the teacher's desk.

She was looking for me?

"He's starting over. He needs supervision, discipline." Reeve stiff-fingers Robbie at his desk. "Get to work, wanker."

Robbie goes, "I only cooperate with Johanna."

I say, "Then get to work, wanker."

Reeve smiles at me.

God, wipe me off the floor.

She orders him, "Use proper English and punctuation. Don't be lazy."

Robbie thumbs his nose at her, then lowers his head and begins scribbling on a clean sheet of paper. Reeve gets up and comes toward me. She's wispy. I expect her to rise like a balloon with a string. Then I'd reach up and pull her down.

She clenches my upper arms in both her hands and pushes me out the door. Without taking her eyes off me, she says, "Keep working, Robbie. We'll be back." She steers me across the hallway and keeps going until I hit the wall. "What have you done to me?" she asks.

"What do you mean?"

"I can't stop thinking about you."

My heart thumps.

"You bewitched me," she says. "You did some kind of juju

spell." Her eyelids glimmer in iridescent pinks and blues, a sequin on each tear duct. She can't. Stop thinking. About me?

"It's mind control," I say. "You will succumb."

She pooches her lips. "I'm so mean to you."

My tailbone still hurts and I found a bruise where she pinched me. "No, you're not."

"Yes, I am." She drops her hands and steps back. "I don't want to be."

"I know."

"No, you don't." She looks off to the left. "It means I like you." The trace of a smile on her lips. "Isn't that stupid? It's so wrong."

"No, it's not."

She shakes her head.

"The liking me part. That's right."

"There's this party at Amanda Montero's. Do you want to go? You'll be risking your life if you say yes."

"Yes," I say.

"I mean it." Her face and voice are serious. "I'm not a nice person."

I look into her very soul. All I see is beauty.

Reeve says, "Don't say I didn't warn you."

Robbie fills the doorframe and announces, "I'm done." He walks up to me and thrusts his papers in my face.

"Watch it." Reeve jabs him in the gut. "You almost hit her."

I absently scan the papers and think, It's nowhere near long enough. "When's Amanda's party?" I ask.

"Friday night." Reeve clubs Robbie on the arm and he steps back, out of our space. I automatically think, Don't hurt him.

"You want me to pick you up?" I ask.

"No. God, no. I'll come and get you."

This is happening, right? It isn't a hallucination, or a mental stimulation. "When?"

Reeve pushes Robbie toward the exit. "Like, nine o'clock?"

Wait. "I have to work Friday."

"Then forget it."

"Only till ten. Or ten-thirty."

"Can I come to the party?" Robbie asks.

Reeve stops and slugs him on the arm. "Don't be a moron."

His expression doesn't change, but something does. Reeve's eyes soften. She blinks up at me and says, "Can he come? We could put him on a leash and tie him to a tree."

Okay, this is weird. A date with both of them? "Um, sure," I say.

Reeve smiles at me, apology and tenderness and sexiness in that smile. She goes, "Did I forget to mention, you go out with me, you get benefits?"

Benefits? Or burdens? Never mind, I think. I'll take any piece of Reeve Hartt I can get.

The three of us head outside, where the bus is slowing at the light. "Let me give you a ride," I tell Reeve. "I'll drop you at the corner or something."

"No."

Robbie says, "You can drive me."

"Shut up." She kicks him. "Okay. But leave us off at the 7-Eleven. And promise you won't go to my house—ever again."

"I promise."

Her arm grazes mine, igniting a skin fire. A car length into the parking lot, Reeve skids to a halt and Robbie plows into her.

There's someone in my car. Leaning out the passenger window, Novak flicks an ash off the end of her cigarette.

Reeve says, "On second thought."

I catch her arm.

She twists out reflexively and shoves Robbie backward.

"Wait." I grab her arm again.

She chops my hand down.

*Ow. That hurt.*

Reeve's face pales. She hustles away with Robbie in tow.

"It's fine," I call. "Reeve—"

"Just forget it," she barks over her shoulder. "Forget it."

"Was that Reeve?" Novak has her shoes off and her feet up on my dashboard. "Who was the guy with her?" she says.

My eyes stray back to Reeve and Robbie, loping to catch the bus. "Her brother."

"Flatliner is her brother? God, Johanna." Novak flicks her ash. "You sure know how to pick 'em."

I snap, "What does that mean?"

Novak sits up straight. "Reeve Hartt's a cold, hard bitch. And you're too good for her."

I get in and crank the ignition. "Who the hell are you to be giving me advice about who I should date?"

Novak's head lolls back. "You're right. I'm sorry. I just can't believe you like her." She tosses her still-lit butt out the window. "Does she like you?"

"I know it must seem impossible to you."

Novak casts me that withering look. "You're taking everything I say wrong." As I back out of the space, she tells me, "I'm moving in with Dante. I have no choice. His mom says I can sleep in the basement with the cockroaches."

If that's supposed to make me feel guilty . . .

"It'll be cool," Novak adds quickly, forcing a smile. "There's a futon down there, and a TV. Mold and mice to keep me company."

Dante'll sneak down. It won't be that bad.

"Could you do me a favor?" she asks. "Drive me home? Not my home. To my parents' house."

"Where's your car?" I slow at the intersection.

"Dante has it. He totaled his on Sunday."

"What?" I turn to Novak. "Is he all right?"

"Yeah. Oh yeah." She clutches a knee to her chest. "He fell asleep and jumped the median, then hit a retaining wall. He walked away. The wall didn't."

"Geez," I say.

"So I gave him my car."

"You *gave* it to him?"

"Loaned it. Whatever. What's mine is his."

I hope she doesn't tell her parents that. "I'm glad he wasn't hurt." I guess.

She opens her purse and lights up another cigarette. There's something she isn't telling me.

"What?" I say.

She billows a cloud of smoke from her open mouth. A sneaky grin creeps across her lips. "So, lonely lesbo has a fuck buddy."

I hit the speed bump hard. Damn. Straight.

Soon.

# Chapter 14

Reeve isn't in school the rest of the week and I don't see Robbie either. I don't even know if we're going to the party or not. Why didn't I get her phone number? How did we leave it? Did she really ask me?

There's no wall clock in Bling's. I rearrange the watch display over and over to check the time. 9:58. 9:59—she's here.

She picks up a digital watch and tries it on. "Pretend you don't know me," she says.

My stomach somersaults. She wanders over to the hair scrunchies as a horde of girls surges in, dispersing in pairs. Robbie's in a corner playing with his string.

I check the time. Ten exactly.

Shondri has a line at the register. The store is small and cramped with this many people in it. Now Reeve is trying on shades.

I slip between bodies down the main aisle, attempting to look inconspicuous. Forcing myself not to scream, *Everybody out!*

Reeve catches my eye and smiles. I can't wait for these stragglers. Behind the counter, I press the button for the metal grate to lower.

"What are you doing?" Shondri asks.

"It's closing time."

"Johanna, we have customers."

"But I have to leave. I have curfew and, uh . . . I'm grounded." I've never been grounded in my life.

Shondri's eyes slit. "You mighta told me that."

I hunch my shoulders. "Sorry."

Reeve disappears behind a rack of earrings, then materializes on the other side. She mimes, *Don't stare.*

"Go on," Shondri says. "I'll close."

"Are you sure?"

"Do I got a choice?"

I rush to the storeroom for my bag and when I come back, Reeve and Robbie are gone. I skid out into the mall and see Robbie at the photo booth. "Hey!" I call. "Where's—"

Hands cover my eyes. "Trick or treat," she says.

"Definitely treat."

She's in front of me. "Ready?"

*I've been ready forever.*

"Where's your car?" she asks.

"This way." I start for the northwest entrance, by Target.

"Butt crack!" Reeve calls. She takes my hand, just like that. Like it's the most natural thing in the world.

My eyes drift down to her wrist, to the watch.

She forgot. She'll notice later and go, Shit. She'll return it to Bling's.

So there's no problem. And if she really wants it, I'll buy it for her.

Amanda Montero lives in Glenarm Canyon, in one of those cozy cabins that cost a million dollars. It's weird how geography dictates status. The poor neighborhoods, the ghettos, are built on a floodplain. The middle class is mesa. The upper crust, geographically speaking, claims the summit.

Why would Amanda Montero want to use my apartment? Her house is a four-star resort. There are signs and arrows directing people to the party out back, in case the strobes and blasting bass aren't enough. We, Reeve and I, and, oh yeah, my other date, Robbie, make our way up the driveway.

Reeve looks amazing tonight. She's wearing this straight, full-length skirt with buckles and grommets that's made out of nylon, like a backpack. Not new. Everything she owns is vintage cool. I have on my black pants and white shirt from work. So glam.

People glom together on the patio in cliques. Three or four girls in bikinis lounge at the pool. Brr. It's chilly in the mountains at night.

The pool is shaped like a scalloped oyster. A waterfall splashes down fake boulders, making me think of Fallon Falls. If we'd kept going up Terra Haute Road, we'd have come to Fallon Falls. Maybe I'll take Reeve there later? Throw Robbie off the cliff?

"I didn't know it was a pool party," I say to Reeve. The

only parties I've ever been to were at Novak's, where I immediately gravitated to the greenhouse.

"It's whatever," Reeve says. "You know."

One of the bikini chicks leaps to her feet and bounds over to us. Her boobs jiggle. "Oh, you are so leaving," she says to Reeve.

Reeve goes, "I was invited."

"By who?"

"Britt."

Amanda's eyes narrow. I survey the area but don't see Britt.

"You fucked my little sister," Amanda says.

Reeve goes, "Only 'cause she wanted it."

"You lying bitch."

My eyes dart back to the pool. One of the girls is Nameless, from Rainbow Alley. Is that Amanda's sister?

Amanda says, "She's *not* a dyke."

"Okay. You'd know."

Reeve and Amanda have a stare-down.

Amanda blinks over to me. "You can't bring him here."

Reeve says, "He's staying."

Robbie, she means. Why is she looking at me?

Robbie drones, "Fooood," and elevates his arms like Frankenstein, goose-stepping toward the wet bar. There are bowls of chips and coolers of drinks.

Reeve calls at his back, "Wander off into the hills where no one can find you!" Her fingers intertwine with mine and she says, "This is Johanna."

I say to Amanda, "We've met."

"We have?" Her eyes scorch me. "Do you go to our school?"

We've both gone to Jefferson High for four years.

Amanda points at me. "We had yearbook together last year. Right?"

"I don't think so," I say. "I'm pre-med."

Two guys sneak up behind Amanda, one pressing a finger to his lips. He grabs her arms while the other guy snags her ankles. They swoop her into the air and she squeals.

My hand absorbs the rapture of Reeve's fingers woven through mine. She has a tight grip.

She gazes up at me. "Are you really pre-med?"

"Do we even have that?"

She laughs. I smile back. Her attention wavers over to Robbie, who is standing at the bar shoving chips into his mouth by the fistful. "He is so bent," she says. "What am I going to do with him?"

"How come you're responsible for him?" I ask. "Can't he—"

"You wouldn't understand," Reeve snaps. She releases my hand and stalks off toward the pool. I stumble blindly behind.

She stops suddenly and turns to me. "Are you sorry you came with me yet?"

"Not at all."

"I guess you heard. My lucky number's ten."

I laugh. Not the reaction she expects, I guess. Somewhere in the back of my mind, at the instinctive level, I know I should be jealous. Am I?

Reeve's eyes graze the ground and she swings her right hand close to my body. Her wrist winds under my wrist and she tickles the tips of my fingers with hers. Tingles of desire radiate through my body.

Reeve says in a low whisper, "Let's go somewhere."

*Fallon Falls.*

She hooks her fingertips under mine and leads me to the pool. The party's gearing up.

"Reeve? Reeve!"

She slows.

"Hey."

It's Britt. Her eyes flit to our linked hands.

Reeve says, "This is Johanna," clenching my hand tighter.

"I know," Britt says. She has these blue-gray eyes like a snow cat's. They stare at me intently. What? Is she trying to telepath a message, like, Lay off? I telepath back, Reeve might've been yours once, but your number's up.

"You could've told Amanda you invited me." Reeve's voice is cold.

Britt's mouth drops. "I did. Melia's been telling everyone—"

"I know what Melia's saying. She should shut up. We have to go." Reeve tugs me ahead.

I turn to see Britt drilling me with eye daggers. It feels . . . satisfying.

She's negative zero.

We cross the pool deck and round the faux waterfall. Behind us, I hear someone screech, "Nooo . . . !" Then a splash. People shout and laugh.

Reeve seems to know her way around here. She creaks open an iron gate to a cobbled path leading down an incline. It's only wide enough for the two of us, so our arms press together. Around a rock ledge past a hidden alcove is a hanging garden.

Reeve says, "Do you want to sit or stand?"

For what? There's a patio set, an arched trellis with a spray of climbing roses. Reeve follows my eyes to it, then leads me that way and we duck under a spiny branch.

The roses are red. The archway is dark.

Reeve lets go of my hand and straightens to her full height. She's wearing her plats, and she's only, like, three or four inches shorter than me. Her eyes are subtle, brown eye shadow, white mascara, natural lip gloss.

"I don't know you at all," she says.

*Oh, Reeve. I know you.*

She adds softly, "But I want to."

With both hands spread, she touches her fingertips to mine. We stand a long moment with our hands out, wing tips pressing. Our palms never touch. As if on cue, our fists come together.

Reeve says, "Do you kiss on the first date?"

I let out a nervous laugh. "I don't know. This *is* my first date." Feminazi doesn't count.

She widens her eyes.

"Except for the hookah."

Her eyes go black. "That didn't happen. We weren't ready."

*You mean you weren't.*

Reeve smiles tenderly. A sensuous smile that stirs the night.

"Do you?" I ask. "Kiss on the first date?"

"I do," she says, sounding serious. "I definitely do."

I lick my lips. My mouth is dry and I swallow dust. Reeve angles her chin up and closes her eyes. I think, If I close my eyes, I'll miss. I'll kiss her forehead, or her nose, or . . .

Reeve pushes down our fisted hands and rises up to meet me. In sync, we come together.

Her lips part slightly and so do mine.

Velvet night against my mouth, her lips are moist and warm. She opens her mouth and I do too, then she twists her lips, her lip gloss a lubricant. She sucks my upper lip between her teeth and holds while I tremble with the Earth.

My hands unclasp from hers and wrap around her, pulling her into me. Her hand slides up under my hair and her rigid fingers drive down the base of my skull.

It's hard to breathe, hard to stand. My hands move to her lower back, to bare skin where her shirt has ridden up. I flatten my palms against her and crush her to me.

A little "Oh" escapes from my mouth. Reeve makes a sound, a long "huhhh." The tips of our tongues curl and touch and tickle.

Reeve's head jolts back. "God," she says. "I'm going to come."

I'm shaking so hard, I think I might die. "Is that bad?"

Reeve fingers my cheek, the back of my neck. I lean into her, covering her hand with mine, taking it and kissing it.

My eyes close. This is Joyland. My alternate universe I never dare inhabit. Until now.

It's real. I'm finally alive.

My eyes open slowly.

"Wow," she says.

"Yeah."

"That wasn't your first kiss."

"It was."

She arches her eyebrows and her eyes glisten. I can kiss! I'm a good kisser.

She touches my lips with the tip of her index finger and I kiss her fingertips. "You're my first everything," I say.

120

Her face changes. For a moment I think she might cry, and if she does, the depth of my desire will burst apart with her. She takes a step back, away from me. "We better go see what Robbie's up to."

"Reeve." I clench her arm and she reacts with a jerk.

Licking my lips, I lean into her. My arms enclose her, but she twists out, pressing her hand against my hip. She says, "Let's not get carried away."

Too late. I'm flying. I thought she wanted me.

She adds in a quiet voice, "I want you to savor your first time, okay? There's only one first time. Don't lose it."

I won't. I'll never let her go.

# Chapter 15

Robbie could be one of those idiot savants, I think, like in *Rain Man*. I read through the last part of his essay, as much as I can decipher. His spelling and punctuation suck, but the content is moving. And disturbing, of course.

**My best momen was when I kill everyone. Not Reeve. I learnd if you elimnnate the sourc of diseeze the symptms go away. but you always have the sicness inside you.**

*Does Reeve feel that way? Does she think she's got a sickness? I hope not.*

I open the door to leave for work and trip over a box on the landing. Taped to it is a note: "Enjoy these. ♥ U."

Novak's loopy writing. I bring the box inside and set it on

the coffee table. Inside is a DVD player. She must really be moving out. A couple of DVDs are stuck in the side.

One is *Fantasia*. The other is—

Porn. Under the player are three more DVDs. They're all porn.

Girls on girls! Are these Novak's? I might watch . . . *one.* Now I wish I didn't have to go to work.

I surveil the entrance my entire shift, assuming, hoping, Reeve will appear. Certain she'll come by and return the watch.

Shondri says, "I'm giving you a promotion." She hands me my paycheck. "Assistant manager."

"You're kidding." I stare at the check stub. Ten cents more per hour.

"Don't let it go to your head."

That makes me laugh. Still, I've never been promoted. All I can think is, I want to tell Reeve!

How does Reeve spend her off time? She has girlfriends. Britt, others. I've seen her holding hands or nuzzling with them at lunch. I always imagine they're me and then I take that scene to Joyland.

This one time I caught Reeve in a passionate kiss with Britt. I came in early for a make-up test or something and they were outside on the quad before school. Britt was moaning and breathing hard, then she went, "Ow!"

"You bit me!" Britt said.

"Did I?"

"I'm bleeding. You did that on purpose," Britt whimpered. "Why'd you do that? I never did anything to you."

Reeve said, "You asked for it."

Britt crumpled to the ground and started to cry.

Reeve would never make me cry. She *couldn't*.

I didn't see Britt for a while after that, and I'm pretty sure they broke up soon after.

God, this is driving me crazy. Why doesn't she come in?

Closing time and still no sign of her.

*I'll drop by her place. I know I promised, but* . . .

As I turn onto 68th Street, the house comes into view. At night, the trash and tires and abandoned furniture look like a haunted junkyard. I pull to the curb across the street and park.

The streetlamp nearest me has been shot out and the pole tagged. This whole ghetto street scene creeps me out. I spot a dim light on inside her house.

The front door suddenly crashes open, scaring the bejeezus out of me. Reeve storms out. "I told you, no!" she yells back inside. "I won't do it. I'm not doing it anymore."

A woman's voice rises in a screech, "I'll die! You know I need it."

That guy shadows the doorway, bracing himself with both hands in the doorframe.

Reeve shouts, "You go buy her shit! You fucking got her hooked again."

"Watch your language, young lady."

Reeve spits at him.

He laughs and fades into the background.

The woman—Reeve's mom?—staggers out, grabs Reeve by the arm, and wobbles. She's, like, completely anorexic. She's wearing saggy stretch pants and a bra.

Reeve catches her in a fall. "I won't buy for you, Mom," she says. "I won't do it."

Her mother's reply is faintly audible. "Fuck you."

"Fuck you! Your life is fucked."

Her hand flies out and slaps Reeve's face hard enough to snap Reeve's head back. Geez. Her own mother.

"Bitch," Reeve goes. Then louder, "Junkie bitch!"

The woman hauls off to slap her again, but this time Reeve blocks her wrist, pushes her mother in through the door.

I can't just sit here. Can I?

Reeve appears again. The guy follows with a thin brown cigarette dangling from his mouth. Reeve hops down off the porch, straight toward me, and the guy comes after her. "Where do you think you're going? Hey, dyke!"

"Cram it."

From inside, Reeve's mom yells, "You have my permission to do what you need to do, Anthony!"

Reeve pulls up short.

The guy approaches her from behind, cups her shoulder, and she knocks his hand off. He bends down to kiss her neck, but she whirls and kicks him in the balls.

*Good.*

He doubles over, then screams, "You fucking cunt! You cunt-licking—" He hits her with his fist square to her jaw.

Reeve crumples to the ground. My Reeve.

My fingers grab the door handle and I charge out. Reeve rises up and kicks him again, but I can see him lunge for her head. I yank him off her from behind. He's about my height, greasy, stinking of booze and b.o. He has tattoos up and down his arms and shoulders.

"Who the fuck are you?" He wrenches away from me. His eyes have no pupils.

"Johanna," I answer. My voice is surprisingly calm.

"Oh yeah. The dyke's bull dyke."

Reeve aims to kick him again, but he catches her ankle, twists her leg.

"Stop it!" I push him off and kneel to her. "Reeve."

He launches onto the porch muttering, "Fucking freaks," and vanishes inside.

I hold her face, fingering her chin with my thumbs where blood is dribbling and her lip is swelling. I wrap my arms around her. "It's okay. I'm here."

She thrusts up both arms. "What are you *doing* here?"

My mouth opens.

"Don't ever come here." She shoves me backward, onto my butt. "Go home," she says, scrabbling away from me. "Go back where you came from."

"Reeve . . ."

She rises to her feet and storms off.

I stand and stumble toward the street. *Don't leave her here!* my brain screams. *She'll die!*

"You don't know me."

I turn. "What?"

She's out of breath. "You never will. I don't ever want to see your ugly face in mine again. You disgust me."

She's traumatized; she doesn't mean what she's saying. "I can help you. I'll phone someone. The cops or—or social services."

"Don't do anything!" she shouts in my face. "Just get out of my life!"

I plant my feet, or try to. "There are people who can help, Reeve. Who want to, if you'll let them."

"Like you? Is this the way you help?"

A car alarm blares and diverts our attention momentarily. I take her hand and say, "I love you."

Her face shatters into a million pieces.

She jerks back her arm. "Don't."

"Too late." I open my hand to her.

She slaps it down. "Just go away." She sprints for the driveway before I can think what else to do.

I stall for a second at the gate. *Stay. Go.*

*Reeve, I want you. I need you. I need to get you out of here.* I concentrate so hard, she has to hear.

I feel her calling out. Her fear and longing and total sense of hopelessness. The guy's silhouette swoops across the window like some bird of prey and my blood runs cold.

# Chapter 16

My film notes jumble into hieroglyphics—useless to study for my final. The way she lives. The violence, the brutality in her life.

How long has she been taking it? Forever? Her father, her mother, this guy. How many assholes have come and gone in her life? I knew people were terrorized. Child abuse. Spousal abuse. I've never actually known anyone who lived it.

*God, Reeve. You're so strong.*

I push my notes away and lay my head on the table. I will it to be different for her. Please, God, if there is a God, hear me. Help her. Show me how to help her. I need to take her away from there, shelter her and care for her and show her real love.

I hardly ever cry. When my mom died, when Tessa left, I cried. That time I got lost walking home from Fallon Falls and no one came to find me. I was scared. I'd taken a different trail through the trees and it didn't lead me to the road. I climbed and climbed, thinking I'd come out at the top of the mountain or someone would come looking for me. No one did. I had to find my own way.

I'm not crying now. I'm . . . seething. Yes, I'm angry at life, at God. *Think, Johanna.* I need a strategy. Power. I can find a way.

I prowl the parking lot, the quad, the cafeteria, first floor, second floor, Arts wing, B2. The door's locked. She doesn't have a locker—or if she does, I've never seen her use it. You have to pay for a locker. You have to bring your own lock.

The halls are filling and among the surface swell, a recognizable head of hair bobs by. "Robbie!" I race to catch up with him as he veers into the media center. When I touch his back, he freezes.

"Robbie, it's me."

He turns slowly. His face is blank, impassive. Where is he?

"It's Johanna."

"I am here to cooperate," he says like a machine.

"Whatever. Do you know where Reeve is? Is she in the pit?"

He stares at my mouth.

"Downstairs," I say. "The pit of Acheron."

He smirks.

"Is she?"

He stands there with that stupid smirk on his face, so I reach up and slap him. Not hard.

His eyes go dead.

"God. Oh God. Sorry. I'm sorry, Robbie."

He looks at me. "Medic," he says.

I slit-eye him. "Just tell me where she is, *please*."

"Here."

I peer around him. There are computers and books and TVs in the media center, and people, but I don't see her.

Robbie says, "Did you turn in my senior project?"

*Shit.* "No. I'll do it today." I was thinking I wouldn't turn it in yet. I wasn't sure it'd be acceptable to Mrs. Goins. I was thinking I'd rewrite it.

"I have to graduate," Robbie says. He reaches out a hand and my first impulse is to brace for an attack, but he only places it on my shoulder. Then, with his other hand, he touches my face, my cheek. It's . . . creepy.

He clamps a hand around my neck.

My life flashes before me.

Robbie deadpans, "Turn it in."

The bell rings for class and he heads into the media center.

Okay, he's kidding. He has a morbid sense of humor. I feel my neck to make sure my trachea is intact.


A batch of curled memos and announcements, a couple of sealed business envelopes fill Mrs. Goins' mail slot. I stuff in Robbie's essay. I should've thought to put the pages in a report cover. Wait, I have one.

My Film Studies report. I remove it. I search the mailroom for a blank sheet of paper and find a stack in the trash from the Xerox. On a clean side, I make a cover page.

I wonder again why his name is different from Reeve's. I re-arrange his three sheets to put the good stuff first. The part about killing his mother is at the end. My hope is that whoever reads and evaluates the essays never gets beyond page one.

The maze of vents and pipes echoes and knocks and winds in-terminably through the school's underbelly. I take a wrong turn and lose my bearings. Water gurgles through a pipe.

B2 was unlocked when I tried it again, so I'm pretty sure she's down here. The pit looms ahead. The door's been re-placed, along with a padlock. Oh no. Someone discovered them. "Hello?" I call.

Nothing. The door's locked. I rest my forehead on the frame and say, "Please, if you're in there. Let me in." *Let me in, Reeve.*

I don't know how long I stand there; stand in silence.

When I get upstairs, people are herding into the gym for a morning assembly. I forgot about it. The cops have hauled in a wrecked car from an accident that happened earlier this year. It's scrap metal. A mother talks about how her son finally died after being in a coma for six weeks and I think of Carrie. She should just die. Dying would free her and let her mom move on.

Would dying be better than living in a hell on Earth?

Reeve's not at the assembly, not at lunch, not in Mrs. Goins' room last period. It's wishful thinking; the project's over.

If she thinks I'm giving up, she doesn't know me. She does not know Johanna Lynch.


Carrie's mother rails at Jeannette, shouting so loud she's waking the dead—but not the comatose. Carrie has a new bedsore. Jeannette strides past me into the foyer, looking harried.

I sign in and check the status chart. Oh my God. Frank has passed. Sweet old Frank. Rest in peace, Frankie-wanker.

Carrie's mother hangs over my shoulder. "You are to make a note on my daughter's chart to call me if *anything* changes. I mean, *anything.*"

"Okay."

She whirls on Jeannette, who's come up behind her. "Someone used Carrie's lip gloss. I want you to find out who and fire them."

"Evelyn . . ."

She pivots and slams out the front door.

I widen my eyes at Jeannette.

Her shoulders sag. Blowing out a long breath, she says to me, "I've been thinking about what you asked. Your friend in the abusive situation?"

I nod.

"I was wrong. I wasn't thinking clearly. If it was me, or one of my children, I'd want someone to care."

*I care.*

"Make the call."

Make the call. Make the call. The mantra burrows into my brain. If I make the call, what will happen? Take 1: The cops show up. They restrain that guy, Anthony. They drag him from the house and lock him up. Take 2: As the cops are leaving, they see what a waste case the mother is. They take her too. Reeve and Robbie have to move. I never see Reeve again.

It's selfish, I know, but there has to be a way to help without losing her.

My final in Film Studies is an essay question on Unit Five. "Name three films that serve as examples of film as institution and explain how each reinforces and/or resists cultural paradigms and values."

Why can't we just watch *Dumb and Dumber?*

I b.s. a brilliant answer.

My last final of high school—you'd think I'd be happier to have it over with. I feel emptied. Reeve is right. Firsts are better. Firsts are filled with mystery and expectation; firsts are beginnings.

At my locker, a body crunches into me and smothers me in a hug. "We're graduating. Can you believe it?"

Novak clenches my arms and holds me away from her. Then she pulls me to her and kisses me on the lips.

I wrench out of her grasp so hard I hit my head on the locker door. "Why'd you do that?"

She laughs. "Chill, lesbo. I'm just happy." She opens her arms to embrace me again, but I stiff-arm her away. "Go kiss your fabulous boyfriend," I say.

133

I take off running.

"Johanna!"

The memory of Reeve's lips on mine, my first kiss. The memory I need to sustain me until the next time. Novak. She ruined it.

"Hold up, Banana."

I charge down the hall, desperately needing to get away from it, from her, from all of it. High school, loss, grief.

I race around the corner and plow into Mrs. Goins. She drops an armful of folders. I stoop to help her pick them up.

"I received Robbie's project," she says. "I assume you put it in my box?"

My breath is coming out in great gulping heaves, but I manage a nod. I'm on the verge of tears.

"Are you okay?" she asks, peering over her glasses as we stand.

I swallow hard.

She asks, "Did you read his essay?"

I shrug, hoping that'll be enough response.

"It's . . . unsettling," she says.

"But it's done, right?"

She shifts the load in her arms. "I suppose. We talked about it this morning at the staff meeting."

"So he'll graduate, right?"

She hesitates.

"You said if he wrote the essay, he'd graduate. He *has* to graduate."

"Oh, he will."

Thank God.

"Johanna, do you know if any of what he wrote is true?"

Make the call. Make the call. "We didn't discuss it. I got it done for you, okay?"

My feet carry me to the staircase and down the steps. Get away, escape. B2.

The padlock is mangled. As my fingers curl around the doorknob to the pit, a nuclear reaction bubbles the blood in my veins.

She's here.

# Chapter 17

I open the door slowly so I don't freak her out. A conversation halts mid-sentence.

She glances up from the loveseat, where she sits cross-legged, eating a burger. "Oh snap, it's Johanna of Arc," she says.

Robbie's on the floor, a few feet away from Reeve. He sits up fast and slams his instrument case shut.

I step into the room.

Reeve says, "Who let the dogs in?" and Robbie goes, "Who who?" like a routine they've rehearsed.

I ease the door shut behind me.

Reeve watches Robbie remove his string from his pocket and begin threading it through his fingers. A crumpled Mickey D's wrapper lies beside him.

"Stay out of his way," Reeve says. "I mean it, Robbie. Don't mess with him."

I've intruded again. I always feel that way when she and Robbie are together.

She bites off a nibble of burger. "You don't give up." Reeve meets my eyes.

"Not on you."

Her chewing slows and she lowers the hamburger to her lap.

I'm about to say, Reeve, talk to me, but Robbie blurts, "I'll kill him. I'll kill both of them."

Reeve snarls, "Drop it, Robbie."

He sulks.

I wish he'd go. I want to be alone with her. Robbie winds the string around his index finger so tight it balloons the tip purple. "Robbie," I say. "You're graduating. I talked to Mrs. Goins."

His head whips up and he grins so wide I see all his teeth.

Reeve says, "You can hang your diploma on the wall. Oh, wait. You don't have a wall."

Robbie ignores her, unwinding his string.

Reeve pushes to her feet, hands the rest of the burger to Robbie, and ruffles his hair. "Go do that somewhere else, gradu-asstard." To me she says, "What do you want?"

She knows what I want.

Robbie snarfs the burger in one bite, then scrunches the length of string in a wad and jams it into his pocket. He stands, grabbing his case.

"What time is it?" he says at the door.

I look at Reeve.

She says, "How should I know?"

My eyes fall to her bare wrist.

He exits. Reeve moves behind me and kicks the door shut. "I—"

She reaches up and presses a finger to my lips. "You cannot fall in love with me," she says.

Our eyes hold. I clasp her wrist gently and kiss the fleshy part of her finger. "I already am."

She pulls her hand away. "You don't even know me."

"I know you kiss on the first date."

She blows out an irritated breath and flops down on the loveseat. She doesn't look at me. I smile. *Look at me.*

"I don't care about knowing you," I say. "I mean, I do, but it won't change the way I feel about you." *I've been in love with you since the day I was born, or reborn.*

She buries her head in her knees.

I approach her slowly, lowering myself onto the cushion. "You have to get out of there, Reeve. That house. Those people."

"Anthony's my dad's half brother. My uncle." She twists to face me. "He might be more."

What does that mean? I start to ask, but she throws me this defiant look, so I drop it. "You can't be in that house," I say. "It isn't safe."

"I live there. What am I supposed to do? Run? Been there. Done that."

"I could make a call."

She sits up straight. "Don't. Please." Her eyes plead. "They've been called. Everyone's been called. The cops get called regularly for yet another"—she air-quotes—"'domestic disturbance.'"

I'm confused, or ignorant. "Then why doesn't somebody do something?"

"Like what? Arrest us?"

"Not you. Him."

"You think it's about him?" Reeve shakes her head. "Johanna, Johanna, Johanna."

Don't mock me, I think.

She pushes to her feet and I reach out to her. "I just want to help you. Tell me what to do."

"Nothing," she says. "It's too late. There's nothing you can do. The damage is done."

Damage can be undone. No one's died. "There has to be a way."

"Nope." She perches on the edge of one of the plastic tubs, extending her legs and flexing her toes. Her feet smell a little, but so what?

I scoot over to sit directly across from her, taking both her hands away from her feet and pressing them between my hands.

She studies our hands together. Mine are so much bigger than hers.

"Come live with me," I say.

Reeve throws back her head and laughs.

"What? I'm serious."

"Girl, you move fast."

Her arms retract, but I hold on.

She adds, "One kiss and you love me and want me to move in with you. Have you set a date for the wedding?"

"May twenty-third," I say.

She smiles and shakes her head.

"What?"

"You're something. But I'm not sure what." She angles her head to peer sideways up at me.

A streak of fire ignites my lower belly. I want to kiss her so bad.

Gently, I pull her toward me. She rises off her butt, then I do. We stand in unison. I slide my arms around her waist and she doesn't resist, so I nuzzle her neck and see her skin prickle. Is she cold? Excited?

I moisten my lips. I raise her chin and she closes her eyes.

Sparks fire off every nerve ending from my lips to my face, to my ears, head, neck, toes. The kiss is explosive.

I pull us onto the loveseat. I stretch out the length of it, drawing her close to me, still kissing. We lie together and kiss. Somewhere in that universe of time, I whisper, "I love you, Reeve Hartt."

She responds by kissing me harder and longer and deeper. She loves me too. She's just afraid.


All the way home, the feel of her mouth on mine is so visceral I almost come. When we had to break it up, Reeve looked as dreamy and lovesick as I felt.

There are four voice mails on my phone at home. Reeve, I pray. Please be Reeve.

Three calls from Novak. Three desperate messages: "Johanna, call me. Please."

The phone rings as I'm stripping off my underwear and bra to drop into bed. I let it ring, then think, It might be Reeve.

I get up to answer.

"Hey, caught you."

*Shit.*

"Are you going to hang up on me?" she asks.

I exhale exhaustion and weariness and need.

"I know I was wrong," she says, "to kiss you in public. I should've waited until we were alone. And naked. Don't hang up!"

Please. I can't hear this.

"Where'd you go today?" she asks. "You, like, blended into the woodwork. Not that you would. I mean, you stand out. Oh, forget it. The reason I called is this list my mother wants me to make for my graduation party. She's still going through with it, like she's a martyr or something. She doesn't want to pay the caterer's cancellation fee, that's the only reason."

I can't care about her life anymore.

"So the list. You and Dante. I told her you and Dante. That's not good enough. It's never good enough with her."

Novak has lots of friends. Why is she bothering me with this?

"Johanna?" She hesitates. "You are coming, aren't you?"

Reeve's hair is coarse and tangled. A little dandruffy. I wish she'd let me shampoo her hair. I'd massage her scalp and . . .

"You can bring Reeve," Novak says, channeling my thoughts. "Hey, I'll put her on the list. Do you know her address?"

I close my eyes and resume our make-out session in the pit.

"Johanna?"

I think I gave her a hickey.

"You are coming. Aren't you?"

Definitely coming.

A knock sounds on the door. "There's someone here," I say to Novak. "I have to go."

"Wait! I need to tell you something else."

I set down the phone.

I fumble with the deadbolt and chain, finally unlatching the locks and yanking open the door.

"Well, I'm glad to see you're taking precautions," she says, shoving my shoulder. She smiles and flips her student ID at me. "This is an unscheduled inspection of the premises," she says. She pockets the ID. "I understand you're harboring a fugitive. Or will be."

My heart leaps. Will I?

Reeve swerves around me and enters the apartment. She surveys the room. When her eyes catch mine, they cling. See—neither of us can let loose of the other. Is she really moving in?

"Johanna. JoHAAANNA." Novak's voice.

I roll my eyes at Reeve. "Just a sec." I trip over the box Novak left and almost take a header. "I have to go," I tell Novak.

"Who is it?" she asks.

Reeve's watching me.

"I have to go." I don't wait for Novak to hang up.

"I hate her," Reeve says.

"Who?"

"Novak. Your *friend?*" She makes it sound like it's more than it is.

"Why do you hate her?"

"She uses you." Reeve checks out the kitchen, the hallway. "She's a rich bitch. They're all the same."

"She has her good points." Why am I defending Novak to Reeve?

"I can't stay." Reeve backs toward the door.

I grab her. It happens so fast; she reacts by slamming into

the wall and extending her arms to fend me off like I'm going to hurt her.

"No, Reeve—" I hold up my hands.

She shrinks into herself.

"Stay. Just for a while."

"I can't. I snuck out. If Anthony sees I took the van . . ." Her eyes dilate like a trapped animal's.

"Come tomorrow, then," I say. "I'll pick you up somewhere. I'll make you dinner."

She waffles her eyes. "You cook?"

"If you want to call it that. I cook, I clean, I'm the perfect housewife."

Reeve smiles a little. "You're the perfect everything," she says. "That's your problem."

"No, I'm the perfect nothing."

The space between us narrows. I lean in to kiss her and she doesn't back away. She doesn't come to me either.

I let her decide, yes or no.

She glances to the left.

In that split second before, though, I see desire. I feel want.

I say, "No pressure, okay? When you're ready."

*Please be ready. Be ready soon.*

# Chapter 18

The midday sun slants through the window and I shoot upright in bed. What will I make Reeve for dinner? Beyond nuking a frozen entrée or cutting open a bag of salad, I can assemble a sandwich.

No one's home downstairs in the main house. Martin's laptop is open and Tessa's crocheting is sitting on the table. "Guys?" I call, even though I can't feel a heartbeat in the house.

I move through the living room to the bedrooms. As I pass the bathroom, a change in heat and humidity shifts my focus. I backtrack. The shower door is open and a wet towel is heaped on the mat.

"Tessa?" The showerhead drips.

The door to their bedroom is open. The bed is made, shams aligned, closet doors shut tight. "Martin?"

They got hungry; they're at the store. Martin's the cook in the house, so maybe he ran out of broccoli or butter or whole grain bread.

I return to the dining room. It must've been a last-minute decision for Martin to leave his laptop on. The screen saver hasn't kicked in and I look at what he was working on. Some list of names.

There are cookbooks galore that Martin brought with him from Minnesota. I select a skinny one: *Quick Mexican Dishes.* I flip through it and the pictures make me hungry. There aren't too many ingredients. Tortillas. Cheese. I can handle Mexican. As I turn to leave, I spy a book on the top shelf and grab it. *Making Love to Food: A Guide to Sexual Cooking.*

Oh, baby. Forget the fajitas.


I have to grocery-shop. Damn. I haven't deposited my check. The cash for my car insurance is still in my bag.

Except, it isn't. I dump the bag and can't find the envelope. I check all the usual places—pockets, drawers, divan cushions.

I had it, I know I did. Martin keeps a stash of cash in a cookie jar, which I only know about because one day these band geeks came to the door selling candy and Martin was making dumplings or something; his hands were covered with flour. He said, "Mojo, would you buy ten candy bars from these guys? There's money in the loaded potato."

That's what he calls the cookie jar. Martin won't mind. I'll replace the money as soon as I get paid.

I leave Martin an IOU: "I unloaded 40 from the potato. Pay U back. J."

Writing out a grocery list makes me think of Mom, and I don't want to. I want—need—to be happy.

On my way home from Safeway I think about calling Reeve to make sure she's coming. I mean, she never said yes. We didn't set a definite time.

*Stupid.* What if I'm going to all this trouble and she doesn't think I'm serious? She'll have to learn that about me—I'm always serious about her.

As I'm slicing a mushroom from cap to stem, the way the book shows, the phone rings. It startles me and I cut my finger. "Hello?" I answer, sucking the blood.

"It's me," she says.

My pulse races. "What time are you coming?"

"Did I say I was?"

All the blood drains out of me.

"Kidding. I'm calling to ask what time you want me."

I'm really bleeding. "Any time." I stanch the bleeding with pressure from my thumb. "Come now if you want."

There are voices in the background, yelling, a TV blasting. Reeve's voice lowers. "Can Robbie come too?"

He wasn't exactly in the plan.

"Never mind," she says. "Forget it."

"No, it's okay." I shouldn't have hesitated. "It's fine. Of course he can come." Snuff the candles, fade out of Joyland.

"Are you positive?"

That I want *her* here? "Yeah. Positive." I hope I sound enthusiastic. "I'll need to make more food."

"No shit. He eats like a pig."

Great.

In a low, sultry hiss, Reeve goes, "Thankssss."

I say, "Hurry."

I run downstairs to unload another twenty from the potato.

Along with a jumbo can of refried beans and grated Mexican cheese, I splurge and buy a set of six dinner plates. Something nicer than Tessa's Corelle ware. The mushroom and puff pastry dish with marinated asparagus will have to wait. It was a recipe for two, anyway.

When Reeve shows up, she's alone.

"Where's—"

"He isn't coming." She cups her hand on the doorknob over mine and closes the door. "He's asleep."

If that's autism, THANK YOU. Reeve's hair is up in a clip and her neck is exposed and so are the top of her breasts. I feel light-headed and horny.

Inches away, she breathes in my hair and we empty our lungs at the same time. Her eyes skim me up and down and come to rest on my chest.

I couldn't decide what to wear. Jeans. Duh. I couldn't pick a top. The sexiest thing I have is this chiffon negligee Novak gave me when she cleaned out her closet before Christmas. I was only trying on the negligee to dream, to imagine what could be.

Reeve's eyes rise to my neck, then skid down my arm. I reach across my front and slide the spaghetti strap back over my shoulder. I should've put on a bra, at least.

Reeve is wearing a bra. It's visible through her black, see-through blouse. Her jeans are cut so low and fit so tight I don't even have to imagine every mound and curve of her.

She can't seem to take her eyes off my chest.

"Um, I wasn't quite done getting dressed."

She lifts her eyes to mine. "You look done to me."

I laugh. God, I sound like a goat. Reeve fingers my chin, draws it to her, and kisses me.

She curls a hand behind my neck and kisses me harder.

My knees buckle and Reeve catches me collapsing. She laughs. So do I.

"What are we having to eat?" She trickles a hand down my arm as she moves past me into the living room. "I'm starving." She dumps her purse off on the coffee table.

"I was going to make this puff pastry thing. Before Robbie . . ."

She whirls on me.

"Quesadillas," I say.

"I love Mexican food."

What if she hated it? I didn't even think . . . My strap slips off again and I slide it up.

"What can I do to help?" Reeve rubs her hands together.

All the plates and silverware are out. My hair is still wet from the shower. Did I even comb it?

No, I had to try on this sexy nightie.

"I'll set the table," Reeve says. "You finish . . . whatever." Her eyes glom on to my chest again.

As I travel past her toward the back, we touch hands. If it's going to be just the two of us, I'm not ready. I want to put on makeup and do my hair.

Ten minutes later I come out to find the table set and the salad on. Reeve found the candles I bought and is dripping wax into Novak's ashtray. "I couldn't find your candleholders," she says, swirling the wax carefully in a circle.

"Because I don't have any?"

She places the lit candle in the center and ignites the other off its wick. "There." Her fingers spread apart. "Perfect."

The table looks beautiful.

"Drink before dinner?" she asks. She twists around and grips a bottle of wine by the neck.

"Where'd you get that?" I ask.

"I never come empty-handed," she answers.

I lift a water glass off the table and hold it out.

Reeve uncrinkles the foil seal. "Do you have a corkscrew?"

"I don't know. What does one look like?"

"Like a corkscrew?" She cocks her head.

She's so funny. "Martin probably has one," I say.

"Who's Martin?"

"Bro-in-law. Be right back." I set down my glass.

She follows me to the door. And out.

"It's just downstairs," I say.

"I'll come with you."

I don't know why I feel strange taking her into the house. Novak goes in and out like she owns the place.

"Who lives here?" Reeve asks as I roll open the sliding door.

"My sister, Tessa, and her husband, Martin."

"You never told me you had a sister."

Our time together hasn't been wasted with inconsequential chatter. "Family," I intone. "You know." I flip on the kitchen light. In the dining room the same scene as before, except that Martin's laptop has powered down.

"Weird," I think aloud.

"What?" Reeve scans the area.

"Looks like they went somewhere suddenly. Like, just picked up and left." I haven't put on shoes and Reeve must've kicked hers off upstairs. Her toenail polish is dark blue.

"Did you used to live here?" she asks. She does a three-sixty in the dining room.

"Yeah. When Tessa moved back, I moved out." In the kitchen, I tug open the utensil drawer and scavenge around for a corkscrew.

Reeve says, "Do you hate your sister?" She fixes on me.

"I don't . . . hate her."

"You don't . . . love her." Reeve widens her eyes.

"We just don't . . . connect. Not like you and Robbie." I find what looks like a corkscrew and say, "Let's go."

Reeve says, "You want him? You take him."

I don't really want to talk about sisters or brothers or anything family. Reeve ventures deeper into the living room.

She's gazing at the ceiling, the walls, the windows, seeming to absorb all the architectural details. A swirling plaster ceiling and crown molding. Aubergine. Hate the color.

"This is nice," Reeve says. "You have a nice family."

I shrug. "They're okay. Can we go?"

"A nice house and a nice family." Her voice sounds odd. "And you're nice. Too nice for me."

My blood chills. "Reeve, I'm not that nice, but I am that hungry. Why don't we eat now?"

Reeve rushes by me, muttering, "I'm out of here."

She tries to close the sliding door in my face, but I stick my arm through the opening and get crushed. I suppress the wail of pain. "You can't go."

She flies up the stairs. I chase her to the top and into the apartment. "We haven't even had dinner."

She snatches her purse off the coffee table. "Later. Never."

I have to stop her, hold her, make her stay. I grab her wrist and she wheels around. Her arm swings back and a fist comes right at me, knuckles smashing into my cheek and knocking me off balance. I see her mouth drop and her hand unclench. This high-pitched sound escapes from her throat.

"Why . . . ?"

The door slams. Vertigo hits me and my legs give out. I'm down. Pain shoots up my face and eye socket. My fingers come away from my cheek wet, smeared with blood. It's my blood.

I take off after her. I don't make it to the bottom of the stairs before I fall and crunch to Earth. "Reeve, wait . . . please." My voice sounds far away.

Acid burn of tears. Every nerve ending hurts.

A car swerves into the driveway, headlights flashing off my face, and I burrow my head in my arms.

The thunk of a door. "Johanna."

I'm still on my hands and knees, shielding my eyes; an urgent voice in my head mingles with bewilderment. I push to my feet, or I'm helped. "Johanna." Martin's soft voice in my ear. "I'm sorry."

His hair is disheveled and his eyes are bloodshot. He rakes a hand through his hair and says, "Tessa lost the baby."

# Chapter 19

No reason, Martin said. She was working, not even standing up. She was helping a woman fill out a Medicare form when she started to bleed. She'd lost a lot of blood by the time Martin got there.

The image of it cleaves my brain like a chasm to understanding. Tessa sitting there, feeling the wet. Knowing what it is.

"She's staying in the hospital overnight for observation," Martin added. "Nothing serious."

Nothing serious. Except her baby died.

The candles melt down to gooey gnomes. I blow them out, then sit at the table in the dark, thinking. Trying not to think.

The left side of my face throbs and I get up to look in the mirror. Dried blood is caked on my cheek and eyebrow. My hair towel from earlier in the evening is on the floor, still damp. I pick it up and dab at the wound.

The gash isn't deep, nothing serious. I haven't lost anything. *Reeve?*

Don't think about it.

My left eye is swelling.

I lie in bed but can't sleep, so I get up over and over again to look at myself. The longer I look, the more I morph. The image of me, Johanna Lynch, my external reflection. My injury merges with the way I see myself.

Then I focus and remember what's important. My sister's in the hospital. Reeve got away.


I wait in the living room for Martin and Tessa. I hear the door open and Martin say, "We'll try again."

"No," Tessa whispers hoarsely. "I can't keep doing this. I can't have this on my conscience."

"What, honey?" Martin sets her carryall on the table.

I stand at the sofa.

"You're creating life," he says.

Tessa bursts into tears.

I should leave. This is between them.

Tessa takes off for the bedroom. She sees me but doesn't stop. I want to run to her, hug her, tell her how sorry I am. Martin casts a shadow over me. Clenching my arms, he says, "Johanna. My God. What happened to you?"

Instinctively, I cover the side of my face. "I fell down the stairs."

His eyebrows arch. "Do you need anything?"

"I'm fine." My eye is swollen shut, but it doesn't hurt. "How is she?" I stare after Tessa.

Martin drops his head to his chest.

"Sorry, stupid question. Does she need to talk or anything?"

"She needs to rest. Doctor's orders." He clamps a hand on my shoulder, sort of steering me out. "I'm sure she'll let you know when she's ready to talk."

No, she won't. She hates me.

As I'm studying my face in the mirror up close and personal, the phone rings. Reeve, calling to apologize?

"Hey, lesbo. You're alive."

I slump into a chair at the table, where the candle gnomes have hardened.

"I'm moving today," Novak says. "I have gobs of stuff for you. Clothes, books, shoes if they fit. I cleaned out my closet. . . . You're probably really busy, huh? I thought I'd drop these things by. . . ."

I feel alive. For the first time.

"Are you busy?"

Tessa's baby is dead and I'm alive.

"Johanna? I don't blame you for not speaking to me. I'm sorry. For anything and everything I ever did to you, I'm sorry."

A smile curls my lips and I lift my head. Actually, I'm happy. How can I be happy?

Novak says, "I need you."

That engages my brain. "What do you need now?" I snap.

She hesitates. "I have all this stuff for you, but I can't fit it in my car. I thought maybe I'd drop some off, then you could follow me back with your car and we could load up the rest."

My face is a tie-dye of blue green purple black yellow amber tan. Sort of cool.

"If I don't get everything out of here, I'm afraid Mom will sell it or give it to the Goodwill. Dante has to work—"

"Tessa lost the baby."

"What?" Novak gasps. "When?"

"She just had another miscarriage."

"Oh my God," Novak says. "Johanna. My God. Poor Tessa."

"I know," I say. "I need to be here."

"Of course you do. I'm so sorry. Tell Tessa I'm sorry. Martin too." Novak inhales audibly. "Oh my God," she says in an exhale. "Is there anything I can do?"

I press the wound to see if it changes color. "You have to move. You're busy."

"I'm not too busy to—"

"I have to go be with Tessa."

Novak says, "Call me later. You know, if you want to talk." She adds, "How's it going with Reeve?"

I hang up.

# *Joyland: Take 9*

I open the gate and walk up the crumbling sidewalk. I ring the door-
bell and Anthony answers.

"Is Reeve here?" I say.

He ogles me. "Who nailed you, bitch?"

"You did, asshole." *It might as well have been your fist,* I think.
*It should've been your face.*

Reeve comes to the door and the guy explodes in gaseous fumes.
"Johanna. My love." She takes me in her arms. "I'm sorry. I'm
sorry, I'm sorry, I'm sorry." She kisses my eye and my cheek and
my lips. "I love you so much. Forgive me."

"You know I do."

"I need you. I need you, I need you, I need you."

"I know."

"I love you, I love—"

*I press a finger to her lips. She doesn't have to say it. I know it.
I've always known.*

"Come away with me," I tell her.

*We float to the car and drive off. We drive off the edge of the
world.*

. . .

Eye shadow I have. Three shades of brown. Neutral lip gloss.
No foundation or whatever it's called. I brush on sparkly
cheek highlighter, which must be Novak's. It only enhances
the cut and the mass of swollen flesh over my cheekbone.

I should probably stay home until I heal. *When will that be?*

I am fascinated with my face, a need for people to see me,
stare at me. Look at me.

Why hasn't Reeve called? She doesn't need to apologize; it
wasn't her fault. Not really. I was so sure Reeve would stop by,
the way she does without warning, that I called in sick for
work last night. "The flu," I told Shondri. I faked a cough.

"I'm real sorry," Shondri said.

"I'll be in tomorrow for sure."

"Don't come in if you're sick. I can handle it."

"No," I promised her. "I'll be there."

I check myself out in the rearview mirror as I'm driving to
school. I look tough.

Mrs. Goins is the first to say anything. "Johanna." She
stops me in the hall. "My gosh. What happened to your eye?"

"I fell."

She frowns.

"It was an accident."

"My gosh," she says again. She keeps staring at me.

Now I feel too visible. "I'm late."

"Maybe you should see the nurse."

"I'm fine." I scuttle off down the hall, sensing her eyes on me. Now everyone is looking. People turn their heads.

Novak is camped out at my locker. Why does she have to come to school today of all days? She scrambles to her feet when she sees me. "Oh my God." She covers her mouth with her hands. "What the fuck?"

"I fell." I nudge her out of the way to open my locker.

"You fell?"

"I tripped on the stairs." I yank my lock and swing the door open.

"You klutz. When?"

She's standing too close.

I step back. "Friday or Saturday. I forget."

Novak's eyes fuse to my face. "Are you all right?"

"Yeah. Why wouldn't I be?"

She can't stop looking.

Go away, I think. You're not the one I need to see. My locker is empty. Classes are over. Why am I here?

I guess I'm hoping Reeve still has finals.

"Johanna." Novak opens her arms to me.

*No!* "I told you. I'm fine."

# Chapter 20

The media center is empty. I take that back. One person hunches over a PC, clicking away like a time bomb. As if on cue, she glances up, watches me as I wander toward the silent reading area and over to the beanbag chairs.

I drop into one and shut my eyes. I mentally call Reeve: *Are you here? I need to see you, touch you, tell you it's okay. I need to—*

I feel a presence and open my eyes. "What?" I ask Britt.

Tentatively, she lowers herself into the beanbag next to mine. She leans forward.

"What?" I say again.

"She did it to me too."

"Did what?"

"Marked me."

I make a face. Ow. "What are you talking about?"

"You know."

No, I don't. Marked her. How?

"She's mean," Britt says. "She's got this ugly place inside her and you never know what'll open it and set her off. She'll keep doing this to you."

"You're jealous. You had her; you let her go."

Britt just sits there, staring. Then glancing away like she can't look.

I push to my feet and sling my pack over my shoulder. I need to find Reeve.

The second I step out into the quad, a hand shoots out to clamp my wrist and I'm yanked backward so hard my shoulder pops.

His case clubs my leg. "Let go, Robbie."

He holds firm.

"You're hurting me."

His hand loosens. He looks crushed. "I just wanted you to come," he says.

"Come where?"

His eyes meld to my swollen cheek.

"I fell. Is Reeve in the pit?"

He doesn't answer. He turns and walks off.

If Robbie's here . . .

B2 is open. Robbie hits the light and illuminates the underworld. He doesn't check to see if I'm behind him, but it's like he knows I am. Like he can smell me.

When he opens the door to the pit, Reeve jumps up from the floor. A human shield, Robbie, blocks my entrance, and her exit. He pushes Reeve onto the loveseat.

"See?" he says, yanking my wrist to pull me in. "I told you."

Reeve meets my eyes and swallows hard.

"You did that to her," Robbie says accusingly.

"I know what I did." Reeve's eyes never leave me as she gets up, gazes into my eyes, moves toward me.

"Reeve . . ."

"Don't." She jabs my shoulder with the base of her hand. "I know you didn't mean it."

"Yeah?" she mutters. "What if I did?"

Robbie says, "She didn't mean it. She loves you."

I blink over at him. He's fixed on Reeve. She turns away. Did she tell him that? I say to Robbie, to Reeve, "I love her too."

Robbie steps around me, out the door. Out of our space.


We lie together on the loveseat, touching each other's faces and eyes and lips. Tracing contours and lines and shapes. Reeve keeps kissing my eye.

She doesn't say she's sorry, but she doesn't need to.

I tell her about Tessa, the baby, how and when it happened. The first baby too. Reeve listens as she touches my forehead, my eyebrow; she kisses my eye. I tell her I understand about her hitting me. She can't help it.

She watches my lips as I talk. She says, "You're so stupid."

"What?"

"To love me."

"You love me too."

"I'll hurt you. I'll continue to hurt you. Ask Britt. Ask everyone."

"You can't hurt me," I tell her. Fuck Britt. And Melia. Fuck numbers one through . . . whatever.

"This doesn't hurt?" She presses a finger to my cut. Involuntarily, I flinch.

"See? You don't believe in reality? Physical evidence?"

"I believe in truth."

She runs a fingertip across my eyelashes. Her eyelashes are scant, both eyes now. "We didn't even eat first," she says.

"I *know*," I say. "Come over later."

"You didn't drink the wine, did you?"

I click my tongue. "No. I saved it. I knew you'd be back."

"Oh, you knew." A smile tugs her lips. "You know me so well."

I kiss her nose, her eye. "Plus, you forgot your shoes."

"Tell me about it. I drove home barefoot and stepped on broken glass in my driveway."

I get up to check out her feet. "Are you hurt?"

She pushes me back down. She rolls on top and kisses me hard.

Time dissolves.

"Do you have my shoes?" she asks, coming up for air.

"I'm holding them for ransom."

She gazes at me, into me. She slithers her fingers down the length of my arm. "Are you okay?"

"Yes," I say. "More than okay."

"I should have forced Robbie to come. He would've protected you."

We kiss again. Time washes away.

Robbie bursts in and says, "School's out." His case clunks on the floor.

Reeve and I both stagger to our feet, then giggle as we

steady each other. I glance over at Robbie, expecting him to smile, to be happy for us.

He looks . . . brain-dead.

As we wind through the labyrinth, one sentence circulates in my brain: Robbie would've protected you.

I've been physically hurt by two people in my life. Reeve, which doesn't count because it isn't her fault. And Robbie, when he dislocated my shoulder.

It wasn't his fault either, but there's a difference. Given time and love, Reeve could learn to control her rage. She has the capacity, I know.

I'm not so sure about Robbie.


"What's his name?" Jeannette plumps the pillow while I hold up Carrie's head. Her eyes are partially open but unresponsive.

Because only guys smack girls around?

"It was an accident," I tell her.

She motions for me to set Carrie down. As I do, a breath leaks out from between her lips and Jeannette and I both freeze.

But it's only a reflex.

Jeannette smoothes Carrie's silk comforter across her chest and shoulders. "It's always an accident, Johanna. Oldest excuse in the book."

This conversation is over. "I'll sit with her for a while."

"Don't touch anything. Evelyn has a photographic memory."

Jeannette's gaze penetrates me, like she can see into my core. "I'm fine," I tell her. My core is solid.

## *Joyland: Take 10*

I feed her my last bite of chocolate mousse and she closes her eyes in ecstasy. "Rapture," she breathes. As I slide the spoon slowly out of her mouth, I place my lips against hers and taste.

Butter and cream. I lick the inside of her mouth and around her tongue. We kiss across the smoldering candle. Without detaching our lips, she comes around the table and slides onto my lap.

She clasps my face in her hands and kisses me hard, bends my head back on my neck. I think my neck will snap. Come with me, Reeve, I think. I can't die without you.

She slips my spaghetti straps over my shoulders, runs her hands down my bare arms, and presses her lips to my neck.

My arms curl around her waist. Bare, naked skin, soft and velvety. Baby fuzz. Her cami is silk, slick, and cool. My hands journey up underneath and I feel her ribs, her spine, her bra. I trace *both hands around her sides to the front. I locate the snap. As her breasts spring free, she says, "Kiss it."*

. . .

"What are you doing here?"

I jump.

Evelyn says, "Do you have permission to be in here?"

"I, uh . . ."

She reaches across Carrie and yanks her hand out of mine. Tucking Carrie's arm under the covers, she says, "Who are you? I've seen you here."

"Johanna," I answer, standing. "I volunteer at the hospice."

"As what?"

That's a good question. "I was just keeping Carrie company."

"She doesn't need company." Her mom adjusts her head on the pillow and adds, "In case you didn't notice, she's asleep. She needs to rest."

She needs to die, I think.

"Please leave."

Not a problem.

In the public ward, Mrs. and Mr. Mockrie have their beds rolled together. So sweet. They're both sleeping. Quietly, I pull a chair up and sit, drinking in their peace.

## Joyland: Take 11

She says, "Will you marry me?"

"Yes." I don't hesitate.

Her luminous smile radiates sun and moon and stars. She is my galaxy, my gravity, the center of my being.

We decide to wear white, to symbolize the purity of our love. We buy matching wedding gowns, strapless and snug at the waist, flowing, milky rivers of white satin to the floor. Our veils are lace. Through the snowflake pattern, we gaze into each other's eyes.

At the last minute, in the bedroom getting dressed, we decide to walk down the aisle barefoot. She slips a garter up my leg and pauses, moving both her hands around my left thigh. She falls to her knees. She lifts my dress and kisses me, there, between my legs. It tingles. She crooks her finger and I look. She's left a lipstick print on my thong.

"Mark me," she says.

• • •

166

"Aggie? Where are you?" Mr. Mockrie struggles to sit up.

"She's right here." I take his hand in mine.

Tears bubble in his eyes and I pat his shoulder. "She's here, Mr. Mockrie. She'll always be with you."

# Chapter 21

I stop at Taco Bell on my way home from the hospice, then remember I have quesadilla ingredients for an army. When the
cashier at Taco Bell stares at me, I just smile. Let her think
what she wants. My black eye, it's like . . . a badge of honor, or
proof I'm alive.

Reeve left two messages on my voice mail. "Hi. It's me. I
hate leaving messages."

Two: "Don't call me here. I don't want that bastard trash
talking to you. I think I can get out later, like eleven? Will you
light a candle for me?"

"A cathedral full of candles, Reeve."

I wrench on the shower and step in. My face pulses as
hot water expands every pore. I close my eyes and Fallon
Falls appears. I'm standing under the plunging cascade of
water, my face and body pounded by the force of unhar-

nessed energy. Reeve comes into view. Reeve disappears. Physically and emotionally drained, I'm too tired to even get to Joyland.


A dusty box of tea lights is left over from Tessa's days in the apartment. I light one for each window, then all the others for the planks of every step. When I switch off the inside lights, it looks totally romantic. I sit hugging my knees on the landing, waiting for Reeve.

I hear her first. She says, "Don't disappear. Let me know when it's time to leave."

"It's time to leave."

Robbie came?

At the bottom of the stairs, they stop. "Hi," I say, standing. "You made it."

Reeve doesn't say anything. Robbie goes, "Are we having a séance?"

Reeve backhands him in the chest.

"Come on up," I say.

Robbie asks, "Do you have rat traps? Are there spiders?"

"He's afraid of creepy crawlies," Reeve says. "He's a wuss."

"No rats," I tell him. "No roaches or spiders."

Reeve has to shove him up the stairs. He peers cautiously into the apartment, sniffs the air, and puckers his nose.

"Scrubbing Bubbles," I tell him. I smile at Reeve.

She pushes him in and Robbie goes, "Graup," or something. "You live here?"

Reeve says, "Look out for the bat."

He covers his head.

Reeve cricks a grin at me. She snakes a hand behind my head and pulls me in to kiss her.

A light-year later Reeve yells, "Don't go in there!"

I jerk around to see Robbie in the hall.

"That's Johanna's private space. You have no right." Reeve takes off after him.

"Don't worry about it." Shutting the apartment door behind me, I call, "Go ahead and look around. You guys want something to drink?"

Robbie stumbles back into the living room, his jaw slack. "You live here?" he says again.

Reeve shoves him a little. "Shut up. You sound like a tard."

"Could I move in?" he asks.

I look from Robbie to Reeve. "Anytime."

Reeve says, "Don't give him ideas." She retrieves an object from her bag. "I didn't have anything to wrap it with," she says, handing it to me.

It's heavy. "You didn't have to get me anything."

She looks into my eyes. "Yeah," she says. "I did."

Oh, Reeve.

"Open it."

The box is long and black, with a silver emblem. Pretty. I set it on the coffee table and lift off the top.

"Oh my God," I gasp.

"They're sterling silver," Reeve says.

Two candlesticks, a matched set.

"Oh my God," I say again. "Where did you . . . ?"

I don't finish. These had to cost, like, a hundred dollars. Where would Reeve get . . . She takes my face in her hands and kisses me.

"I'm dying of starvation," Robbie says. He finds the bowl of chips I planned to set out, along with the jar of salsa. *Don't think about where she got the money.*

Robbie sinks to the low divan, his knees hitting his chin.

As I'm replacing the candlesticks in the box, Robbie says, "Can we watch these movies?"

"What . . . ?" Shit. The DVDs.

Reeve says, "Go ahead. Put them out."

"What?" Oh, the candlesticks. "I don't have any long candles." I hurry over and snatch the DVD Robbie plucked up off the floor. His eyes glint.

Reeve says, "Damn. I should've bought candles. I knew I should have bought candles." She fists her leg, hard.

"It's okay." I scramble to gather all the DVDs and toss them into the coat closet. "Next time."

Reeve says, "Johanna?"

I turn. She's come up behind me with a glass of wine.

Robbie says, "Where's mine?"

"You don't drink," she informs him.

"Yes, I do."

"No, you don't." She sips, then spits it back into her glass. "I forgot." She raises her glass and chinks mine. "To firsts," she says.

"Firsts," I repeat. We drink together.

Robbie sprawls the length of the divan, looking pissed.

"He's on meds," Reeve says.

"No, I'm not. But you should be," Robbie growls.

Reeve lowers her glass and glares at him. Then her face softens. She walks over and hands him her glass of wine. "Okay. But don't get wasted. I may need you to drive home."

He drives?

Reeve returns to the kitchen for another glass, while Robbie gulps his wine, dribbling it down his shirt. He doesn't even notice.

"Shove over." Reeve throws his ankles off the end of the divan and Robbie flails to sit up. She flops down next to him. "Cheers." She raises her glass.

I sit on the coffee table across from her. "Cheers." We all clink.

The wine smells spicy and tastes like . . . cranberries? I'm not really a connoisseur.

Reeve eyes me over her glass. God, why did she bring him? I want to attack her.

I stand and say, "I'll start dinner."

"Let me help." Reeve bounces to her feet.

She shadows me to the kitchen, tickling the back of my neck, saying, "He'll pass out after one glass. Plus, his brain shuts down at ten."

"How can you tell?" I ask.

She thumps my back, playfully. I open the refrigerator to retrieve all the ingredients, but Reeve nudges me out of the way. "I'll get everything." She kisses me first and I melt.

The TV comes on at some point and there's heavy breathing and moaning. I glance over and go, "Crap." I missed a DVD, or he found them. I hustle across the room and wrench the remote out of Robbie's hand. "We're not watching TV."

He pouts.

"How's your sister?" Reeve asks from the kitchen, where she's sawing a tomato with a dull knife.

"I don't know," I say. "I haven't seen her." I haven't talked to her, haven't run into her. She hasn't come up to have a conversation with me.

"Tell her I'm sorry about the baby," Reeve says.

"I will. If I talk to her." Where'd I leave my wine?

Reeve opens the refrigerator and pulls open the vegetable crisper. She says, "I can't stop thinking about how it would be to lose a baby. I mean, if you really wanted it. Not like an abortion, where you choose. Mom tried to abort us."

"What?"

"Where's the cheese? You have cheese, don't you?"

"Um, yeah. In the door." I'm stunned. "How do you know?"

"About the abortion? She told us."

God.

"It was too late by the time she went in to have us aborted. She's so stupid. Do you want kids?" Reeve asks.

I take a gulp of wine. No. Yes. I don't know. I say, "I'm an avowed lesbian."

Reeve laughs. "Yeah. I used to think I was bi, for about an hour." She yanks open a silverware drawer and withdraws the meat cleaver. "Do you want this chopped or shredded?" She poises the knife over the head of lettuce.

"Whatever," I say.

Reeve adds, "I told you me and Robbie are twins, didn't I?" My double take is classic. "How?"

She screws up her face. "The sperm meets the egg. . . ."

"I mean, you have different last names." I mean, he's autistic.

"Not to mention how much we look alike." She chops lettuce, while my brain scrambles to catch up. She says, "My mom's a whore. She turns tricks for money."

I don't get the connection. I sit in a chair at the table, wine in hand, watching Reeve butchering that head of lettuce.

"She was sleeping with so many dicks, there's no telling who our father is."

Unbelievable. Twins.

"I sort of look like my dad, or at least the guy Mom says is my dad. She was sleeping with Anthony too, so she gave him credit for Robbie." She exaggerates a smile.

Is that even legal? I want to ask her about the autism, but instead I say, "Do you want kids?"

"Oh yeah. Ten at least."

I can't tell if she's serious.

"I did it once with a guy," she says, looking up and meeting my eyes. "Does that disgust you? You being so avowed and all."

I stick out my tongue at her and her eyes gleam.

"Did it count?" I ask.

Her eyes go blank. Ripping the tortilla package open with her teeth, she spits out the corner and says, "What's Robbie doing?"

I swivel my head. His glass of wine is empty, clutched in one hand on his chest while the other arm hangs limply to the floor. "Zoning. Sleeping."

"I had to bring him," she says in a lowered voice. "I'm sorry." She searches a couple of cupboards for something.

"What do you need?" I ask.

"Cookie sheets. An aluminum tray. Whatever we're going to broil these on."

"Under the stove." I get up to show her.

She bends to the oven drawer and clangs pans around, then withdraws a blackened cookie sheet I've never used. I watch her assemble the quesadillas like she's done it every day of her life.

"Do I just put it on broil?" Reeve asks, studying the oven dial.

"The oven doesn't work."

She spins around.

"We'll have to nuke them."

Reeve just looks at me. "You might've told me that before I put them on a cookie sheet."

My face flares. "Sorry. You can use plates."

Reeve goes, "Then I'll have to do them one at a time."

"Yeah."

"And they won't be crispy."

"No."

She lets out a short breath.

She had a plan and I screwed it up. I suck as a girlfriend.

The quesadillas cook fast, anyway. Reeve hands the plates to me and I transport them to the table. The lettuce and tomatoes add a gourmet touch. "They look awesome," I tell her.

"They would've been better broiled."

"I know. I'm sorry."

Reeve goes over and shoves Robbie awake. As he stumbles to the table, I pull over a step stool so he can use my chair.

"No." Reeve pushes me off roughly. "He can sit on the stool." Is she still mad about the oven?

Robbie and I switch. He's groggy and I feel the same way, though my stupor is probably from the wine. Reeve refills my glass and hers. She pours Robbie a little. "To our first meal together." She raises her glass and clinks mine. She clinks Robbie's.

Robbie says, "To DVD porn."

Reeve ignores him. "To Johanna," she says. "My first avowed lesbian."

I crack up. Really? We drink.

"To Reeve," I toast. "My first . . . everything."

Robbie swipes his nose with the back of his hand, coughs, and a loogie flies out of his mouth and onto my quesadilla.

Reeve looks at my plate, then up at me. She bursts into laughter.

Her laughter makes me laugh.

She says, "He's an asstard, but what can I do?"

# Chapter 22

## Joyland: Take 12

Reeve strikes the last chord and holds it while the crushing roar of the crowd detonates eardrums. She throws her head forward, bending at the waist, flinging her arms out to the side and letting her guitar swing free on the strap. As she unfolds, the people scream their adoration. She nods to Robbie beside her.

He blows a discordant riff on his saxophone and the notes trickle into space.

I push the button to engage the hydraulic lift.

A square of stage shifts where Reeve is standing. Smoothly, it descends. Roaring cheers echo down into the chamber where I wait.

When Reeve hits the bottom, I'm there to meet her. She removes the guitar over her head and I say, "You were awe—"

She pulls me to her and kisses me hard, rough. Her tongue jams into my mouth. I catch my breath and inhale her. She's hot. She's thirsty. She digs her mouth and teeth into me and my flesh smears *her sweat. Our knees buckle as we kneel together, kissing, tonguing, groping every inch of bare, slick skin.*

*Strobe lights flash above us. Raw, shooting streaks of blue and green and red. They ripple over our bodies. The noise is a drug.*

*I feel the jolt, the surge. Motors whir and we're rising. We're high, higher, Reeve's mouth is on mine, her body stretched out, legs extended. We're naked, horizontal, and exposed. I'm vaguely aware of the motion up up up, then off. We're on the stage.*

*The audience is manic. We're making love in front of a hundred thousand cheering people. We do it. We give them a show.*

*The sky glitters with stars and moons. Robbie blips a sparkling riff, then disappears. It's only me and Reeve, one star. We are the night.*

. . .

Light streams through my miniblinds and I bolt upright. I check the time: 9:36. I forgot to set the alarm.

Wait.

There's no school today. I fall back down. School is over. I blow out relief and bliss.

I survived high school. Is there a club for high school survivors? A special-color ribbon? I really don't think I'll be looking back with fondness ten or fifty years from now. No medals or trophies or awards of distinction. My best moment has come at the end, when I finally connected with her.

I saved the best for last.

Novak calls as I'm reheating Reeve's leftover quesadilla for breakfast. Last night, Reeve and I had only started kissing and getting into each other when Robbie announced, "It's time to go." Reeve pushed me away so fast, it was like a car bomb exploded in her brain.

"We're going to pick up our caps and gowns today, right?" Novak says.

"No," I answer automatically. "I'm going with Reeve and Robbie."

Where did that come from? We didn't discuss graduation.

Novak doesn't speak for a minute. "So, do you hate me now?"

I suppress a weary sigh. "No."

"I didn't know what I was doing, okay? I was temporarily blinded by lust or insanity. Make that overwhelming guilt."

"About what?" I ask.

"All those times I had someone and you didn't."

A claw rips my gut. "So it was a pity kiss? Wow, thanks."

Novak huffs a breath.

"I have to go," I say.

"Johanna, wait. God!" she cries. "Mom hired this party planner and a decorator and a live band for my grad bash."

A live band? Just like in my sex dream. Hey, am I prophetic?

"Won't she be surprised when, like, two people show up?" Novak laughs.

I chew off a hunk of quesadilla and zone. If Reeve deposited DNA on her tortilla, we are officially exchanging body fluids.

"I sent Reeve and Robbie an invitation. Do you think they'll RSVP?"

I swallow my bite. "How'd you find her address?"

"I have my ways. Mooahaha."

"What ways?" I don't want Novak talking to Reeve—ever.

"Student directory? Duh." Novak rambles on and I'm gone. We both still had most of our clothes on, on the bed. Reeve kept her eyes closed when we kissed. I tried, but my natural instinct is to open my eyes, to see her.

"How's Tessa?"

That brings me back. "I don't know. Fine, I guess." Martin hasn't been up to report on her status. She certainly hasn't reached out.

Novak blurts, "Couldn't I come live with you? Just for the summer?"

Before I can reply, she adds, "I'm sorry. It's just . . . I hate it here. I'm lonely. Dante's never home."

Imagine Reeve living here with me. We'd spend every moment together, in Joyland, where we'd ride along the beach and dash under waterfalls.

"Okay, thanks for listening," Novak says. "I'll let you go. I didn't mean to make this your problem."

"Novak—"

"I love you, Banana," she says, and the line goes dead.

*Please, Novak. Please get out of my head. And elsewhere.*

What am I going to do today? I call Reeve.

Her mother answers. "Who is this?" She sounds drunk.

"Johanna. A friend of Reeve's," I say.

"What kina friend?"

I think I hear Reeve's voice in the background. "A friend from school." Her mother goes, "It's a frien' a yours. Since when do you have frien's?"

A guy laughs.

Reeve's voice: "Give me that, bitch." There's muffled scuf-fling and Reeve comes on. "Yeah?"

"Hi. It's me."

She says, "What are you doing?" Kind of mad.

"Calling you?"

"That was a good idea, wasn't it?"

My stomach plunges. Reeve doesn't say anything else.

"Are you busy today?" I ask. "Do you want to come over?"

She covers the phone or something, but it doesn't mute her voice. "Do you mind? This is private."

"One of your cunt lickers?" he says.

There's a crack and a squeal. Reeve yells, "Robbie, no!" She comes back on. "Don't call me here." The phone cuts out.

The horror of her life grows in my chest like cancer.

I head to my room, seething. I need to get her out of there. Take a drive. Pick her up and maybe drive to Fallon Falls. As I'm clomping down the stairs to leave, Tessa slides open the patio door and steps out. She has on shorts and a grungy tee of Martin's that reads: DINOSAURS DIED FOR OUR SINS.

"Are you leaving for school?" she says. "It's late." She checks her watch.

"School's over," I tell her.

"It is?" She blinks like she's been asleep, or out of it. "I guess it is that time already. Do you have a watch?"

"Yeah. Why?" Pretty cold. I want to ask how she is, but I can't get the words out.

We stand there. A cloud passes in front of the sun and the temperature drops ten degrees. Tessa clutches her coffee mug with both hands and drinks from it. She glances up and starts to cough. I want to pound her back, comfort her, tell her how much I love and miss her.

She chokes out, "What happened to you?"

The wound is scabbed over and the bruise is receding. Still yellow-gray around the edges.

"I fell down the . . ."

Tessa says, "Why didn't you—" at the same time I say, "It was the same night you—"

We both stop. "I'm so sorry about the baby," I say.

She says flatly, "Thank you. Isn't that what I'm supposed to say?"

I don't know. Is she asking me, or telling me. . . .

"Johanna, I—"

My key ring falls off my thumb and chinks on the flagstone. I bend to scoop up the keys. When I straighten, Tessa's looking at me, into me. "I can't believe you're not going to your own graduation. It's an accomplishment," she says. "It means something."

I shrug. "Not to me."

"Not to you," Tessa repeats. "What is significant and meaningful to you?"

"Besides being gay? Besides coming out to you and you not even caring enough to call me and talk about it?" My voice sounds shrill.

Tessa swallows hard. Her cheeks flush red, like mine always do when I'm embarrassed or mad.

My throat closes completely. I have to get out of here.

* * *

I veer into a 7-Eleven to use the pay phone. *This* is significant and meaningful in my life, Tessa. I dial Reeve's number. The mother answers and I hang up. Your love and acceptance. *That* would have been significant.

All you had to do was call. Say, Johanna, I got your letter.

I get in the car and drive. When someone writes, "I have something really important to tell you," you respond. When they write, "Last time you were home I wanted to talk to you about it, but I was too scared. I don't know why. I know you love me. You'll love me no matter what. Right?" You confirm, Tessa. I poured out my *heart* to you.

What was your reaction when you read, "Okay, here goes. I'm gay"? What did you think? For weeks, months, I sweated it. I still do, every day. Are you deliberately making me go through this hell? You've never once brought up the subject the whole time you've been home. Significant and meaningful? What's *your* definition, Tessa?

I look up and I'm sitting at the curb in front of Reeve's house. Consciously, I channel my anger into courage to get out and go up to Reeve's door. As I'm locking the car, Reeve storms out of the house, her mother on her heels. "I told you I need a fix *today*," she screeches.

"I heard you!" Reeve heads for the van. I wave to flag her down, but she shouts, "I'll follow you!" and jumps in the van.

I get back in the car and shift into gear. Reeve backs out the driveway and squeals a wide arc in the street, then waits for me to pass her. About half a mile down the road, right before the highway ramp, I pull into a Ramada Inn and Reeve drives up behind me. We both get out.

"What do you want?" she yells, stalking up to me and whacking my shoulder.

I take her hand. "You." I pull her to me, pressing her face to my shoulder. "It's okay," I say into her hair. "I'm here."

She doesn't struggle. "Why?" she asks.

"Why what?"

She smacks me again. "Stop saying that. Why?" she repeats. "That's what I want to know. Why do you care?"

I trace the side of her face with my knuckles. "Because I love you. And you need me."

"You're wrong. And you're stupid." But she snakes her arms around my neck.

"And you're warm," I say.

And you're mine.

# Chapter 23

Reeve points across the street to a Village Inn. "Can we go there? I'm hungry."

"Have you ever been?"

She frowns. "No."

"Then, yeah. It'll be a first for both of us."

She smiles into my eyes.

I ache to hold her hand crossing the street, but if someone honks or hurls a slur . . . Reeve doesn't need that right now.

At VI the hostess shows us to a booth and we scoot in across from each other. I feel lighter, buoyant almost, like a boat. Reeve moors me.

"You have to get out of there," I tell her.

The waitress comes and Reeve orders coffee. Reeve opens the menu and says, "I don't have any money."

"I'm buying," I tell her. "Order whatever you want."

She studies the menu while I study her over it. She's not wearing makeup and her eyes seem smaller, more recessed. A carafe of coffee arrives and Reeve pours us both a cup. "Are you getting breakfast or lunch?" she asks.

I'd check my watch if I was wearing one. "Whatever you're getting."

Reeve drinks her coffee black and I make a mental note: Learn her habits. The waitress returns and Reeve orders French toast. "Same," I say.

I lean across the table and reach out my hands. "I'm serious about you moving in."

She pulls the rack of jellies over in front of her and sorts through them. "We haven't even had sex yet."

"We will."

She doesn't glance up, but her lips twist. Her face is kind of pale and splotchy. The few eyelashes she has left are white blond.

"I know what you're going to say," I continue. "Bring him. Robbie can move in too."

"Just move in." Reeve skids the jellies to the wall.

"I'll help you move."

She blows out a breath between her teeth.

"What?"

She sits back, crosses her arms, and steels her face. She looks so fierce and bold. I scoot out the end of the booth and around the table to slide in next to her, to put my arm around her, both arms. She lists, resting her head on my shoulder.

"You don't understand," she says quietly. "You don't know everything."

"I don't care." Only now matters. What we do with our life together.

Reeve doesn't speak, so I press my temple to her head to will her thoughts into my brain.

The waitress brings our food. She looks at me and says, "Are you sitting on that side?"

I go, "Is that okay?"

She sets our plates in front of us and replies, "I don't care, but it's a family restaurant."

Reeve and I look at each other and crack up. I'm staying put.

The French toast is awesome. I can't remember the last time I ate a real breakfast.

"Are you going to graduation?" Reeve asks, sawing off a corner of bread.

"I don't know. Are you?"

"Are you kidding?" She chews and swallows. "It's the biggest day of Robbie's life. The whole family's coming." She pours more hot syrup over her stack and adds, "Even my dad might show."

"I thought he was gone."

She eats in silence.

"You have to come," Reeve says in this pleading voice. "I want you to graduate with me."

"Then I will."

She freshens her coffee from the pot and says, "We have to go to Novak's party too."

"No."

"Yes." She whaps my arm. "We're both going. I want to see that bitch's face when I fuck you in her bed."

I hesitate . . . then laugh.

Reeve takes my face in her hands and kisses me. In broad daylight, in the Village Inn.

We drive back to my apartment to hang for a while. Get naked? Do it in *my* bed I hope I hope. Tessa and Martin are out back planting flowers or shrubs. Martin usually does the yard work, cleans the house, cooks. He's the total package.

Reeve says, "Is that your sister?"

I tighten my grip on her hand and tug her toward the stairs. "Do you know when we can pick up our caps and gowns? Like, how much time do we have?" I start up the stairs, but Reeve slips out of my grasp. She heads for Tessa.

*Shit.*

Tessa straightens, arms at her sides, digger pointed at the ground.

Reeve says, "I'm sorry about your baby."

Tessa's eyes fuse to mine. What is that expression? Horror? Outrage? She aims the sharp point of the digger at Reeve, or me.

Martin pops up from behind the forsythia bush. "Hey, Mojo." He looks at Reeve.

"This is Reeve," I say, threading my fingers between hers. "My girlfriend."

Martin's eyes bulge. He sticks out his hand and shakes Reeve's. "I'm Martin, the evil bro-in-law."

Reeve says, "I'm sorry about your baby."

Martin cuts to Tessa, then back to Reeve. "Thank you."

Tessa, with the digger.

Reeve adds, "I was in your house while it was happening."

"What?" Tessa says, sounding shocked.

"We're out of here." I go to grasp Reeve's hand, but she's way ahead of me. She's halfway up the stairs. On the landing, she crosses her arms and taps her foot. I reach around her to unlock the door.

Reeve charges inside and whirls on me. "They didn't even know who I was. Didn't you tell them about me?"

"No. I mean . . ." I expel a breath. "My sister knows I'm gay, but—"

She storms down the hall and slams into the bathroom. I say through the door, "Reeve, I'm sorry." I'm not sure what I'm apologizing for. "We don't talk that much. Not about significant things. Meaningful things."

The door swings open and Reeve lunges out at me. She smashes me against the wall, her face on fire. "Bye."

She heads out.

"Don't go!" I chase her down. "Reeve." I catch her as she grabs for the doorknob, flinging my arms around her waist from behind and pulling her into me.

We stand pressed together, front to back. She's trembling. "I'm sorry. I don't think about introducing my friends to Tessa anymore."

"Is that all I am? A friend?"

"Of course not," I say. "I love you."

"Am I the only one?" she asks.

"Yes. Completely." First, last, and always.

She turns and kisses me so hard she cuts my lip on her teeth, then pushes me back. I taste blood.

Her face disintegrates and she shrivels into herself. I hold her; kiss the top of her head gently. "I want us to be together. Always." She needs tenderness, reassurance. "I love you," I say softly.

"I don't trust Robbie to be alone with Anthony. I shouldn't have left him there. I have to bail," she says.

"It's okay." I rub her shoulders and gaze down into her eyes. "Maybe I can get out later."

My hopes soar. "I'll be here." I smile and see her relax.

Hand in hand, we descend the stairs. I walk Reeve to the van and we linger on a goodbye kiss. When I return, Tessa is looming at the edge of the patio. "I want to talk to you," she says.

Well, finally. I cross my arms, bracing.

She says, "I can't believe you told a complete stranger about my personal life."

"She's not a complete stranger, obviously. Reeve Hartt, by the way. That's her name. She's my girlfriend."

Tessa saws her jaw until it pops. "The baby was our business. My private business, Johanna."

My arms uncross and dangle at my sides. "Sorry." It comes out a murmur.

Tessa's eyes pool with tears. She rushes to the sliding door, rolls it open then closed behind her.

I think, God. I'm the worst sister in the world. No wonder she's given up on me.

# Chapter 24

Shondri calls the next morning and asks if I can come in to work. "Yes," I tell her. I need the money bad.

She adds, "My kid has a doctor's appointment at eleven. You think you can handle it alone for an hour?"

"Absolutely." I didn't know she had a kid. "I'm on my way."

There's a knock on my door as I'm slugging down my last Fresca for breakfast. I open the door cautiously, scared it might be Tessa ready to rip into me some more.

"Oh my God." I throw my arms around Reeve. "Hi." Robbie's with her.

"You should ask who it is," Reeve says.

"I knew it was you."

She kisses me. I pull her inside and the kiss prolongs.

Robbie makes a gagging sound in his throat, like paper tearing, and Reeve and I start laughing in our kiss.

"Yikes," I say. "I have to go to work."

Reeve undoes the top two buttons on my white shirt. "Better," she goes.

Damn. Dammit. I have to go; I need the money for my insurance. "If you guys want to hang here for a while, that's cool. I'll try to get off early."

"Can we watch porn?" Robbie asks.

I just look at him.

Reeve says, "We're going with you."

"What?"

She fists me in the arm.

"To work?"

"Is that a problem?"

"Um . . ."

"We'll help out, won't we?" She elbows Robbie.

Okay. Wow.

The phone rings as we're leaving and Reeve says, "Don't you want to get that?"

I shut the door behind us. The only person I want to talk to is here. Novak called last night and left a message. She needed to see me. She needed to talk. She needs, needs, needs.

In my peripheral vision, I see Tessa and Martin on the patio, sitting next to each other in new chairs. Adirondack chairs with footrests. There's a new gas grill too.

I'm only doing this for Reeve. I tell her, "I want to introduce you officially. And Robbie too."

"Robbie!" Reeve calls to him. He's plodded off in the direction of my car. "Stop." He obeys.

They're deep in conversation, or at least Martin is. He's reading to Tessa from the gas grill directions.

"Um, guys?"

He and Tessa swivel their heads.

"I want you to meet Reeve and Robbie. Well, you've already met Reeve. But officially, this is my girlfriend, Reeve Hartt. And her brother, Robbie Inouye."

Martin loops his legs off each side of the chair and stands.

"They're twins," I say. Don't ask me why I think that's significant and meaningful. Because it is to Reeve?

Martin balls a fist and holds it out to Robbie. "Word up, homie."

Robbie knuckles him back.

"Nice to see you again," he says to Reeve, smiling.

She blinks. "Yeah, you too."

Tessa forces a thin, unconvincing smile.

Martin says, "You guys want to stay for lunch? I'm going to fire up this puppy and barbecue ribs. If I can figure out how to get the propane tank attached."

"No, thanks," I reply. "I have to go to work."

Martin fakes a pout. "How about you two?"

Tessa lowers her head and looks away.

Robbie says, "Okay."

Reeve grabs his sleeve. "We're going to work with Johanna. But thanks."

"Rain check," Martin tells them. "You're welcome anytime." He engulfs me in a hug, and Reeve too.

It makes me think he and Tessa talked about it—about me. He's showing support and acceptance.

Robbie says, "Just screw on the tank, dude." He shows Martin where on the gas grill.

"Dude," Martin goes. "Any moron could've figured that 'un out, eh?"

Everyone laughs but Tessa.



"He's cool," Reeve says as we round the corner of the house.

"Yeah, he's a good guy." Tessa found her soul mate. I smile. So have I. "You want to ride with me?" I ask Reeve.

"Absolutely. Since we took the bus."

She rode the bus clear over here to see me? What if I wasn't here? I told her I'd always be here. And I was. Score one for me.

The mall echoes our footsteps as all the stores and stalls are being readied to open. At Bling's, the grate is halfway up, so I duck underneath and Reeve and Robbie trail behind.

Shondri is loading the register. "These are my friends, Reeve and Robbie," I tell her. "Reeve is my girlfriend." I toss Reeve a quick smile, thinking, I just came out to Shondri. "They're here to help."

Shondri says to me, "Can I talk to you?"

My heart drops. Reeve takes the hint and shoves Robbie down the aisle.

Shondri says, "They can't work without applying and getting hired and filling out W-2s."

"They're not *working* working. They're just helping out. They're not getting paid." Do they expect to be paid? I'll just pay them out of my check.

Shondri eyes me, then shifts her gaze to them. "Is he the one smacking you around?"

I huff in disgust.

"Today you got a fat lip."

Do I? I feel it with my tongue and it is swollen. Reeve kissed me hard.

"It's . . . herpes," I say. "It flares up."

Shondri's expression doesn't change.

I tell her, "You could try them out. See if you want to hire them. We need help, right?"

Shondri watches Robbie pick up a ponytail holder and stretch it as far as it'll go, then snap it at Reeve. She throws one at him.

Shondri cracks a roll of quarters over the cash drawer. "My kid's got the flu bad. I've got to leave."

"I can handle it," I say. "If you want to go now, we can hold down the fort."

Shondri says, "I just need to be out of here by ten-thirty for the doctor." She slips the register key into the secret drawer. "It's on your head."

What does that mean?

"Show them how to set up the displays."

"Okay." I walk to the back, feeling weird about this. Why? I say to Reeve, "You're in. If you do good, Shondri might hire you."

"Yeah?" Robbie perks up.

Reeve screws up her face, like, Who'd work here?

Exactly. "Do you want me to put your purse in the store-room?"

"I'm fine." Reeve squeezes her purse to her side.

Robbie has his case. I look at it, then him. He clutches it to his chest.

I stash my stuff, then show them the drawers where the inventory is stored; I tell them to reload the hooks on the walls and the racks on the tables. Robbie props his case against the wall and begins arranging the fake fingernails and stick-on jewels.

Reeve fills a spinner of earrings, while I do watches and bracelets. She meets my eyes once and winks. God, could I do her in the storeroom?

Shondri bustles by. "That looks nice," she grumbles at Reeve.

Reeve smiles. "Thanks."

Shondri never told me my displays looked good. I take my promotion as a sign she's satisfied with my work, though.

As soon as we open, it's a mob scene. Tweeners everywhere. I home in on this suspicious-looking group of grungy guys, all wearing lowriders and chains. The girls are sneaky. They finger the necklaces and talk on their cells. They leave without buying anything. A second wave flows in. Were they summoned by the cells? Sometimes they work in teams.

A commotion out in the mall draws my attention.

Mall security is there and . . . Oh my God. Oh no. A security guard has Robbie by the arm.

I dash out.

"What else did you take?" the guard says. Robbie yanks two scrunchies off his wrist.

"What's going on?" I interrupt.

Over Robbie's shoulder, I see Reeve. She slips a pair of earrings from her purse into her back pocket. I try to get her to look at me, but she gazes off into the mall.

The security guard goes, "Follow me."

"No." I snag the guard's arm. "It's a mistake. They work here."

"Oh, really?" She arches her eyebrows. "Then why were they leaving?"

God. Oh God.

"Please," the guard insists. "Follow me."

Reeve fixes on me.

"You have it wrong," I say. "I made them do it."

My story is lame. I asked Reeve and Robbie to come in and steal for me because I worked at Bling's and I didn't want to lose my job. I'm a terrible liar.

There are two security guards in the office, a lady and a man. The lady says, "Jim, I can handle this. Why don't you go on back."

I feel like hurling.

She eyes each of us—me, Robbie, Reeve. Reeve's head is down. "What's in the case?" she asks Robbie.

"Nothing," I answer for him. "I mean, there's an instrument. Robbie has a lesson today. He didn't put anything in the case."

"Is that true?" she asks Robbie.

He's suddenly a deaf-mute.

"They're innocent," I say. "They only agreed to do it because they're my friends."

The guard twiddles a red pen between her first and second

fingers. She taps it on her paper. "You can go," she says. I get up and snag Reeve's arm.

"Not you." She points the pen at me.

I sit.

Reeve and Robbie stand and leave quickly.

The guard says to me, "This is really stupid."

Tears well in my eyes. "I know."

"I'm going to let you off this time."

"You are?"

"You need to leave the mall and never come back."

But my job . . .

"Did you hear me?"

A long moment passes.

"Now would be a good time."

I scramble to get up. My heart hammers in my chest and my stomach hurts. I need my keys, which are in my bag, in the storeroom at Bling's.

Shondri's on the phone when I reenter. She looks right through me and her eyes go vacant.

I let her down. God, punish me.

Outside, I drive around the mall twice, but there's no sign of Robbie or Reeve. A raindrop splatters on the windshield and a hot tear streaks down my cheek.

Damn. I needed that job.

# Chapter 25

She calls just as I'm about to crash. "You're so stupid."

I take the phone into the hall, sit on the floor with my back to the wall, and flatten my feet against the opposite wall. Tessa used to shimmy up the wall by pushing with her feet and wriggling her back. She called it the spider. As a kid I was always too short, but Tessa would put me in her lap and we'd spider together.

"That was crazy," Reeve says. She lets out a small laugh. "What did your boss say?"

"Nothing."

"You didn't get busted, though, right?"

"Right," I lie. "I quit. I hated that job anyway."

"Did security give you her number?"

"What?"

Reeve goes, "She's a dyke. She had our backs, girl."

She did? I guess I was too freaked out to register her on my gaydar.

"She wanted you bad."

"Oh, sure."

Reeve laughs softly. The laugh fades and she says, "I want you bad."

I stutter a breath. "Can you come over?"

She doesn't answer. "What time tomorrow can we pick up our caps and gowns?" she says. "Do you know?"

"No." I tongue the blood blister under my lip.

"We have rehearsal in the morning, so maybe we pick them up afterwards?"

"We have rehearsal?" I say.

"Where do you live, girl?"

"Here. Come over."

"I can't," she says. "We got back late and Anthony . . ." Her voice lowers. "Never mind."

If he hurts her, I'll kill him. I will.

Reeve says, "I'll check the schedule, if I can find it. I can't believe we're graduating Saturday."

"I could pick you up tomorrow. At the 7-Eleven or something."

"No. I'll come to you."

We don't speak for a minute, just cling to our connection.

Reeve says, "I'm in the closet."

"Oh, right." She's the out-est person I know. People sometimes delude themselves into thinking they're safe, that they blend, or pass. Everyone knows. Even if they suspect, you're tagged. "Your secret's safe with me," I say.

Reeve exhales audibly. "Someday I'll show you my closet.

It's deep and dark and there are secrets nobody knows. Secrets no one will ever know."

"Keep your secrets," I tell her. "You're starting life over with me."

When Reeve breathes out, I breathe in. I close my eyes and will us together.

She says, "I can't use the phone after nine. What time is it?"

I don't know. I'm sitting in the dark so I'm guessing it's after nine. "What happens if you get caught?"

"You don't want to know."

My imagination fills the blank spaces. Don't hurt her. Please, God.

"I'm pushing my luck. Better fly."

"I love you," I say.

She doesn't say it back, but she's thinking it. I know she is.


I forget, or never knew, that you have to pay ninety dollars when you pick up your cap and gown. If you don't order early. If you forget to order, or if you live day to day, in Joyland, for Reeve, with no plans for the future.

Reeve says, "I didn't forget. I just wasn't sure we were graduating. I skipped a lot this year. And Robbie . . ." She glances over at him. "Can you cover us? I'll pay you back."

I have my checkbook in my purse, but I still need to pay my car insurance, and my final check from Bling's will be minuscule now. If I even get one. The guy taking money for grad gear doesn't call the bank to verify my balance, thank God.

The ladies who are fitting robes in the gym can't get Robbie to drop his case. He shifts it from hand to hand, holding tight. Now I imagine he has a shitload from Bling's in there.

We aren't the only people who waited until the last minute and have to settle for leftovers. Our gowns are faded and shabby; mine's too short; Robbie's is frayed. While Reeve's getting hers from a rack in the back, Britt appears.

"Is she making you pay yet?" Britt asks.

"Huh?"

"All she does is take and take and take."

I click my tongue at Britt.

She says, "Don't say I didn't warn you." She slings her robe hanger over her shoulder and exits.

I go find Reeve. "Can we leave these at your place?" She folds her gown over her arm.

"Do you plan to spend the night?" I ask.

She says, "If only."

Robbie sniffs his cap. What does he smell? Our school colors are jade and pewter. We're going to look like a sea of algae.

"I'm stoked," Reeve says as we meander down the main hall from the gym. "I never thought we'd make it." Her eyes glisten. "We'll never walk these halls again."

I snake an arm around her waist and she rests her head on my shoulder. "Are you going to miss it?" I ask.

"Yeah," she says. "Aren't you?"

"Seriously? No," I admit.

"Not the school part, yeah. But the rest of it . . ."

The rest is what I'm terrible at—feeling a part of anything.

In the quad, seniors mill around and some girl calls out to Reeve. Reeve takes my hand and heads in that direction. All the years I dreamed about this, being together with her. The reality is even better than the fantasy.

The girls are the LBDs. Reeve says, "You guys know Johanna."

They all look at me like, Who? Except Britt. The rest of them check me out, sort of undress me with their eyes—not an unpleasant feeling.

One of the girls asks Reeve, "Are you still going to Florida State?"

Reeve says, "Sure. How about you?"

The conversation dulls in my ears and I stare at Reeve. She didn't tell me about going to college out of state. We haven't talked about the future. Yet.

Britt studies my face, then smiles. It isn't a happy smile. More . . . sympathy, or pity?

*Pity you, Britt.*

Robbie's case bumps my leg and I turn. He bumps me again. I mouth, Quit it.

He bumps me again.

I fake-jab an elbow into his gut.

Reeve is talking to the LBDs about Pride Day. When is it? Where should they meet? This beam inside me lights. I've always wanted to go to Pride, and now my first time will be with my girlfriend.

On the way to the car, I ask her, "Are you really going to Florida State?"

She eyes Robbie ahead of us and her whole body seems to deflate. "What do you think?"

\* \* \*

My arms are full of robes and I feel weighted down with the re-
alization that Reeve feels trapped. Novak rushes out the sliding
glass door and flings her arms around me, almost flattening me.
"Oh my fucking God, we're graduating! Here, let me help you."

We get wrapped up together in the billowing plastic
cleaner bags. "Thanks."

Novak stoops to pick up one of the caps. "I just talked to
Tessa." She clomps behind me up the stairs. "She's having her
tubes tied."

I stop dead on the landing. "When?"

Novak shrugs. "She didn't say."

All Tessa used to talk about with me and her friends was
how she was getting married as soon as possible and having
kids while she was young, not like our parents. Back when I
worshipped her, when she considered me a friend. She'd spider
up the wall, the phone cradled to her ear. "I want six kids, at
least." She'd wink at me.

Martin made lists of baby names: Emanuel, Aidan, Jake—
wait. That's what he was doing on the laptop the day Tessa—

They were having a boy.

"Let me get the door." Novak takes the keys from my
hand.

Tessa is giving up on something she desperately wants.

Novak opens the apartment door and we step inside. I
heap the robes on the divan while Novak removes my bag
from my shoulder.

"Stop it." I snatch it out of her hands. "What do you
want?"

"God. Why are you so pissed at me?"

"Why am I pissed? You kissed me." You used me, I think.

"Dante dumped me," she says. Immediately, she adds, "Don't look so shocked."

Do I?

"We both knew it was coming." She flips her hair over her shoulder. "He was just waiting for the right time and place, when it would hurt me the most." Her eyes are puffy and she looks demolished.

"I'm . . . sorry," I say. "What a jerk."

"I don't know what to do, Johanna." Tears film her red eyes. "He wants me out today. I know I can't live here. I just need someone to talk to." She blinks and a tear spills over the rim. "Just talk to me."

God. God, Novak.

She buries her face in her arms and bawls.

At the hardest time in my life, when I was coming out, she was there for me. The whole time Mom was dying. She was the only one. Novak.

"Novak," I say softly. "Come here."

## Joyland: Take 13

*Night descends and the dark is profound. I'm falling, falling down a canyon wall into a river of syrup. She flows around me, through me. Her lips on mine are sticky sweet and I melt into the riverbed.*

*We're dragonflies on lily pads, mermaids swimming free. Her body wraps around me and fills the emptiness inside until I'm full to bursting at the gills.*

*My fingers tangle hair; the long, golden, silky strands twist around my fingers, pulling tight, fingers turning purple. I close my eyes and dream. She takes me into Joyland.*

• • •

# Chapter 26

Reeve calls to tell me she and Robbie will be at my place by nine to pick up their caps and gowns. "I love you," I say.

It's *you* I love.

She wears short shorts and a tank. She smells like heavy perfume or incense, and I bury my face in her hair. She whispers, "Me too."

I knew it.

Robbie has on a dress shirt that's yellowed and wrinkled, like right off the rack at Goodwill. Reeve says, "I should've come earlier so we could celebrate in private."

*God.* I kiss her to delirium.

A knock sounds on the door and I panic.

Robbie says, "I'll get it."

"Don't—"

He opens it to Tessa.

She delays a smile before going, "Hi." She doesn't enter. She stands at the threshold and looks at her watch. "Graduation starts at eleven, right? Do we need tickets?"

I blink to Robbie, then Reeve.

"Because when I graduated, family members had to have tickets. It was limited seating."

I say, "It's outside on the football field."

Reeve adds, "If you want to be in the bleachers, you should get there early. Otherwise, people stand or sit on the grass."

Tessa stares at me. What?

"Here." She holds out an envelope.

More money? I never asked for money. All I wanted . . . On the front is printed: CANCELLATION NOTICE. Shit.

"You're not driving without insurance," Tessa says.

*Watch me.*

"There's usually a thirty-day grace period, so you should be okay. Where's the money I gave you?"

It takes every ounce of willpower not to glance over at the candleholders. I say, "I have it."

Tessa says sternly, "Pay the bill, Johanna."

I toss the envelope on the divan.

She goes, "Is that what you're wearing?"

I scan my outfit. I have on shorts too, a tee, and my Converses. "Yeah." *What do you care?*

Tessa's eyes infiltrate my brain, where a steel grate slams down. "Could we get some pictures of you in your cap and gown?" Her attention shifts to Reeve. "All of you?"

I turn away. "We weren't going to get dressed until we got to—"

"Pictures would be cool," Reeve cuts in. She heads toward the bedroom. "Where is everything, Johanna?"

"In here." I hung our gowns in the coat closet. Robbie wanders out of the kitchen with the bag of Doritos. "You want some?" He extends it to Tessa.

"No. Thanks." She presses a hand to her stomach.

I notice then she doesn't look well.

Reeve takes the bundle of robes from me and sorts through them. She hands me mine and Robbie his.

Tessa says, "Do you need any help?"

She looks so pale and sad. "No," I say. "But thanks."

Reeve asks her, "Which side does the tassel go on?"

"Left," Tessa answers. "Then you flip it to the right at the end of the ceremony."

"Cool." Reeve smiles at her.

Tessa says to me, "Come downstairs when you're dressed. We can take pictures in the backyard." She stalls in the doorway, like there's more. "Is your family coming?" she asks Reeve.

"Oh yeah. Try and stop them." Reeve removes her cap from the bag.

Tessa says, "Maybe we could all sit together."

Reeve shoots me a panicked look.

"There'll be too many of them for you all to sit together," I say.

"Right." Reeve doesn't take her eyes off me. "They won't even all fit in the bleachers."

Tessa's eyes pierce me. *What, Tessa? Say it.*

"How do you get this thing on?" Robbie garbles through a

mouthful of chips. He's gotten himself all twisted up in his robe.

Reeve drops her cap on the divan to shake him loose.

Tessa's footsteps sound on the stairs.

I say out of nowhere, "She's going to have her tubes tied."

Reeve says, "Really? Why?"

"She doesn't want to get pregnant again."

"Duh. I mean, why doesn't Martin get a vasectomy?"

Robbie goes, "Ow. You stuck me."

Reeve snaps, "Stand still or I will."

"They shouldn't give up yet," I say. "They're still young. They should keep trying."

Reeve locates a straight pin in Robbie's hem. "When's she having the operation? Maybe you can talk her out of it."

"I don't know. She didn't tell me. She told Novak."

Reeve says, "She told Novak before you?"

I remove the plastic bag from my robe and think aloud, "She likes Novak better."

Reeve turns and asks, "When did you see Novak?"

I unclip my cap from the hanger. I separate the little plastic bag with the tassel, wishing I hadn't brought up this subject.

Reeve waits for an answer.

"Yesterday."

"She came here?"

This conversation can't continue. "Do you tie the tassel onto this knobby thing?"

Robbie says, "My zipper's stuck."

"Stop pulling." Reeve slugs him. "You broke it." She fists him again and I feel it in my chest.

"Here, let me help him." I take Reeve's balled fist and squeeze it gently. "You get dressed."

"Congratulations." Martin hugs me, then Reeve. With Robbie, he goes, "Dude," and they strike knuckles.

Martin drops his gaze. "What do you have there?"

Oh God. The case. Is Robbie actually bringing it to graduation?

"Is that a sax?" Martin's eyes gleam. "I played the sax in band. Can I see it?" He holds out his hand.

Robbie gives him the case.

Just like that. Martin squats to open it. "I think I still have mine in the garage. Alto or tenor?" he asks. He snaps open the clasps.

Robbie crouches down beside him. "It's not a saxophone."

Tessa calls, "Hurry up. Martin, what are you doing?"

Robbie relatches the case, stands, and grasps the handle.

Martin goes, "Show me later."

Robbie nods.

Tessa lines us up by the forsythia bush, whose yellow flowers are in full blaze. She snaps two or three pictures, then rearranges us. She says, "Can I get a couple of each of you alone?"

I hate having my picture taken.

"Smile," Tessa says.

I look more natural when I don't smile.

Martin goes, "I want in." He runs behind us and snakes his arms across our shoulders.

Tessa centers a shot.

Martin says, "Let me get one with you and Johanna."

Reeve must feel my muscles tense, because she says, "We better go. What time is it?"

I say, "We're already late. You guys go ahead; I'll meet you at the car."

I rush upstairs for my bag and keys. As I lock the door, Martin calls up the steps, "We'll give you a shout-out when you're on stage. Wave so we can get a picture."

Tessa says, "Johanna?"

I launch off the last step and head for Reeve and Robbie, who are halfway across the yard.

"Johanna!"

Reeve flings out a stiff arm to block me. "Go see what she wants." Reeve widens her eyes at me.

*Only for you.*

"Congratulations," Tessa says.

"Thanks." We stand there awkwardly.

Tessa picks up a box off the gas grill and hands it to me. It's wrapped in our school colors. I glance over my shoulder at Reeve, who's waiting by my car. "Open it," Tessa says. "You have time."

Quickly, I rip off the wrapping to find a blue plastic case. It's hinged. I open it, and gasp.

"Oh my God." It's a gold watch with a diamond-studded crystal. Are they real diamonds? "You didn't have to do this."

"Put it on."

Now?

Tessa takes the case from me and unhooks the watch from the velveteen base. "This isn't the original case. I lost it in the move." Her nails are manicured and polished, which they never are. "Mom gave me this for my graduation."

A lump rises in my throat.

Tessa flips my wrist over and adds, "I know she'd want you to have it." She clasps the watch.

I can't even look at it or I'll start bawling.

"It's too big," Tessa says. "I can take it in and get the band adjusted."

"No." I back up a step. "It's fine. I like it loose." My arm drops and the watch is gobbled up by the sleeve of my robe.

Tessa hugs me. Not tight. She lets go. I try to say thank you or thanks or I love you or I'm sorry, I miss Mom, don't you, don't you wish she was here? Do you hate me, please don't hate me anymore. Please, Tessa, please?

# Chapter 27

It's a hundred degrees and I'm sweating in my robe. Ahead of me, perspiration beads up on Robbie's neck. He has bare spots in his hair, like mange or something. Like cigarette burns?

I can't see Reeve. Novak passes at the head of her row during "Pomp and Circumstance," but she seems lost in her own little world. Where's Reeve?

The bleachers are packed. I search but don't see anyone I know, not that I expect to.

The speeches are endless. Mrs. Goins accepts an award for her years of service and she almost breaks down. At the end, she opens her arms and says, "I'll miss you most of all."

My throat catches. Mom said that to me. Tessa was moving her out of the house to the hospice and Mom was looking at her things, touching them for the last time. Mom clasped my hand and said, "I'll miss you most of all." I think it hurt Tessa's feelings. *But Mom meant both of us, Tessa.* She did.

The roster of names goes on. When I get my diploma, Mrs. Goins hugs me and says, "Johanna. I'll remember your kindness and generosity."

"You will?"

A flashbulb blinds me.

Then it's over. We stand as a class and flip our tassels. I look around at all the people I know, and don't know, and a wave of panic sweeps over me. Real life starts now.

"We have to get over there." Robbie points.

I can't see through the forest of robes. Robbie begins knocking people aside with his trusty case.

Reeve has already found her way to the family area, where her mom slumps next to her, looking strung out. Anthony's there, his slicked-back hair. He blows out a stream of cigarette smoke and says to Robbie, "The retardo graduates."

Anthony smiles at me and my skin crawls.

There's no one else in their family group. Anthony keeps smiling at me.

Reeve says to no one in particular, "We have to go turn in our robes."

Anthony flicks a long ash onto her cap.

Robbie yanks Anthony's wrist up so hard it makes him yelp. "Don't!" Reeve says. She chops down Robbie's arm. Robbie brushes the ashes off her cap.

Anthony stubs out his cigarette in the grass and says to me, "I hope you're coming to the party."

I look at Reeve, but she's gazing off into the distance.

"Reevie"—he fingers my tassel—"if she's too much woman for you, I'd be happy to share."

Reeve doesn't hit him or kick him or spit in his face. She's fixed on an object, a moving object, coming our way.

Something tickles my neck and I flinch. Anthony has lifted my hair and is blowing on my neck. Blech. Get away.

Reeve says, "He's here." She ducks her head and shoots past me.

"Who?"

People have spread blankets on the grass and kids are running around. The zipper on my robe scritches and I glance down to see Anthony pulling it.

I lurch away, then charge off in Reeve's direction, feeling violated. "Reeve!" At the end of the folding chairs, she stops.

"You okay?" I ask.

She wheezes. "I can't see him. I don't want to talk to him."

"Who?"

"My dad."

I check over my shoulder. A skinny guy in a skullcap gives Anthony a high-five handshake. Robbie is rubbernecking the crowd and I hold up a hand to signal him.

Reeve yanks down my sleeve. "I don't want him to see me. Get me out of here."

I take Reeve's hand and we jog to the main building. At the gym, Reeve falls back against the brick wall, breathing hard. "He's come for us. He'll take us. He said he'd come and he did."

She doubles over and dry-heaves.

"Baby." I rub her back. "No one's going to take you."

"Where's Robbie?" She straightens fast. "Oh my God. I left Robbie."

I snag the back of her robe as she tries to bolt. "Robbie saw us. He's coming."

Reeve raises her eyes to me. "You don't know what my father will do. What he did to us."

I know enough. I wish I didn't. "It's over, Reeve," I tell her. "No one's going to hurt you again."

"You don't know that." She pushes me. "You don't know anything. You can't just say that and it fixes us."

I grab her wrists and draw her to me. I hold her hard. She starts shaking and I tighten my grip. I hold her until the earthquake ends.

"Where's Robbie?" she asks again.

I peer around the corner and Robbie almost decapitates me. He swishes by me in his billowing robe and halts in front of Reeve. They don't say anything to each other. Robbie flattens his back against the wall beside her, crushing his case to his chest.

"I killed him," he says. "I killed them both."

Reeve goes, "Sure you did."

He could splinter their skulls with that case.

Reeve says, "It's so hot." The noonday sun is directly overhead. "Let's take these off." Reeve unzips her robe.

Robbie unzips his. Mine is halfway unzipped already and I finish the job. We step out of the robes and I begin to gather them. Reeve says, "He knows we have to turn these in at the gym. Just leave them here." She kicks them into a heap. "Someone will find them."

I'll lose the deposit. But I never really paid it.

"We can't go back out there." Reeve shudders.

"We won't," I say. "We'll figure out—"

"The party." Robbie fits his cap on the end of his case. "That rich bitch's party."

"No," I say. "We're not going to Novak's."

Reeve looks at me. "Why not?"

My eyes fall. "I just don't want to go."

He says, "I do. It's the best place. We'll be safe there."

Reeve knuckles Robbie on the head. "Smart thinking, brainiac. Sometimes your mental powers scare me."

Robbie says, "The retardo graduates."

She laughs. I love Robbie for making her laugh.

But I really don't want to go to the party.

# Chapter 28

A hundred cars cram Novak's circular drive. We have to park in the cul-de-sac.

Reeve says to Robbie, "Leave your case here."

Robbie squashes it to his chest.

"No one's going to take it," I tell him.

His eyes bounce around the car.

"I'll lock the doors. It'll be safe."

Reluctantly, he sets the case on the floor by the backseat.

The patio is a feeding frenzy. You can't see the band, but you can hear the reverb. The three of us hang at the fringe for a minute and, surreptitiously, I seek out Novak.

Robbie splits off and Reeve calls, "Where are you going?"

"I smell meat." He sniffs the air, then raises both arms like a zombie.

Reeve says, "Get me something too."

He weaves through a clot of blue-hairs toward the food tents and we lose him. "The whole fucking school's here," Reeve mutters.

She slides her hand into mine and smiles up at me. Her eyes shine. She's gone heavy on the makeup, green and silver, our school colors. "I always feel safe with you," she says. "That worries me."

"Why?"

"It just does. You might be the first person I've ever trusted."

I wrap my arms around her and close my eyes. I will the sick feeling inside to go away.

"Lesbo!" Attacking from behind, Novak swings me around and smothers me in a hug.

I peel her off.

Novak thrusts her fist into the air and whoops, "We did it!" She laughs in my face. Her shoulder glances mine and she says in my ear, "Thanks for last night."

Warning flares go up. Where's Reeve?

Novak touches my hand. "Meet me at the greenhouse?"

I step away, and see Reeve glaring at Novak. I reach for her but can't grasp her hand.

"I'm hungry," Reeve announces. "I'm going to find Robbie."

Novak's arm hooks around my neck. "Kiss me."

"Stop it," I say between clenched teeth. "Please," I plead with her. *Please, Novak.* I run to catch up to Reeve.

She's found Robbie in a food tent, where he's bent over a steaming vat of Swedish meatballs. He plucks out a meatball with his fingers and goes, "Hot." He pops it into his mouth. He shakes the steaming gravy from his fingers back into the pot.

A caterer in a white shirt smirks. Reeve slams the metal lid on Robbie's fingers. "Get a plate," she orders. "Get a couple. And forks too."

"What's she on?" Reeve says to me.

"Who?"

"The love of your life."

I just look at Reeve. "I don't know. You name it. And she's not."

Reeve goes, "What's going on between you two?"

Heat rises up my neck. "Nothing. We're friends. I told you."

Reeve narrows her eyes like she doesn't believe me. Then they go imploring like she wants to—needs to. Robbie shoves a plate in her face and says, "The meatballs taste like caca."

That sort of breaks the tension. Reeve and I inch along the buffet line, filling our plates. We're so close, I think. She trusts me. Nothing, *no one*, can be allowed to jeopardize that.

The first wave of people have finished eating and Reeve leads us to an empty table out on the lawn. People drink or dance or lounge around the pool. Robbie wolfs down his food. We eat in silence, watching all the people. I wonder what Tessa and Martin are doing. Are they here?

Reeve says, out of the blue, "So, where's the greenhouse?"

"What?"

She balls a fist.

The greenhouse, relative to where we are . . . ? "Over there somewhere." I wave my fork.

Reeve pushes back from the table and stands. "I know we weren't invited, but you don't mind if we come along with you." She yanks Robbie up by his arm.

"I wasn't going . . . I'm not go—"

She takes off, with Robbie in tow.


Don't be here don't be here please don't be here— "Shut the door!" a voice calls. I wait until Reeve and Robbie are inside.

She slouches against the far wall, an open bottle of vodka clutched in her hand. Bottles are littered across the dirt floor. "Welcome to my grad bash." Novak hoists the bottle to her lips.

If she drank all of this by herself, I think, she could die of alcohol poisoning. God, Novak.

"What are these?" Reeve asks. Her fingertips graze a blossom.

"Orchids," I tell her. "Novak's mom raises orchids."

"As opposed to children," Novak says, and laughs hysterically.

Robbie coughs behind me. I look at him and he plugs his nose. Yeah, it's pungent in here. Fertilizer and mold and booze. Sweat is filming on my skin.

Reeve moseys down the aisle, touching each of the orchids. A rectangular table splits the greenhouse in two. There are pots of orchids arranged on the table.

I cross to the other aisle to get to Novak. "You've had enough." I wrestle the bottle out of her hand. She grabs a beer beside her and I take that too.

Novak says, "When is it ever enough?"

I scan for Reeve. She's picking a tall purple and white orchid. *No, don't pick them!*

"Come on. You need to get up and walk." I try to pull Novak up, but she's limp.

"Joho." She smiles up at me. "Johanna, Johanna, you are a banana." She cracks herself up.

I yank on her arm.

Novak says, "Can I stay over with you?"

Across the table, Reeve's eyes meet mine.

"I promise to be a goo' girl this time. You know I'm good."

I mental Novak: *Pleeease.*

"You slept with her?"

"No," I huff. "It wasn't like that. We talked. Dante dumped her and she needed to talk."

"She stayed overnight?" Reeve says.

Novak goes, "You kissed me first."

I whirl on her. "Stop. You promised."

Reeve makes a sound in her throat.

"It wasn't like that," I say.

"You did it, Joho. You finally got me."

"Shut up," I snap at Novak. I catch Reeve's eye again. "Nothing happened."

"You slept in the same bed?"

Novak goes, "Naked."

"Shut. Up. We were not naked." I need to get to Reeve. "Novak was upset and she didn't have anywhere to go." I gauge the distance. I'm closer to the door, so I veer in that direction, stiff-arming Robbie out of my way. "Her mother kicked her out."

Reeve moves in the opposite direction, toward Novak.

"Lesbo's *damn* good." Novak clunks her head against the glass of the greenhouse. "But you know that, huh, Reeve?"

Reeve stops. She kicks Novak in the stomach. Novak grunts and doubles over.

"Reeve!" I yelp.

Reeve kicks her again in the side.

"Stop it!"

Then in the face. "Reeve!" I charge and push her away.

Novak groans. She crumples over and curls into a ball. I'm grasping Reeve's arm, but she kicks Novak hard again.

"Goddammit." I spin Reeve around. She fists my face. I feel my neck snap and something come loose. She slams me again.

The Earth trembles and Robbie's there, clenching Reeve's wrist, then both of them, forcing her back.

Reeve lets out this keening wail and wrenches out of Robbie's grasp. I step over Novak to get to her, to Reeve.

Reeve starts trembling uncontrollably and I say, "It's okay." I draw her into me.

Behind me, Novak writhes on the floor, moaning. She could die. She could pass out and die.

"I'm here, baby." Blood drips off my arm, onto the floor. "I only love you." My blood, spurting from my nose, smearing in her hair. I hold her tighter, squashing my nose into her head. "I'm sorry. I should've told you." I sniff and blood runs down the back of my throat. "She doesn't mean anything to me." My eyes shift down to Novak. "She's nothing."

Novak hauls herself up to her hands and knees. Her hair covers her face and she pukes.

Robbie goes, "Dude." He staggers backward. I steer Reeve ahead of me, out the door. I hear Novak hurl again.

Reeve's focused on me, her eyes wild.

"It's okay," I tell her. There's blood all over her hair and in my mouth. "It'll be fine." I press my wrist to my nose to stanch the flow and a sharp object scratches my face. The gold watch. "Let's go," I say. I take Reeve's hand and tug her toward the car.

"Where's Robbie?" She stops.

Where'd he go?

"We have to find him," Reeve says.

"I will," I say.

She blocks me. "You can't go." Her eyes skim down my front, my face. She swallows hard. "I'll go," she says. "We'll meet you at the car."

With the bottom of my tee, I wipe off Reeve's arm where blood dripped. It soaked into her shirt, but only the side. I want to kiss her so bad.

She touches the watch.

"It's yours," I say. What's mine is yours. *Just love me.* I unlatch the wristband, or try to. It's stuck. Reeve backs away before I can get it off.

*Joyland: Take 14*

*The dark is bitter, thick and viscous. The dark fills every crevice and crack in my nails as I scrape bottom. I'm alone in this bottle of ink, this bottomless well of sticky pitch. I open my mouth to cry out, "Where are you, Reeve?"*

*She answers, "I'm here."*

*Her voice is so faint.*

*I claw through the murky tar as it hardens.*

*"I'm here." Her voice sounds clearer.*

*"Here."*

*Closer.*

*I reach her. We clasp hands. She's clean and washed, the water-fall cleansing her skin pure and white. I swim up next to her and feel the release, the warm, sweet rush of water. The darkness falls away, the ink rinses clear and free. A diluted pool of grayish scum swirls at my feet and down the drain.*

*She plucks a rose petal from my hair.*

*The petal liquefies in her hand and drips blood off her fingers. She cries.*

· · ·

# Chapter 29

My nose is broken. Overnight the bridge swelled to a bulb and the bruise radiated out and under my eyes. I stare at myself in the medicine cabinet mirror for a long time.

I deserve this. For what I did. I'm so . . . so weak.

Reeve, I'm sorry. I'm so sorry.

I don't know how long I stood looking at the busted back window of my car. Apparently, Robbie got his case. He and Reeve disappeared and I drove home feeling lost.

Then I remembered—Novak. I left her dying there. She couldn't die, could she?

Even though she promised—she *promised* not to tell—she didn't know what she was saying. She was hammered.

Betrayal all around. From all of us.

I think about driving to Reeve's house and reassuring her. *I'll always be here for you, baby. I'll never leave.* I'll explain how

I really do understand her need to test me, to see how far I'll go with her.

*All the way, Reeve. All the way.*

I go back to my bed. But for the life of me, I can't conjure up Joyland.

By afternoon, the bruising has spread down my whole left cheek. It symbolizes something—trust? Intimacy? You can trust me to take what you dole out, Reeve. I gaze into the mirror and think, This is a phase of our love. We're taking it to the next level.

I'll give Reeve time to regroup, or whatever, then I'll go to her. I need to focus on the future, next year. If Reeve wants to go to Florida State, I'll find a way to make that happen. I'll go with her. Robbie can tag along and I'll watch out for him. Why hadn't Reeve and I talked about the future? Because she doesn't feel like she has one and my future is her, the only thing I want in life.

A knock sounds on the door. "Johanna?" Tessa calls.

I don't want to see her.

She pounds harder. "I know you're there."

I shouldn't have parked in the driveway.

Tessa's dressed in flimsy drawstrings and a tank. I have this flashback to her last night home before college, when we stayed up all night to talk. All those nights. She's not talking now; she's slack-jawed. "What in heaven's name . . . ?"

I shrink behind the door.

Tessa muscles it open. "What happened to you?"

I say, "I fell."

"No, you didn't."

I open my mouth, then shut it.

"Come out here in the light." She takes me by the wrist. Her eyes squinch and she winces. "Your nose." She reaches up to touch it, but I move away. "We need to get you X-rayed."

"No. It's fine."

"It's not remotely fine. You're hurt. Who did this to you?"

"That's none of your business," I say flatly.

"I'm making it my business," she says. "You're my sister. I love you."

"Oh, really? Could've fooled me."

Tessa looks crushed. Her eyes pool.

The sliding door opens and Novak emerges. She glances up, shielding her eyes against the sun.

"What's she doing here?" I say. She limps over to one of the Adirondacks and curls into it, hugging her knees to her chest.

Tessa says, "She called last night and said she was in trouble. I told her she could stay here."

"She can't." I go to close the door. "Tell her not to call me again."

"She didn't call you. She called me. Reeve was here too."

I pull the door open. "When?"

Tessa rubs her eyes and stretches the skin across her temples. "I don't know. Two. Two-thirty. She was standing at the bottom of the stairs. When I came out, she left."

How long was Reeve here? Why didn't she come up? "Did Reeve see Novak?"

Tessa expels a weary breath. "I don't know. What does it matter?"

"It matters because Reeve might believe I brought Novak home."

Tessa bites her bottom lip and says softly, "Oh, Johanna."

It rips me. But I shut the door on her, the way she shut me out.

The bruising seeps down my face like ink. Now the left side of my mouth is swelling and turning black. Maybe more than my nose is broken? Foundation or concealer is never going to cover this. I need a mask, like the Phantom of the Opera.

It's a random solution, but I wonder if any costume shops are open. Even if they are, I don't have the money.

My watch sits next to my purse, which means I took it off at some point and laid it on the table. There's still blood smeared on the crystal.

I could pawn it, or sell it on eBay.

No. It was Mom's watch.

*Mom, can you see me from heaven? Please don't look.*

I need to get away from here, get out of my head.

At the bottom of the stairs, a wave of dizziness slows me and I steady myself on the wooden railing. I feel something carved in the wood. I lift my hand. Two words: I CANT

Who did this?

"Johanna. Hey." Novak springs like a cat.

I launch off the bottom stair and race for my car, throwing my bag across the front seat and cranking the ignition. A whoosh of air draws my eyes to the busted-out window.

"Joho!"

I shift into Drive.

"Wait."

She limps around the garage, clutching her stomach. My stomach hurts too, Novak.

Reeve did it, the carving. I CANT.

*She doesn't mean that. We have to talk.*

The gas gauge wiggles on E, but I can make it to Reeve's. I exit at Vasquez and run a yellow light. The same thought keeps winding through my brain: "I can't" is different from "I won't." "I can't" is not a decision.

She's still scared.

I see them as I turn onto 68th. Two cop cars parked in front of Reeve's house. What's going on? I pull to the curb across the street and wrench open my door. As I charge toward the driveway, an officer steps out from between the cruisers.

"You can't go in there," he says. Another cop is stringing crime-scene tape.

"What happened?" I ask.

He eyes my face. "What happened to you?"

I touch my nose and feel the bulge. "Nothing."

"Right." He shakes his head. "Are you acquainted with the residents of this house?"

The picture window is shattered, shards dangling from the window frame. "Where's Reeve Hartt?" I ask.

"Who is this Reeve Hartt?" The cop takes out a little notebook.

"Reeve and Robbie. They live here with their mom and . . . Anthony."

He flips a page. "That's Anthony Inouye, the uncle? Is there anyone else?"

"Not that I know of. Where are they?"

"Did you know them?"

Did I? What does that mean, Did I?

A movement in one of the police cars snags my attention. Behind the metal grate separating the front and backseats is Anthony. He meets my eyes and a chill slithers up my spine. He does that nasty flicking with his tongue.

The officer says, "The detectives may want to question you. Wait here."

He turns to leave and I run to my car.


This is stupid, just driving around. I do a U-turn in the Ramada lot and retrace my route back to 68th. At the last second, I change my mind and steer into the alley between blocks. I drive slowly, counting houses.

The chain-link fence in back of Reeve's house is trashed. The kitchen window is broken too. There's that yellow and black crime-scene tape everywhere.

Next door, the neighbor is outside on a plastic chair, watching a kid scrape dirt with a spoon. I park in the alley and approach her.

"Do you know what happened next door?" I ask. "Why the cops are there?"

She's not much older than me, I think. She flips through a fashion magazine. "There was a party." She dog-ears a page. "I couldn't get my baby to sleep because the music was so loud. Then there was yelling and crashing around, which is nothing new with them."

The kid is filthy, like he's been eating dirt. The girl squints up at me. "You must've been at the party."

"Me? No." Why would she think . . . ? I cover my nose with a hand.

She pages through the magazine and says, "I come out for a smoke and see Robbie tearing out the door with this knife and he takes off running. He's got blood all over him."

"Robbie?" I glance over at the house to see a man with a camera exit the back door.

"The ambulance comes, then the cops. That's all I know." She slaps her magazine closed, scoops up the kid, and disappears inside.

My vision blurs as I stumble back to the car. I feel queasy. My chest constricts and I can't breathe, like a panic attack. I make it to the car, but my aim is off and I can't stick the key in the ignition. I lie on the seat, convulsing.

I close my eyes to visualize her. Her emotions pour into me and I shiver. Her terror, hopelessness.

I CANT.

Somebody died. No no no. Don't think that way.

A final spasm ripples through me, then calm. Control.

I push on the seat to right myself. Think, Johanna. Make calls. Find her.

# Chapter 30

I slam into the curb and almost hit the mailbox. My eye is swelling shut.

"Hey." Novak jumps up from the bottom of the apartment stairs. "I want to apologize—" She stops. "Oh. My. God."

I flatten my hands over my face. Tears threaten.

Novak says, "Did she do that to you?"

My panic attack returns full force.

"What? What, sweetie?" Novak clenches my arms.

I steel myself because I need to be strong for Reeve. "I have to find her. I don't know where she is."

Novak says, "You're shivering. Sit down. Tell me what's going on."

My legs give out and I drop to the step. I press my fingers over my eyelids and they burn, my nose throbs. Think.

Words pour out: "There were cops at her house. An ambulance."

Novak eases herself down in front of me on the grass. "Just now?"

"I went over there. I drove around. I don't know where she is, or what happened."

"Okay," Novak goes. "She'll call you. Right?"

I CANT.

"You promised not to tell. Damn you!" I clutch the stair rail to haul myself up.

She scrambles to her feet and takes off running.

*Nice. Leave me to drown.* She's right, I really know how to pick them. But not Reeve. She needs me now more than ever.

Maybe, maybe she did call. A glimmer of hope lifts my feet up the stairs.

There are no messages on my phone and I barely make it to the divan before my knees give out.

"What time did this happen?" Tessa asks. I didn't shut the front door, and she and Novak are coming inside.

Novak says, "I don't know. Ask Johanna."

Tessa suddenly looms over me. "Tell me everything you know," she demands.

I slit-eye Novak. How could she run to Tessa? I can handle this. I don't need Tessa.

Tessa says, "Johanna, I can help."

"I don't think you can." I push to my feet and my head explodes.

"Johanna!" Novak yells.

"What!" I scream back.

She says, "Let Tessa help."

I look at Tessa. "No," I say. "I'll call the cops myself and find out."

"Novak told me someone was hurt, there was an ambulance," she says. "The police won't release information to you."

The conversation with the neighbor replays in my head. "Robbie had a knife. He was all bloody."

Tessa says, "Whoever was hurt was transported to a hospital, right? Do you know which one?"

"How many are there?"

Tessa says, "Thirteen, not counting all the urgent-care facilities around."

Thirteen?

"We're wasting time!" Novak cries.

She's right.

Tessa hustles out the door. "We'll find them," she calls. "Come on. We'll figure this out."

I stumble after her, elbowing Novak away.

Inside the house, Tessa opens her carryall and yanks out a thick black notebook. Page after page of resources and referrals, people and places and phone numbers to call for help.

She works at a free clinic. She'd have this.

"What's the address?" Tessa asks.

"Of what?"

"Their house." She opens to a listing of hospitals.

"I . . . I'm not sure." There's no house number on the front. "It's 68th Street."

"23 something West 68th Street," Novak pipes up. "I sent Reeve an invitation to my party."

Tessa says, "North Suburban's closest." She punches numbers on her cell. "Turn on the TV news. Yes, hello. I'm looking for someone who might have been brought into Emergency this morning? Thank you." Tessa slides onto a barstool at the counter and looks at me. "What's their last name again?"

"Hartt. Reeve Hartt," I say. "And Robbie Inouye."

The TV blasts in the living room.

Tessa says into the phone, "Hartt. Or Inouye." She asks me, "How do you spell that?"

Martin staggers in from the back, yawning. "What's up?" He rakes a hand through his messy hair.

"Someone got stabbed," Novak says behind him.

"We don't know that," I snap.

Martin asks, "Who?"

Tessa holds up a finger for silence. Bookmarking a page with her finger, she flips through a section of laminated sheets in the notebook and I see they're children's services and halfway houses, shelters and abortion clinics.

I never really knew what Tessa did at the free clinic. Fed poor people and vaccinated children?

"Okay, thank you." Tessa presses a button on her cell. "They might've gone to St. Joseph's. Or Denver Health." She pages back to the hospitals.

Martin settles a hand on my shoulder and asks, "What happened to your face?"

Novak reaches for my hand, but I won't let her. "Don't worry, Joho. We'll find her."

There is no "we." There is only me. And only Reeve.

I lower my head and close my eyes. I send her a silent message. *I'm coming. Hold on.*

"They're at St. Joseph's." Tessa shuts her cell.

Novak says, "They took Dante there after he totaled his car." She heads for the door and I snag her arm.

"You're not coming," I tell her. "This is partly your fault." I say to Tessa, "Nobody's coming."

Tessa says, "Johanna—"

"Stay out of it."

I race upstairs for my keys and bag, feeling a little dizzy. My face and hair are wet by the time I reach the car. When did it start to rain?

Tessa's waiting by my car.

I shoulder her aside and lock myself in. Jamming the key into the ignition, I crank and nothing happens.

I try again.

"Damn. Dammit." I'm out of gas. Rain is pouring through the broken window in back. I ball my fists and punch my eyes. *Ow.*

Now what? Think. THINK. My head hurts so bad.

I open the door and Tessa says, "We'll take my car."


We park in the visitors' garage and follow the signs to Emergency. The receptionist tells us, "I'm not allowed to give out information on that party. If you'll wait in the lounge, a doctor will be in to speak with you."

"What does it mean when they aren't allowed to give out information?" I ask Tessa.

"We're not family. It's not our information."

The signs point toward a corridor and as we turn the corner, I see her. "Reeve!" She's at the drinking fountain. She raises her head, pivots, and hurries off the other way.

I chase her down. I spin her around and lift her off her feet. "Reeve. Oh my God." I hold her so tight.

She says in a raspy voice, "Go away. Get the fuck out of my life."

Her carving fills my brain. I CANT.

"No, Reeve. I can't."

.

Robbie said he'd kill her. In his essay, he wrote, "May 23 I kill my mother."

Tessa is talking to an older lady who seems to be with Reeve. I don't see Robbie or their mom. I hear a few details: A bunch of Anthony's friends showed up with drugs and booze. The party got out of hand. Someone had a knife.

Reeve seems dazed, so I clutch her hand and lead her outside. There's a covered gazebo in the visitors' area. As we sit on the pentagonal bench, she looks at me, at my face, and visibly shrinks.

I lift her onto my lap and wind her legs around my waist. "It's okay, baby," I say.

"No, it's not." Her voice is hollow. "It's never going to be okay."

I rub her thin arms. "I'm here. I'm never leaving you."

Her chest heaves. I just want to hold her until she stops fighting it. She doesn't speak, doesn't volunteer information, and I don't want to push her to the dark place. I ask, "Where's Robbie?"

She shakes her head. "He grabbed the knife from Anthony and I couldn't stop him. He's so stupid." She draws her knees to her chest and I wrap my arms around her to hold her on my lap.

"Start at the beginning. You left the party. . . ."

"My dad was there."

"At Novak's?"

"No. At our house. I didn't want him to see me or Robbie, so we snuck upstairs and covered ourselves with a blanket."

No cover . . .

She lolls her head back. "I heard this crash and Mom screamed. Then Anthony yelled, 'Shut up, bitch! Shut that whore up!' She was doing meth and heroin. There was so much noise and I thought I heard a gun go off." Reeve closes her eyes. "When I got to the kitchen, Anthony was smacking Mom around. It wasn't the first time, but it was the first time she fought back." Reeve blinks at me. "She always took it. She kept taking it. My dad hit her too."

I feel my jaw clench.

Her hair is wild and tangled. I go to smooth it down and snag my fingers. "Where's your dad now?"

"Robbie sleeps so hard, you know? I thought he'd sleep through it. I don't know what happened to Mom. It was like, finally, something snapped. She said, 'That's it, Anthony,' and she grabbed a knife. I think she really would've cut him."

She should have cut out his heart.

I rub her arms. "Where were you? What were you doing?"

"Staying out of the way. I used to try to stop it, you know? With Dad too. I'd call the cops or run to the neighbors and they'd call the cops. Mom would get pissed."

"Why?"

"She didn't want to go back to rehab."

Gently, I comb my fingers through Reeve's hair. "You were just trying to save her life," I say.

"She doesn't want her life saved. She thrives on the hurt, same as you."

That stops me. "What?"

Reeve scoots off my lap. "You let me hit you. You *enjoy* it."

"No, I don't." Heat rises up my neck.

"Really?" She cocks her head. "You keep coming back for more."

"It's not the same," I say.

"How is it different?"

My mind scatters. "I don't know. It just is."

"When you figure out the difference, let me know." She turns to leave.

"The difference is . . . the *difference*"—I stand and clamp her arm—"is that you don't *want* to hurt me."

Her head swivels.

"That's the difference, Reeve."

"I don't see it. All I see is . . ." Her eyes sweep across my face.

"My love for you."

She lets out a hiss of air. "You're sick."

I take her hand and she tries to pull away, but can't. At last she surrenders. "Tell me the rest," I say.

"Can we go back inside?"

The rain mists our faces as we stroll toward the building. "So your mom's in surgery?"

She looks at me. "My mom's dead."

"No. You don't know that."

"I was there. They took her out in the ambulance."

Is she serious?

"Robbie got the knife away from Anthony, but . . ." Reeve swallows hard.

"Robbie was all bloody," I finish. "Your neighbor saw them."

Reeve's eyes fuse to mine. "Did my neighbor see Anthony kill Robbie?"

A chill slithers up my spine. "What?" I whisper.

Reeve goes, "He stabbed my mom, then he slit Robbie's throat."

# Chapter 31

Robbie is dead. I can't believe it.

The gray lady is Reeve's social services caseworker. She says to Reeve, "How do I get in touch with your father?"

"Why?" Reeve asks.

"He's your only living relative. He could take you in until—"

"She can't live there," I cut in.

Tessa goes, "Stay out of this, Johanna."

"He molested them," I tell the caseworker.

The caseworker says to Reeve, "I never heard about this."

The halls have cleared; all the doctors, nurses, police officers have gone. "He abused both of them," I say. "He beat their mother too."

Tessa fixes on Reeve.

"She's coming home with me," I tell Tessa and the gray lady.

The caseworker looks like she has a problem with it, but Tessa says to her, "Can I speak to you in private?"

They leave and I hold Reeve. Robbie's dead. He's dead. He can't be.

Tessa comes back alone. "Let's go," she says. I think she means the two of us, but she grasps Reeve's arm too.

I sit in the back and hold Reeve. She's cold and stiff.

When we get home, I steer Reeve toward my apartment, but Tessa blocks my path. "Where are you going?"

Reeve's fingers are icicles.

Tessa says, "Come in the house. Let's figure this out."

What's to figure out? Reeve is living with me. It's cold and wet and I don't want to argue.

Reeve breaks away and opens the patio door to the house.

Novak ambushes us inside. "Hey, you found her."

I shield Reeve from Novak.

Tessa sets down her carryall. "Reeve can have the sleeper sofa, since Novak's in the baby's—I mean, the blue room."

"No way!" My voice echoes through the house. No way is Reeve going to be near Novak.

Tessa eyes me. "Okay. Then Novak can stay with you and Reeve can have—"

"No."

"It's the only solution," Tessa says.

"Reeve is moving in with me."

"We're through discussing this." Tessa heads into the living room.

I shout at her, "We're not through! It's not a solution!" I

follow her to the back. "Why can't Reeve stay with me? Because you're afraid we'll have sex? I'm gay, okay? It's what we do."

Tessa turns slowly, her eyes rise to my face. "That's not what I'm concerned about."

"I think it is."

Behind me, I hear Reeve tell Novak, "My mother and brother are dead."

Novak goes, "Oh my God."

I say to Tessa, "You just want to keep us apart."

Tessa says, "Yes. I want her as far away from you as possible."

*I knew it.*

In a calmer voice, she adds, "Johanna, look at your face. Look what she did to you. I'm afraid to leave her alone with you."

"I can take care of myself. I love her."

Tessa's eyes soften. "You have strong feelings for this girl. You want to be her savior. But the way she treats you, that isn't love."

We look at each other intensely. I say, "She doesn't mean it. She can't help it."

Tessa gives me a slow shake of her head.

"You don't understand," I say.

Tessa opens the linen closet and hauls out an armload of sheets, towels, a pillow. "She's not staying with you." She walks past me. "Reeve, you're here on the sleeper sofa. Temporarily. I hope you don't mind."

I charge past Tessa and reach for Reeve's hand. "She's living with me."

Reeve pulls away.

What? Why, baby?

Tessa says, "Johanna, if you need sheets or blankets—"

"Fuck you," I say. I storm out, slamming the sliding door so hard the glass cracks.

Ramming my throbbing skull against my car's seat back, I squeeze my eyes shut and get sucked into the undertow. From some roiling sea inside me, an angry wave of tears swells to the surface.

Robbie's dead. Their mom is dead. Reeve saw it happen.

What does it do to a person to live with violence every day? With fear? In my entire life I never once woke up feeling afraid. Well, not of physical violence. My biggest fear was that I'd wake up every day alone, that I'd never find someone to love.

But I did. I found Reeve. We're going through a rough patch. I can smooth it out.

It's freaking Siberia in the car with the window broken. I curl up tight on the seat. I wonder if Reeve is crying, if there are enough tears in a person to cry that much out. I remember this one youth service project we did where we went to the inner city to work with kids. It was Martin Luther King Day or something, and we asked the kids to draw their dream. We told them, "If you can see it, you can be it."

What does Reeve see?

She just lost her brother and her mother.

I lost my father and mother, but it doesn't seem the same. They died in peace.

Tessa lost two babies. And her parents.

Reeve's pain can be my pain. I'll take it. I think about what Reeve said, that the reason I take it is because I don't value my life.

That's not true. I've never had anything to live for as important as her. If someone came at me with a knife and tried to hurt me, I'd defend myself. So why didn't I even try against Reeve?

Because I never felt in danger. I only felt . . . in love.

My legs cramp. I roll onto my back and stretch my legs to the window. My life isn't a constant struggle for survival. Occasionally I worry where my next meal will come from, but I know I won't starve. I never worry about having a warm place to sleep at night.

Except . . . Who's got a bed tonight? Everyone but me.


I have to pee. The security light under the house eave is burned out and I trip over an Adirondack footrest, scraping it across the flagstone. If that doesn't wake the devil . . . The sliding door is locked. Thanks, Tessa.

I creep up the apartment stairs quietly so Novak won't hear. *She* didn't lock me out, at least.

Objects in the room take shape. The divan, TV, hallway. I go to the bathroom. Novak isn't in the bed, or on the divan. I switch on the light in the kitchen and see my spiral, the one I wrote letters in, lying open on the table. Open to a page where I wrote out a scene from Joyland.

On the opposite page, Novak left a note:

*Lesbo,*

*You're a horny bitch. There are lots of grlz who'd sleep with you. I'm going home to kiss my mother's ass. I'd like to remove the poker from it first, but she might bleed to death. Sorry. Inappropriate humor considering the circumstances. If I promise to be a good girl from now on, maybe she'll let me stay until I leave for college. How long do you think I can keep that promise?*

About a minute, I think.

*I know I don't deserve you. I took advantage of you and I'm sorry. Tell Tessa thank you, okay? Tell Reeve I'm so so sorry. OMG. I can't believe her mom's dead. And Robbie. OMG.*

*I have to be honest, Joho. I don't think she's good for you. She might feed your caring soul or your nymphomania, but she's damaged. I know love is blind and all, but not to everyone around you who loves you and doesn't want to see you get hurt. Like me. And Tessa.*

She talked to Tessa about Reeve. She told her.

*You've already ripped this up, so it's not going to matter if I say what I'm going to say next.*

"I'm still reading, Novak," I say aloud.

*I'm not sorry I kissed you. You can forget what happened, but I won't. I think we both wanted it. Maybe I'm bi, or* maybe you're just so fucking irresistible you made me gay. Guys suck, okay? They're never there when you need them the most.

There's an arrow (over), and I can't help myself.

You were always there for me, Johanna. I needed you more than I should have. Sound familiar?

# Chapter 32

Novak straightened my room. My shirts are hanging in the closet and my jeans are folded. She made the bed. Why couldn't she leave my place the way she found it? Why couldn't she leave me the way she found me?

I sit up all night, picking off the black tips from all the candles I lit the night Reeve came over. A tendril of desire tickles my belly.

Death drowns it. A familiar sense of loss seeps through my veins.

Reeve is close, right downstairs. All I have to do is go get her.

No. She needs space to grieve. I have to let her come to me. With time and trust, she can be healed.

When I raise my head from the table, I have a crick in my neck. It's morning.

The curtains on the sliding door are drawn, and Martin, most likely, has duct-taped the crack in the glass. That's going to cost me. Tessa's in the dining room, drinking coffee.

"I'll pay for the glass," I tell her, easing the door shut behind me.

She presses an index finger to her lips. The house is still.

"Does Novak want breakfast?" Tessa whispers. "Do you?"

I cross into the kitchen. "Novak went home."

There's a prolonged silence. "Look. I'm sorry," Tessa says. "Not for what you think. I'm doing what's right for you—for once."

"What does that mean?"

Tessa goes, "Shh. Come sit with me a minute." She motions to the chair beside her.

I open the fridge and grab the jug of milk. There's a clean glass in the dish drainer next to the sink.

Sliding into a chair across from Tessa, I sip my milk. She says, "I should've had this talk with you a while ago."

Blood rushes up my neck. Here it comes.

"I feel completely responsible for everything that happened. I should've stayed home to go to college. I knew how dependent Mom was after Dad died and I shouldn't have dumped that on you."

Does she think I did a crap job of it all?

"I just couldn't quit school so near the end—" Tessa pauses. "Yes, I could have. It's no excuse. And your letter—"

A shadow behind her snags my attention. Reeve. I get up to meet her under the archway. My momentum carries us both backward into the living room and I hold her. I kiss her gently on the mouth and she lets me.

I sense Tessa behind me. Always, I feel her judging me.

Reeve detaches and says, "I need to get my stuff from my house."

I say to Reeve, "Novak's gone. She said to say she's sorry about your mom and Robbie. She's gone, okay?"

"When did she leave?" Tessa asks, eavesdropping on my private conversation.

"I don't know." I smooth Reeve's hair. "I wasn't in the apartment."

Reeve says, "Where were you?"

"In my car."

A glint of emotion passes through Reeve's eyes and a tiny smile crooks her lips. An instant of relief, and trust?


Crime-scene tape is strung along the fence and crisscrossed on the doors and windows. Tessa says, "We should've gotten permission, or a police escort."

Reeve goes, "Fuck the police."

Tessa's eyes narrow at Reeve.

"We'll just get some clothes and leave," I say. "We won't destroy evidence or anything."

From the car, Tessa scans the area. "I don't know."

"You don't have to come inside," I tell her.

Reeve gets out and makes a beeline for the back. I'm on her heels. A basement window has been rigged and Reeve fits through easily, but it's a squeeze for me.

The first thing that hits me is the smell. Like vinegar.

Reeve says, "Mom cooks down here."

Cooks? Then I see it—drug paraphernalia. A thump behind me makes me yelp. Tessa. She claws a spiderweb off her face. Reeve pushes a trapdoor and light filters down a laddered shaft.

The air is a relief. I climb up after Reeve and we emerge in the kitchen, where jagged shapes cut eerie shadows. There are splatters of red on the wall. Is that blood? Oh my God. Reeve's breathing is stuttered and shallow.

"It's okay, baby."

Sidestepping a pile of rubble, she says, "Stay here."

Tessa breathes, "Oh, Johanna," as Reeve's footsteps pound on the stairs. "What are you into?"

Her, I answer silently. I leave Tessa behind and catch up to Reeve.

The second floor is destroyed. Doors are busted down or missing and there are gaping holes in the walls. It stinks like vomit. I flip on a light switch, but nothing happens.

Reeve goes, "I told you to stay downstairs." She comes out of nowhere, pushing me back.

"But I want to help."

"I can do it. Don't come any closer." She balls a fist in my face. "I mean it."

This has to be hard for her, returning to the scene where Robbie . . . her mom . . .

Reeve skitters to the end of the hall, crouches on the floor, and starts shoveling clothes into a pillowcase. I trip on a hunk of loose carpet.

"Damn you." She flies to her feet and charges me. She rams me into an exposed wall beam, gouging my spine.

"Let me help," I say.

"No!"

"Why?"

She sets her jaw.

"I . . ." What doesn't she want me to see? I've already seen it all. I glance over her shoulder. "Is that your room?" It's a closet, or used to be. There's no door. A small, square mirror hangs by a string on a nail. The clothes she hasn't shoved into the pillowcase are scant. She has, like, three shirts and a pair of jeans.

This is where she sleeps? In a closet?

"Don't." She squeezes my arms so hard it hurts. "Don't you fucking feel sorry for me."

I meet her eyes. Snatching the pillowcase from her hand, I edge past her to the closet and sink to my knees. I jam the rest of the clothes in as this fire burns in my belly. How unfair is this? How little she has, how she—how anybody—has to live this way.

Me thinking it's so cool, so vintage. This isn't vintage. It's poverty.

I storm to the stairs and throw the pillowcase down to Tessa. "We're taking everything!" I yell.

Robbie had a room—no door, no closet, no plaster on the walls. He slept on a crappy single mattress on the floor. Reeve slept right outside his door.

His case is sitting on the mattress. He's never coming back.

"That's it," Reeve says.

"Do you want Robbie's things?"

She avoids looking into his room. "No."

As we load up Tessa's Subaru, I think, Get the hell out of

here. Torch it. Demolish the whole block. Tessa pulls away from the curb and I yell, "Stop!"

She slams on the brakes.

"I forgot something," I tell Tessa. "Go back."

I don't wait for her. I fling open the door and sprint to the house.

The case, it could be empty. It could be full of—who cares? That case is all he had.

# Chapter 33

Tessa calls this mortuary and schedules a service for Robbie and their mom on Wednesday. Tuesday she goes back to work at the clinic.

I gather up all the candles that still have wicks and wash the sheets and lower the miniblinds. The bedroom isn't pitch black, not at eight-thirty in the morning, but the gauzy natural light with the flickering candles feels dreamy and romantic.

I hear the apartment door open, close, and lock. I feel her coming down the hall. She lingers for a moment in the doorway. I've been waiting so long for her, for this, for the two of us to finally come together.

Reeve says, "Do you mind if I take a shower?"

"Do you want me to help?"

A smile tugs her lips. "I think I can handle it."

I listen to the water run and imagine her taking off her

cami, her shorts, her bra. Testing the water. Stepping into the spray.

I'm already naked under the sheets, and ready. Reeve comes in, clutching a towel to her front. She looks all pink and tingly. She drops her towel and slides in underneath.

I pull her into my arms.

"Johanna," she says, "I know what you want." She presses her forehead to mine. "I want it too, but . . ."

Her hair is damp and combed straight. I curl her hair over her ear so I can look at her face.

"What do you need, Reeve?" I ask.

Tears glisten in her eyes. "I need you to hold me."

I draw her in closer. Her stick-thin arms slide up between us, sharp elbows pressing into my breasts as her head burrows into my neck.

"I can't give you what you need," Reeve says in a small voice. "I'm sorry."

I close my eyes and fight down the disappointment. "It's okay. I understand." She needs time to heal. "You're all I need."

"Sure," she goes. "But you couldn't wait."

I bleed out internally.

She rolls over, away from me, and I release her from my needs. I'd never force her.

I've never wanted anything or anyone so much.

To cut the silence and tension, I say, "The rule is, after number ten you have to start counting over."

"At number two?"

I clench my throat to keep from crying.

We lie together in bed for a while.

"I want to take you somewhere," I say.

"I told you I'm not ready."

"Not there." I slide out from between the sheets. "Get dressed."

She twists her head to look at me.

"Please?"

"Where?"

"It's a surprise."

"I hate surprises."

So do I. We have that in common.


Memorial Hospice is a hodgepodge of structures—on one side, a cottage house converted to a café; on the other, the new addition, with a glassed-in entrance to hide the older building, the public ward.

"What is this?" Reeve asks.

"A hospice."

"What's a hospice?"

I take her hand. "It's a place where people come to die."

Reeve stops in her tracks.

"I come here when I need hope," I say.

She pulls her hand away.

"It's not like that. It isn't—"

"Why would you bring me here?"

"Reeve, no. It's a beautiful place. It's peaceful. I guess I wanted you to see that life doesn't always end the way you experienced."

"You don't know what I've experienced," she snaps.

"I know I don't. I just wanted you to see . . . the other side."

She stares ahead at the front door. "You come here to watch people die?"

"Yeah. Well, no. To share in their final days."

"You're so weird."

I let out a short laugh. "You like that in a girl, remember?"

She shakes her head, but a smile leaks out.

I take her hand again and she hangs on.

Jeannette stands at the welcome desk, talking to the receptionist. When she sees me, she says, "Johanna. I was about to call you."

"This is my girlfriend, Reeve." I get it out quickly, before I lose my nerve. There's an awkward moment as Jeannette's eyes dart from Reeve to me. To my bruised face. It's okay, I want to tell Jeannette. Everything's under control.

At last Jeannette smiles and extends a hand. "Hi."

Reeve shakes it.

Reeve is trembling. God, is it too soon?

"Johanna, let's . . . ," Jeannette says as she cups my elbow, "over here." She leads me to a sunny nook with chairs and a coffee table, and I tug Reeve along. A purple orchid snakes out of a crystal vase and I think of Novak. "Sit." Jeannette motions us down.

Reeve and I take chairs next to each other.

Jeannette says, "Mrs. Mockrie died early this morning."

"Oh no." I cover my mouth.

"An hour later, Mr. Mockrie passed."

Tears well in my eyes.

"She and her husband came in together," Jeannette explains to Reeve. "They absolutely adored Johanna." Jeannette smiles at me, then cringes like it hurts to look at me.

I shield my face with a hand.

"I'm sorry," Jeannette says, touching my knee. "I know you loved them too. We all did. They went peacefully in their sleep."

I try to mental Reeve: See? Death can be a beautiful thing. We could die together.

Jeannette gets up and presses a hand on my shoulder. She says, "Nice to meet you, Reeve."

Reeve just looks at the orchid.

A gurney rolls out from the corridor. ". . . not happy with her physical therapy regimen. Jeannette! I want to talk to you!"

Does Carrie's mother always have to shout?

"You want me to give you a tour?" I ask Reeve.

She turns to face me. "If that's what you want." Her voice is flat.

"Or we could go." I shouldn't have brought her here.

"What's down there?" She eyes the hall.

"The private suites. People with money. Or insurance."

Reeve stands. "Show me those people."

The first room is crammed for a birthday party, or something. The lady, I know, has terminal cancer. She's propped up in bed, surrounded by people and balloons. I turn to tell Reeve, but she's gone ahead. She's stalled outside the second door. "Who lives here?" she asks. "Or should I say, who dies here?"

I see Carrie's room through Reeve's eyes. The posters and

paintings on the walls, the pictures of Carrie. Her pink flowered comforter and frilly curtains. "Her name's Carrie. She was in a car accident that left her . . ." I don't finish because Reeve has entered Carrie's room.

I check the corridor and slip inside. "We shouldn't be in here," I say quietly.

"But this is where you come." Reeve wanders around, looking at everything. The ribbons, awards, certificates. She picks up a framed photo. "Is this her?"

"Yeah. She's pretty, huh?"

"She's hot," Reeve says.

"What?"

Reeve sets the picture down. "I'm kidding. Is she a rich bitch?"

I try to take Reeve's hand, but she slithers out. She yanks open the bedside drawer and selects a tube of lip gloss.

"Don't touch her personal things," I say. "Her mother's the rich bitch."

Reeve uncaps the tube and sniffs it. In Carrie's little vanity mirror, she glosses her lips.

She straightens slowly and crooks a finger at me, like, Come here.

I widen my eyes at her.

Reeve comes over, stands on tiptoe and kisses me. She touches my face and arm sensuously, sending tingles to my feet.

"Reeve, not here." I feel a tug on my bag and shift my gaze to see Reeve has opened it. She drops in the lip gloss.

"You can't—"

"She won't be needing it."

True. But . . .

Reeve shovels out a fistful of makeup and transfers it to my bag.

"Don't."

"Don't what?" She pulls me down to the bed and kisses me. Her lips are slick and hard. She parts my mouth with her tongue and sucks in my lower lip. The heat begins in my brain and smolders all the way down. Reeve's on top of me, her hand up my shirt, fingers crawling under my bra, over the flesh, touching my nipple.

"What the *hell* are you doing?"

I push up and Reeve goes flying.

Evelyn's face is so red I think she'll explode. "You." She points. "How dare you?"

I can't speak.

"Were you in there?" I follow her shaking finger to the bedside table. The drawer is open.

Evelyn rushes past me, stops at the drawer, and spins around. "Give me your purse."

Reeve hands over her purse. *Thank you, thank you. I love you.*

Carrie's mom empties the contents onto the bed. Cash, mascara, my gold watch.

It's okay. I was going to give it to her anyway.

"Now yours."

Reeve grabs her stuff and pushes me toward the door. "We're out of here."

"You have no right," Evelyn goes. "No right." Her voice breaks.

I claw all of Carrie's makeup out of my bag and wedge around Evelyn to replace it in the drawer. "I'm sorry." I fumble around, lining up the tubes. "I'm so, so sorry."

Evelyn hiccups a sob. "Jeannette's going to hear about this."

"I know. I'll tell her."

She makes this raw, retching sound in her throat, then rasps at my back, "Pervert."

## Joyland: Take 15

*The silhouette behind the scrim is angular and nude. The scrim rolls up and I see she's painted plaster. Blue stage lights illuminate the mannequin.*

*She wears a mask of wax; then, on cue, she comes to life. She strips off her mask to reveal round red cheeks and anime eyes. Dressers dance en pointe to clothe her, but she doesn't like the frilly collars and corseted gown, so she pulls a knife and cuts them.*

*I pass her on the right, according to script, to get her attention. I'm not the kind of person she'd notice, in my drab overcoat and checkered Converses. As I pass the huge snow globe, a girl steps out from behind it. "Fair warning," Britt whispers. "She's not your fairy princess."*

*I draw my sword and Britt retreats.*

*We're alone onstage. The lights have been extinguished. Reeve says, "Tell me what you see."*

*My mouth moves, but indistinguishable sounds come out.*

*"Tell me what you see," she demands.*

*I CANT*

*She peels away a second layer and the face is shapeless skin. No eyes, no nose, no mouth.*

*This can't be her, I think. Not the real Reeve.*

• • •

# Chapter 34

The organist is playing a dirge while a man in a gray suit sits on a high-back wing chair behind the pulpit. Tessa's crying.

Tessa cried more at Mom's funeral than I did.

Reeve and I slip into the row behind Tessa and Martin. There are two tall stands, like plant stands, supporting two square objects draped with cloths.

The ashes. Robbie's ashes and their mom's.

The minister gets up and says a prayer while I hold Reeve's hand. It's limp and cold. No one else is here. Wait. A person sneaks in on the other side. She kneels and steeples her hands. Novak.

The minister reads a passage from the Bible, then asks if anyone would like to come up and speak about the deceased. Reeve s⊢ ⊔ks in her seat. I look to Novak, who is blowing her nose. When I die, I want someone, anyone, to speak for me.

I stand and sidestep out of the pew. Everyone's eyes are on me. At the pulpit, I say, "Robbie didn't deserve to die. He never hurt a living soul in his life." Not on purpose. "He was a good friend and a great brother and he didn't deserve this." I feel my throat tighten and I stumble back to my place. I was mostly mean to him. Everyone was.

The organist plays a hymn and the minister hands the urns to Reeve. She won't take them. Tessa and I end up with one each.

When we get home, Martin leaves for work. Reeve heads for the blue room and I follow, but at the door she turns and pushes me back. An arm shoots out to clench Reeve's wrist. It's Tessa.

Reeve says, "I just want to be left alone."

Tessa says, "Then go. But don't ever push her."

Reeve shuts the door on us.


I'm up early to save Reeve. No, I don't mean save. I don't know what I mean.

"She's gone," Tessa says as I pass by the dining table, where she's casting on, beginning a new knitting project. The click-click of her needles takes me back. I used to sit at her feet and ball yarn while she told me about her date the night before.

"Where'd she go?"

"I don't know," Tessa says. She gets up and pours a cup of coffee.

"You're lying." She's *lying*. She lifts her cup to her lips and

I smack it out of her hand. It shatters against the wall and coffee splashes everywhere. Tessa looks at me, through me. Calmly, she crosses the room, but I beat her there and kick the pieces away.

Tessa squats to pick up a shard and I push her into the wall. She bangs her head.

"She's turned you into a monster."

"Where is she!" I screech.

Tessa stands. "Johanna, we need to talk about Reeve."

"Shut up." I tell Tessa, "Don't talk to me. Don't ever talk to me again."


The phone call comes while I'm sitting on the divan, fuming. Feeling wrecked and worried about Reeve. It has to be Reeve calling. I lunge for the phone.

"Hello, Johanna. This is Jeannette."

All the blood drains from my face.

"I've been waiting for you to call me to explain, but I guess that's not going to happen."

Words jam up in my throat.

"All I have is Evelyn's version. If you have a different story, I'm willing to listen."

The jam unclogs, but I can only manage one word: "No." Evelyn got it right.

Jeannette waits, then sighs and says, "You realize I'm going to have to ask you not to return to the hospice."

A candle inside me extinguishes.

*  *  *

Martin pounds on my door and when I answer, he says, "I'll collect this now." He shoves my IOU at me.

"I don't have it," I tell him. "I lost my job. But I'm looking for another one. I'm going to pay you back."

His eyes are black. As he clomps down the stairs, I call to him, "I promise."

He clomps back up. His vibe scares me. "For your information, your sister put you on our car insurance. I told her to take away your keys and make you ride the bus, but she's too nice for that. I expect you to pay *both* of us back."

"I will," I say. "Every penny. As soon as—"

He stomps down the stairs and I close the door behind him, sinking to the divan. All I want to do is crawl in a hole and die.

Day after day I drive by Reeve's house. The police tape is gone, but the windows are boarded up and the health department has posted a green notice on the door. Where is she?

I'm so desperate for human contact I actually call Novak. Her mother tells me she's gone; she moved to California to get ready for college.

She didn't even call to say goodbye.

Time is meaningless and insignificant. I need to look for a job, but it's so hard to get out of bed in the morning. One inconsequential day I'm jolted awake by shouting outside my window, and a door slamming.

I drag to my door and open it a crack. Martin's in the backyard, lighting up the grill. I squint at the TV clock. He's grilling at seven a.m.?

Tessa steps out and pulls the patio door shut. She looks worse than I feel. She's dressed for work, but her jacket is wrinkled and her hair isn't combed.

I glance back and see Martin looking straight at me. As I ease the door closed, I hear him snap at Tessa, "Get Johanna in therapy too. She needs it even more than you do."

# Chapter 35

"Call me Mary-Dean," she says. I think it's a weird name for a
therapist. I don't know why I come, because all I do is sit on
this hard chair and cry. Mary-Dean says, "It's okay to get it
out. We'll talk when you're ready."

I'll never be ready.

At our third session, Mary-Dean says, "Tell me about your
girlfriend. Reeve. Is that her name?"

My brain instantly engages. Tessa's been talking to her
about me. I should've known. "Whatever she told you is
wrong," I say.

"Who?"

*You know who.* I blow my nose.

"The only thing Tessa told me is that you got hurt."

"By her," I mutter.

Mary-Dean says, "How did Tessa hurt you?"

A torrent of tears threatens.

Mary-Dean goes, "Then tell me about Reeve. She seems to be someone you care about very much."

I stammer out the words: "I-I loved her. I mean, I love her."

Mary-Dean leans forward. "What does love mean to you, Johanna?"

That's the question. "You know."

"I want to hear it from you."

"Reeve was—is—my girlfriend. I'm gay." I wonder if Tessa told her that.

Mary-Dean doesn't look shocked. In fact, she smiles. Not fake, not patronizing.

"I love Reeve with all my heart."

Mary-Dean says, "That's a good feeling, isn't it? Falling in love. Does Reeve love you?"

"Yes."

Mary-Dean nods and says, "How do you know? How does she show her love?"

I know where she's going with this. I won't go there. I can't. I stare over Mary-Dean's shoulder at the black-and-white photo on the wall of a mother holding a child. I have to get out of here.


Tessa's appointments with Mary-Dean are on different days than mine. I don't think it's right that she's talking about me when I'm not there, so I go down to the house to confront her. She isn't home. Neither is Martin. He's left her a note on the counter. "Sweetie. Your grief support group mtg is canceled today. Luv U."

Tessa's in a grief support group. Of course. She lost her baby. She lost two babies. And her parents. And me.

Mary-Dean tries again. "Tell me what love means, Johanna. I'd just like to hear your take on it."

I've been thinking a lot about it and I'm prepared. "Love is being there for someone no matter what."

"Even if they hurt you?"

"Yeah," I say. "Especially then."

Mary-Dean studies me. "Why?" She removes her glasses and sets them on the table between us. "Why does love have to hurt?"

"That's not what I said." Is it?

"Do you think love hurts?"

The people I know who've loved and been loved have all been hurt. Mom when Dad died. Novak every time she got dumped. Tessa.

"Yeah, I think there's an element of hurt."

"Physical?"

"Sometimes," I say. "Not all the time."

"But when?"

"When you let it."

"Did you let it?"

I say to her, "Sometimes you don't have a choice."

She says, "Don't you always have a choice? At least about your actions, how you respond?"

These questions make me anxious. Yes, I let Reeve hurt me. No, I don't believe that's showing love. But I love her. With all my heart, I still love her.

"I don't know how to explain it," I say to Mary-Dean.

She smiles and puts on her glasses. "You'll get there."


I land a job at the cineplex. I figure, hey, can't let that Film Studies class go to waste. Mostly, I'm proud of myself for finding the motivation. It's hard to get out of bed every day and face myself in the mirror. The bruises are gone, but I don't feel healed.

On my way out one day, I pass Tessa coming in. "I've got a job now," I tell her. "I'll pay you guys back soon."

Tessa raises her eyes to meet mine. She says, "It doesn't matter."

"Yes, it does." I say more insistently, "It matters to me. I need to pay you back."

"Okay." She nods. I think she understands.

The next session, Mary-Dean hands me a yellow tablet and says, "I want you to make two columns, or two separate lists. Label one 'Gains' and the other 'Losses.'" I must look confused, because she adds, "Write down all you gained and all you lost, with Reeve."

"Now?" I say.

"You can take it with you for homework," she adds. "Sometime soon I want to hear about your mother and father, and your sister leaving. It must've been extremely hard to lose them all so close together."

I break down, and Mary-Dean immediately passes me a giant box of Kleenex.


*   *   *

It's a slow night, Tuesday night, and the ten o'clock shows have all started. In the ticket booth, I take out the yellow tablet and begin with Gains. I think, This'll be easy.

**Love. Knowing love. Loving and being loved.**

Reeve did love me. She still does. *Where are you, baby?*

Nothing else comes to mind right away. But there's got to be more. I flip the page and write: "Losses. What I lost:"

**Money**
**My job at Bling's**
**Mom's watch**
**The hospice where I love to volunteer**

These are coming too fast.

I page back to the Gains list. Love. It outweighs everything. Back to Losses.

**My car window.** It's covered with plastic until I can afford a new one.

**Martin's trust.** He moved, or locked up, the loaded potato.

**Novak.**

But it's not really Reeve's fault I lost Novak. Is it?

I rip out the page. Look at what Reeve lost—her mother, her brother, her home. *You still have me, baby.*

At the next session, I tell Mary-Dean I forgot to do the assignment. She says, "That's okay. What I really wanted to know is where you would put self-respect."

"Self-respect?"

"Would you say your relationship with Reeve gained you self-respect or lost you self-respect?"

"Gained," I answer automatically.

"How?"

Why? When? How? Reeve would be slugging Mary-Dean continuously.

"I guess . . . I feel . . ."

"Did you respect yourself before you met Reeve?"

"Yeah. I mean, I think I'm a good person. My teacher Mrs. Goins said I was kind and generous."

"Of course you are, Johanna. You're a wonderful person."

"So is Reeve." She just didn't have a choice.

We always have a choice—about our actions.

She didn't have to hit me.

I let her do it.

It was wrong. I was wrong. We were . . .

Mary-Dean asks, "Do you respect yourself more now than you did before?"

This question makes me search my soul.

And I don't like the answer.

# Joyland: Take 16

We dash behind the waterfall, holding hands. The rocks are slippery. We balance for a moment, making sure everyone's secure. I'm awed by the power, the majesty, the roar of water rushing off the cliff.

Robbie sits on the shore. We've just been to his funeral. He removes his shoes and socks, stuffs the socks inside the shoes, and ties the laces together. Reeve says, "Don't lose those, asstard."

Robbie says, "The retardo is a high school graduate."

Reeve turns to me. "Scary, but true."

Novak takes my arm. "Remember when we used to come up here?" She has to yell to be heard over the falls.

"No!" I yell back. I say to Reeve, "She never came here with me."

Novak leans around me. "We came here when Tessa lost her first baby."

"No, we didn't."

Teetering on the rock, she goes, "Yes, we did. We made a little boat and put a pink Care Bear in it. A heart bear. We set it in the river, right here." Novak indicates a spot in front of us where water is pooling between the rocks. It forms an eddy, then swirls off toward the falls. "Tessa said, 'My sweet baby girl. Have a safe trip home. I'll see you when you get there.'"

Reeve stares at the box in her hands. Her mother's ashes.

Robbie is wearing his shabby graduation robe. He's holding the other box.

Mom's an angel in heaven. She says, "You're such a comfort to me."

Novak screams, "Oh my God, Robbie! You're alive!" She hurdles rocks to get to him. He stumbles backward but catches her in his arms. Without warning, he kisses her.

Novak looks stunned.

Reeve says, "You're just so damn irresistible."

That cracks us all up.

"You really know how to pick 'em," Reeve says.

"Yeah, I do," I say.

Reeve's eyes fall to the ashes. She looks up at me. "Should I just dump them?"

Robbie is climbing on the boulders behind Fallon Falls and Reeve hollers, "Get back down here! You have to do this with me!"

Novak says, "He kissed me."

Reeve goes in my ear, "Tell her he has herpes."

I laugh. Reeve bumps my shoulder. I lose my footing and splash into the river. The current is strong and Novak jumps in and saves me while Reeve just stands there.

Reeve opens the box and says, "How do you want to do it,

Robbie?" The ashes are in a plastic bag inside the box. "You just want to pitch the bag?"

Robbie lifts out his bag and hauls back his arm.

Novak bounds back from the river, cries, "No! You have to scatter them. You can't just throw the bag in the river. God." She rolls her eyes at me. "That's littering."

"You do it." Reeve snatches the bag from Robbie and slams it into Novak's chest.

Novak arches her eyebrows at me.

Do it, I shrug.

She removes the twist tie from the bag and, reaching in, grabs a fistful of ash. It's gray and sort of greasy looking. She holds the ashes out in front of her. She shouts at Reeve, "What was your mom's name?"

"Gladys," Reeve says.

Novak widens her eyes.

"Not really."

"Consuela Meaty Loins," Robbie says.

We all look at him. He grins.

Reeve tells Novak, "It's Jaclyn."

Novak extends her arm over the water. "Ashes to ashes. Dust to dust. Go home to Jesus, Jaclyn."

Reeve mutters "Bye" under her breath.

Novak opens her fist and the ashes fly back in our faces. We spit and swipe our eyes.

Robbie snatches the other bag from Novak and raises it high in the air. The ashes stream out and spread over the rocks and water and river grass.

They leave a film. It's gross.

*I look over to Robbie, but he's gone.*
*Reeve's gone.*
*Novak.*
*Mom.*
*All gone.*

. . .

It isn't Joyland; it's just a dream. I wake up crying, feeling inconsolable. I stumble to the kitchen and almost trip over it—again.

Robbie's case. I keep moving it from the front closet to the storage room to my bedroom. I don't know why I haven't opened it.

It's time. I thumb up the latches and flip the cover.

There's a threadbare baby blanket rolled up and paperclipped. I pull the clip, find the edge, and unroll the blanket. Inside is . . . junk.

A magpie feather, an avocado peel, a hunk of bubble wrap, two golf balls, a syringe, a rusty razor blade, string tied to string tied to string . . .

Carefully, gently, leaving everything exactly the way he saved it, I reroll the blanket and shut the case lid.

When I get home from work, there's a box at my door. I know the handwriting and my heart leaps. The first item is a picture postcard. This fat, hairy guy in a Speedo at the beach, snarfing a hot dog. A voice bubble is drawn in: "Eat my wiener."

I crack up. Classic Novak.

On the back, her note says: "Banana, I met someone. Her name's Cate. She's a lez and she's into me. What's her damage?"

She met someone already?

"Miss u, you crazy bitch. Come to CA. grlz, grlz, grlz. U'll never go hungry here ☺. U R 4 Evah my BFF. I wanted to give you this for grad, but I didn't get it done in time ☹."

It's wrapped in tissue. I lift out the bundle and open it carefully. Oh my God. It's a jacket, all different colors, soft as cashmere. I put it on and feel Novak next to my skin. A pang of loneliness stabs at my heart.

*Miss you, Novak.*

A quiet knock sounds on the open door. I turn and see Tessa.

"Oh wow. She finished it." Tessa walks in and runs her hand down the sleeve of the jacket. She steps behind me. "She picked the hardest thing to knit, this Meg Swansen Round-the-Bend. When she said she was going to modify the pattern to make it a hoodie jacket, I thought she was insane."

I twist and our eyes meet. "I wanted to say—"

"Johanna, I—"

"Tell Martin I have your IOU money, with interest, and I'll have your insurance money to you by the end of the month."

Tessa nods and smiles. "Thank you. May I?" She indicates the divan.

I slip off the jacket and fold it tenderly, feel the love Novak put into it.

"Johanna, I wanted to talk to you about your, um, revelation. Long before now. But I just didn't know how. That's not true. Well, it's sort of true." What's Tessa talking about? She pats the place next to her and I go sit. She says, "When I got your letter, honestly, I was shocked. I've always considered myself open-minded; I've had gay friends. But when it's your own sister? When it hits so close to home?" She looks at me and I see the lost look in her eyes.

"It's okay."

"No, it's not. I'm ashamed of myself. I should've accepted it immediately and embraced it and been happy about you finding yourself and having the courage to come out."

"Yeah. You should've."

"You'll laugh"—she shakes her head—"but I thought it was just a phase."

I'm not laughing.

"I did write you back, but I didn't know what to say. If I didn't mention it, it'd seem like I was avoiding the subject. Which, I guess, I was. And I knew how important this was to you. I ripped up so many letters. I could never find the right words."

I know how that feels. "I'm sorry."

"What do you have to be sorry about? You should be mad as hell. Here I am, your sister, your only family, and I'd already deserted you once. I know you needed me. And before, with Mom. I'm sorry. I'm the one who's sorry." Her eyes pool. "I just want you to be happy, Johanna. It's all I ever want for you."

I tell her, just so she knows, "It's not a phase."

She lets out a short laugh and sniffles. "I got that." She swipes her nose. "I love you no matter what. I want you to know I'll always be here for you. From now on."

Finally, at last, we hug. We rock each other for the longest time and this huge sense of joyfulness infuses my whole entire being. I have my sister back.

Tessa says, "I want to ask you something. You can say no." She leans away from me so she can look me in the eyes. "I want to sell the house and move back to Minnesota. I want to finish my master's in social work and get certified there. And I want to try to have a baby."

My heart soars. "Tessa, that's great."

She drops her head. "I don't know. Martin's settled here now."

"He'll do whatever you need to make you happy. You know that."

"You'd come with us." Tessa looks at me. "I wouldn't go without you. You'll love Martin's family; they're insane. The university's right there and you could go to college, live with us, or in the dorm. There's a large gay and lesbian population in Minneapolis."

This tiny trickle of excitement burbles inside me.

"Think about it." Tessa lifts a hank of my hair over my shoulder. "We'll make a fresh start." She holds my eyes. "Johanna, can you ever forgive me?"

I just hug her again. She hugs me right back. I feel this weight lift from my shoulders. Then Tessa says, "Why don't you ever wear the watch?"

I let her go fast and push to my feet. "I lost it," I lie. "I'm sorry." I head for the kitchen.

"You lost it?"

"It was loose," I say over my shoulder. "It fell off."

Tessa sighs. "I should've taken it in to get it adjusted."

That stops me in my tracks. "It's not your fault, okay? It's mine. I let it happen. We're both on these major guilt trips. We need to get off this stupid treadmill and move on."

Tessa stands. "You're right. We do. But that's not the only reason I came up here." She approaches from behind and touches my hand. She turns it palm up and sets something in it. A folded piece of notepaper.

"To be honest, Johanna, I'm against this. Every fiber of my being says I shouldn't do it, I should keep you safe, but Mary-Dean insists this is something you need to do for yourself."

What could it be? I unfold the paper and see it's an address.

"She's living there," Tessa says. "At least, she was."

# Chapter 36

The sign in front of the building reads: SAMARITAN HOUSE. Is this a homeless shelter? *Oh, Reeve.* It looks nice, though, like an old converted Victorian, with three floors and balconies.

The door has a double lock and security cameras. I ring the buzzer and a woman says, "May I help you?"

I don't see a microphone to speak into. "I'm looking for Reeve Hartt?"

"What's your name?"

"Johanna Lynch," I tell her.

"And you are . . . ?"

What am I? "A . . . friend."

"Please wait."

I wait an eternity, standing there feeling like I'm being scanned with metal detectors. I check my watch. Ten to ten. Cheap watch from Target. I have to be at the cineplex by eleven.

An older couple across the street are out pruning hedges. They remind me of Mr. and Mrs. Mockrie and my heart aches for that loss.

The front door whooshes open.

My stomach catches.

Reeve flies out the door and throws herself into my arms. "She told me not to call you or see you ever again. She said if I loved you, I'd leave you alone." Reeve crushes me so hard I can't breathe.

Or maybe I can't breathe because she's in my arms, stealing my breath away. Reeve kisses me and the world spins out of control.

Behind us the door opens wider and this formidable woman steps onto the porch. She says, "Honey, are you okay?"

Reeve goes, "Yeah. This is my girlfriend, Johanna." Reeve smiles at me as she intertwines our fingers. The woman gives me a visual shakedown.

Reeve says to her, "Would you sign me out?"

She asks, "Where are you going?"

Reeve looks at me.

Fallon Falls, I think.

"To the park," Reeve says. "I'll be back in an hour."

The woman folds her arms.

"If I'm not, call the cops. God." Reeve rolls her eyes at me.

"One hour." The woman steps back inside.

Reeve pushes me down the steps. "Fucking warden."

"What is this place?" I glance up to see eyes watching us through the front security screen.

Reeve hops on me piggyback, wrapping her legs around my

waist. "A women's shelter. Tessa got me in." Reeve bites my ear and nuzzles into my neck.

At the car, I let her down and go to unlock the door, but Reeve pulls my hand away. "I can't," she says. "I'm not allowed to get in anyone's car. House rules."

I arch my eyebrows. "Since when do you play by the rules?"

A grin sneaks across her face. "Really." Then her eyes get serious.

"It's okay," I say quickly. "How far's the park?"

"We can walk." She loops both arms around my waist and my arm naturally crosses her shoulders. She smells like Ivory soap. Her hair's been cut recently and I can actually feel meat on her bones. Her eyes are beautiful, of course. Blue mascara, three shades of eye shadow.

"I've missed you so much," she says.

I rest my head on hers. "Me too." All the nights I lay awake worrying, wondering about her.

Behind the trees at the end of the block is a sculpture garden. Reeve leads me to a concrete hexagon, which is smeared with pigeon poop. We don't sit on it. We stretch out on the cool grass, facing each other.

"I've been seeing someone," Reeve says.

My heart explodes.

She jabs my shoulder. "You didn't say 'what?'"

I don't want to know who either.

She pinches my arm playfully. "Not like that. A counselor. Or psychologist, I guess she is."

"You have? Me too."

Reeve frowns. "Why?"

I can't look at her without wanting to kiss and touch her, run my hand up her hip and under her shirt. But we *need* to have this conversation.

I roll onto my back. "You know. Abandonment issues. Self-worth stuff, blah blah." I gaze into the sky.

Reeve's eyes graze the side of my face, then she rolls over onto her back too. "Abuse. Repressed anger. My mother and brother getting murdered in front of me."

She makes it sound like a competition. You win, Reeve. Hands down.

A puffy cloud floats in front of the sun and I shiver. "Are you okay?" Reeve asks.

The word "yes" sticks in my throat. "Are you?" I twist my head and look at her.

"Oh yeah. I'm fly."

Her pain is palpable.

"I don't miss her," Reeve says. "She was sick and twisted. Her whole fucking life was using. I don't even know if I ever loved her. That's so wrong, not to love your own mother."

Reeve . . .

"But damn. What did he do? All he ever wanted was to be left alone. Stupid asstard." She balls her fists at her sides.

I push up to an elbow and pull her into me.

"I don't cry," she says in a hiccup.

"I know."

She holds me hard. She kisses my neck, my jawbone, my face. She's soft and sweet in my arms. She kisses my lips.

God, help me.

She stops and says, "Let's get a place together. I have a job now, at Chili's. Where are you working? I assume you are."

Yeah, and I need my job. "I'm still looking."

"You could work with me. Think of it, Johanna. Living together, being together all the time. We could make it; I know we could. We'd get married and have kids. Since they run in my family, maybe we'd have twins." She grins. "Doublemint gum."

"I'm moving to Minnesota," I say.

At the sudden shift in mood, a chill fills the air.

"When?" Reeve asks.

"Soon."

She climbs off me.

"Tessa and I are selling the house. She wants me to go to college in Minnesota and she's going to have a baby. I want to be there for her. You know?"

"What about me?" Reeve's voice is flat. "Were you going to ask me to come?"

My silence is my answer. She scrambles to stand and I clench her wrist. The rage inside her still surges; I can feel it in her muscles and bones. "I just don't think we're ready."

She slit-eyes me. *"You're* not. Speak for yourself."

"Okay, I will. I'm not."

She goes limp and her head drops back. I stand, still holding on to her wrist. "I love you. I do. But we both need to be in a better place, Reeve."

She raises her face to the sky. Oh, Reeve. *I want you so much. But it's not a good love. It's cruel.*

She says, "What time is it?"

I look at my watch. Shit. I'm going to be late for work. "Ten fifty-five."

"We should get back," she says.

"Reeve—"

She presses a finger to my lips. "You're smart, Johanna."

Am I? I want to ask. Or just scared.

"I like that in a girl." Her finger trails down my front.

I take her hand and kiss it. "Are you going to be all right?"

"Me?" Reeve points to herself. "You talkin' about me? Shit, I'm a survivor."

She's stronger than anyone I know. In some ways.

We walk back to Samaritan House together, yet apart. At the curb by the gate, Reeve turns and says, "I have something for you. Wait here." She sprints to the porch and disappears inside.

I unlock the car door and lean against it, waiting. Thinking how I'm going to drive away from here and probably never see her again. Wondering if I have the strength to leave.

She hurries back, out of breath, and hands me an object. My gold watch.

"I took it," Reeve says. "I'm not a nice person."

I click my tongue. "Yes, you are." Sometimes.

"I can't give you back everything I took."

Our eyes meet and hold. She understands.

"It doesn't matter," I say. Some things I have to take back for myself. "I have something for you too." I open the car door and reach into the back.

"No." Reeve steps away.

"You're going to want it."

Reeve pushes out with both arms.

I extend the case. "It's all he had."

"No," she says. "Get rid of it."

"He'd want you to have it, Reeve," I say softly. "To keep it safe for him."

She loosely hugs herself. "You know what it was? His safe place. That's what he called it."

"Maybe it can be yours too."

She just looks at me. "That'd be retarded."

I crack up. So does she. But she reaches across and takes the case. "He didn't bust your window. I did. He'd never hurt you."

"It's okay. I won't be taking my car to Minnesota," I say. We both hold our breath, like we can't say goodbye to him or each other.

"Johanna." Her eyes sweep up to my face. "I'm sorry."

"I'm not," I say. Not for knowing love, loving her.

She backs up, away, hugging the case to her, walking, trotting toward the porch. Through the door, into the building. I look at the watch in my hand and latch it onto my left wrist. Two watches, too heavy, as if I'm weighted down by time. I remove the cheap watch.

"Hey! Johanna."

I glance up. On the third-floor balcony, Reeve leans over the railing. "I forgot to tell you something."

"What?"

She smiles. "Firsts are overrated."

*Thank you, Reeve. Thank you for that.*

I get into my car and crank the ignition. Another place, Reeve, another time. I pull away from the curb and say softly, "See you in Joyland."

# Resources

The Web site links and organizations listed below can provide information and help to those experiencing violence in dating and relationships. In addition, many local resources can be found through schools, police precincts, social services, hospitals, and community support groups.

**Choose Respect: Preventing Dating Abuse**
www.ChooseRespect.org

**National Coalition of Anti-Violence Programs**
www.NCAVP.org: 1-212-714-1184

**National Domestic Violence Hotline**
www.NDVH.org: 1-800-799-SAFE (7233); 1-800-787-3224 TTY

**National Teen Dating Abuse Helpline**
www.LoveIsRespect.org: 1-866-331-9474; 1-866-331-8453 TTY

**The Network/La Red: Ending Abuse in Lesbian, Bisexual Women's & Transgender Communities**
www.thenetworklared.org: 1-617-742-4911; 1-617-227-4911 TTY

# Acknowledgments

Long, long overdue acknowledgment of my cherished critique group, the Wildfolk, who, for twenty-five years and counting, have nurtured and grown writers and illustrators for young readers. When I dumped this mess of a manuscript on them and wailed, "Help! What does this story say to you?" they weren't afraid to tell me it was a beautiful disaster. Emphasis on "disaster." Eternal, heartfelt gratitude to Hilari Bell, Jane Bigelow, Lisa Brown-Roberts, Meridee Cecil, Carol Crowley, Anna-Maria Crum, Laura Deal, Coleen DeGroff, Wick Downing, Amy Efaw, Randy Fraser, Claudia McAdam, Sean McCollum, Pam Mingle, Christine Liu Perkins, Cheryl M. Reifsnyder, Shawn Shea, Bobbi Shupe, Caroline Stutson, and Denise Vega. I love you guys.

# About the Author

Julie Anne Peters grew up in Colorado in a lively, noisy household where she was a regular kid who tormented her older brother and harassed her younger sisters. Past employment stints include teaching and several left-brain ventures involving computers, statistical research, and systems engineering.

But then . . . writing beckoned. Not easily, not instantly, but the voices, the situations, the details began to come, and to insist themselves upon her pages. Julie's books have received young reader awards, critical acclaim, and literary recognition. Even though her first love has always been young adult literature, her early books were easy readers and middle-grade novels. Then came *Define "Normal," Keeping You a Secret,* and the National Book Award finalist *Luna.* Her young adult novels feature the universal truths and particular challenges of gay, lesbian, bisexual, and transgender teens. She wrote *Rage* at the behest of a young friend who was entrenched in an abusive relationship, but only after many months of her friend's persistent encouragement, and after the relationship had ended. Julie says her aim was to portray teen-dating violence where neither victim nor villain is painted in broad strokes and where redemption is authentic.

Julie has often explored the question of how much we're willing to sacrifice for love, in its many guises and disguises. She found it painful to immerse herself in the psyche of *Rage*'s narrator, Johanna, who allows herself to be assaulted and controlled. And while she guesses that we all put on some blinders about the shortcomings of those we love, especially when we love in a head-over-heels way, she feels that Johanna's sexuality probably makes her more inclined to defend the damaged girl she's in love with—perhaps because she feels she has fewer opportunities to find love, or more to prove.

Julie's own relationship with her partner, Sherri Leggett, poses no such trauma, as they recently celebrated their thirty-fifth anniversary. Julie and Sherri share their Colorado home with a never-ending stream of rescued homeless cats and foster kittens.

You can visit Julie Anne Peters on the Web at www.julieanne peters.com.